King T

Book 9 in the
Combined Operations Series
By
Griff Hosker

Published by Sword Books Ltd 2017
Copyright © Griff Hosker First Edition

Cover by Design for Writers

To Stephen Flynn one of my most loyal readers and a gentleman who keeps me straight!

German starting position December 1944

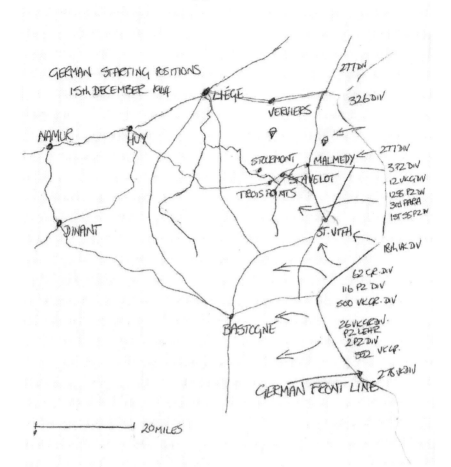

GERMAN STARTING POSITIONS
15th DECEMBER 1944

NAMUR

HUY

LIÈGE

VERVIERS

277 DIV

326 DIV

277 DIV

3 PZ DIV

12 VKG DIV

12SS PZ DIV

3rd PARA

1ST SS PZ DIV

STOUMONT

MALMEDY

STAVELOT

TROIS PONTS

DINANT

ST. VITH

184 VK DIV

62 GR. DIV

116 PZ DIV

560 VKGR. DIV

26 VKGR DIV.

PZ LEHR

2 PZ DIV

352 VKGR.

BASTOGNE

276 VKDIV

GERMAN FRONT LINE

20 MILES

1

Chapter 1

Antwerp November 1944

There were just three of us left from my unit. Three of us who were both alive and unwounded. The wounded were either in hospitals in Northern France or they had already been flown back to England. The dead lay on the island of Walcheren. There were just three of us who had survived the battle of Walcheren and Flushing intact. Sergeant Gordy Barker, Corporal John Hewitt and myself, Brevet Major Tom Harsker, were all that was left from an elite unit. We had fought non-stop since we had landed on Sword Beach in Normandy on the 6th of June. We had helped to recapture Paris and, after spearheading the assault on Antwerp, we had been in at the kill when Walcheren had finally fallen. We had paid a price. Two of our number would not enjoy the peace- should it ever come. We should have gone home but Major Foster had one last task for us. We were to pass on our knowledge to other allied soldiers. They ranged from Engineers to combat troops and from tank crew to paratroopers. I did not think that we would teach the paratroopers anything but, with the promise of leave at the end of it, I accepted the mission. I hoped that I might be home for Christmas although as that was just five weeks away I was not hopeful.

It had taken a few days for us to get to Antwerp. The roads from Walcheren were clogged and there appeared to be little organization. That was not surprising. Everyone had moved so quickly to open the port that little thought had been given to clearing roads. When we had eventually found Major Foster's headquarters he was in a meeting and we had had to cool our heels. We still had the Bedford lorry which we had used on our advance north. It meant we had somewhere to sleep. Accommodation was in short supply. While we waited for the Major to return with our precise orders I had Gordy and John acquire as much ammunition and equipment as they could. Although we were designated as trainers I knew that we would, in all likelihood, be close to the German lines. Others might be demob happy but I would not relax my vigilance until I was back in England and wearing civilian clothes. Dad had thought his time in action had been over in 1918 but he had found himself fighting the Communists in North Russia. I was taking no chances. If we had to fight then we would be ready.

All Belgians were resilient but the people of Antwerp seemed more so. Life was already back to normal. The roads might be a mess and food in short supply but the Germans had gone and they wanted to begin their lives again. They took the damaged buildings and wrecked vehicles in their stride. They carried on as they had before the Germans had invaded and changed their lives. They were determined that it would not change them forever. Food was in short supply but there was no free for all when new supplies were brought in. I was impressed by them.

I stayed with the vehicle and was relieved when Hewitt and Barker returned. They were laden. Gordy grinned, "The Combined Ops flash works a treat, sir. The Green Howards welcomed us to their holding camp like old mates. I found their Quarter Master. He was a good bloke. He comes from Richmond in North Yorkshire. Hewitt here and him chatted about the times before the war when folk went to Whitby for the day. He gave us everything we needed. We have greatcoats, blankets, new canteens, rations and we even got fresh socks and underwear! Hewitt got a good medical kit. We want for nothing!"

"Never mind all that, Gordy, what about ammo and grenades?"

"Yes and yes. The only ammo we couldn't get was German stuff for your Mauser and Luger."

I was not worried. I had taken plenty from the dead and captured Germans. We had met enough to replenish my supplies. "Well done. Now we wait for his lordship. He is in some sort of meeting. As you two are back here I will head to Headquarters and wait for him there. The sooner we have finished this training the sooner we can get home."

"Aye sir, it will be good to get back to Blighty for Christmas."

"Don't count any chickens just yet, Sergeant."

I clambered out of the back of the lorry. Hewitt proffered one of the new coats. "Here sir, do you want a greatcoat?"

"It is just a little fresh, Hewitt. I am guessing that Headquarters will be cosy and warm. You know what the staff are like. I will be fine."

I strode briskly through the streets. The Headquarters building was the old town hall and we were parked just half a mile from it. I was greeted with smiles and nods as I headed there. We had liberated this town. The Belgians had fought alongside us. That made us brothers in arms. I admired their courage. They had used whatever guns they could find and were as brave as any soldier I had met. We had fought with them not far from here when we captured the German H.Q. I wondered what would have happened had the R.A.F. not managed to defeat the Germans at the battle of Britain. Would the Germans have managed to conquer England? Would we have fought as they did? I guessed we would. Britain did not take kindly to invasion. The last successful one had been nine hundred years earlier.

The sentries snapped to attention when I arrived. I showed them my papers and was ushered inside. As I had expected they had a fire going and it was warm with a fug of cigarette smoke in every room. The duty sergeant ushered me into a comfortable apportioned and furnished room. I guessed it had been the mayor's parlour before the war. The Germans had made it into a sort of lounge. There was the shape of a removed painting on one wall. It did not take a Sherlock Holmes to deduce that must have been Adolf Hitler.

"Cup of tea sir?"

"Yes thank you, Sergeant."

He hesitated, "Can I just say, sir, that it is an honour to meet someone who has the V.C. and M.C."

The sergeant looked to be of an age with me. He had the manner of a veteran, "We both know, Sergeant, that fruit salad is more often than not simply a matter of luck."

He shook his head, "I have spoken to the lads who know you sir; Major Foster's team. I know better. You are the real McCoy. I'll get that tea then sir. I'll see if I can rustle up a biscuit too, eh? Nice piece of shortbread."

By the time the tea and shortbread had been demolished Major Foster arrived. He had with him a Squadron Leader.

"Ah, Tom, sorry to have kept you waiting. Busy arranging something for the General. This is Squadron Leader Jennings, He will be sitting in on our meeting. He and I have a great deal of planning to do. Your briefing will not take long. You don't mind do you?"

"Of course, not sir."

I stood and followed them. The Squadron Leader turned, "I know your father, or rather I served under him briefly. I was at a meeting with him last month. He speaks highly of you. He is a proud father. You are the image of him."

"Thank you, sir."

"It's Richard. Yes your old man is a real warhorse. He never slows down. From what I hear you are a chip off the old block."

"I think my grandfather was the same."

Major Foster closed the door behind us. We took seats and the Squadron Leader took out his pipe and began to fill it. Major Foster handed me an envelope. "Here are your orders. You will be based at Liège. The idea is for you to give a talk to the units who are there. We want you to give a sort of lecture. Tell them how you survived behind enemy lines and why you are successful."

"Sir, that just sounds like boasting."

The Major smiled, "You are a Brevet Major now, Tom. You don't need to sir me. And it is not boasting. Look, lots of the chaps seem to think the war is over. The parachute drops on the Rhine and the capture of Antwerp were hard fought but a lot of people think the war will be over by Christmas. That is a nonsense. We both know that. That is why you need to talk to them. You have credibility. You are not a staff officer with a bit of red around your hat. You have been at the sharp end."

The Squadron Leader had got his pipe going. "The Major is right, Tom. Jerry has new weapons in the pipe line. The rockets he has been sending over are nothing compared with the ones he is developing. Our Mossies have been trying to find them so our Lancasters can knock them out. And they have a new tank. It is an upgraded version of the Tiger. Jerry calls it a King Tiger, Königstiger. From what I can gather it is unstoppable. It has seven inches of armour in places! That is like battleship! The gun they are using is the 88 mm and we all know what that is like. It weighs 70 tons and is over 12 feet wide! That is one hell of a machine. As far as I can tell its only weakness is its fuel consumption. It is less than a mile a gallon. There is a tank destroyer called a Jagdpanther; that is almost impossible to stop. If Adolf can produce them in enough numbers we are in trouble. They also have new aircraft too. Your father told me about one which does not have a propeller and is faster than any Allied aeroplane! The Germans are close to a technological superiority. Major Foster is right. We have to end this war before they can bring these new super weapons into production."

"So, Tom, you will have a week of these lectures and then you are off home. The travel warrants for the three of you are in the envelope."

"The Rangers and the Airborne don't need lessons off me, sir. Good God, some of the 6th Airborne spent a week or more behind the German lines after Arnhem."

"And they lost more of their men than you did. You have a reputation of surviving behind the enemy lines and having the fewest casualties." He handed me a map. "Liège is your base but you will also visit a couple of other units. Some are quite close to the front. I will let you know. The weather is so awful at the moment that it is unlikely Jerry will try anything. It is another reason why we are sending you now. The front is quiet. I have no doubt that Adolf will come up with something in the New Year but for now he is busy trying to make the new weapons the Squadron

Leader was talking about." He stood. The meeting was obviously over. He shook my hand.

I turned to the Squadron Leader, "Nice to have met you, sir. If you see my father again, tell him I was asking after him. It is some time since I saw him."

"Well he is based in London again so you will probably see him before I do."

Although it was noon I was anxious to get going. The short days meant that we would struggle to reach Liège by dark. It was over eighty miles. The roads had been badly damaged by bombing, combat and heavy tanks. In addition, we would have to negotiate Brussels. That, too, had been recently liberated. I made sure that we had everything we would need. Apart from the usual weaponry Gordy and John had acquired more parachute cord and camouflage netting. The people we would be lecturing didn't need lessons in fighting but in staying alive behind the lines. That was our expertise. I planned on making our talk as interesting as possible. The extra equipment from the Quarter Master was a bonus.

As we headed south to the capital of Belgium I could not help smiling. Before the war dad and I would have driven along these same roads at fifty or sixty miles an hour. The journey would have been a couple of hours at most. Now we would be lucky to cover twenty miles an hour. The slow lorry, added to the congested roads and road blocks, meant that we were not in for a quick journey. The weather was turning wintry. We had not had snow yet but I knew that would come. The roads were wet and slick but with sleet and rain. Driving the lorry was a challenge and I was glad that we had three of us to share the load.

Gordy had volunteered for the first shift. John Hewitt said, as we passed the buildings where the German sniper had held us up, "If we had had Fred Emerson he would have been more than happy to drive the whole way never mind just the first bit."

Gordy chuckled, "I don't know how he is around women but if he could I bet he would take a carburettor to bed with him."

I felt obliged to defend my mechanical genius, "He just likes engines. Dad told me about fitters in the Flying Corps who were as obsessed with engines. Dad likes tinkering with them."

Gordy shook his head, "Sir, with respect, I bet your dad never named one. Remember Bertha? I mean who in their right mind names a German half-track?"

"You may be right, Gordy."

"So, sir, what do we do while you are talking to these other units?"

"Corporal Hewitt, don't think for one moment that I am doing this alone! You two will have as big an input as I do!"

"Really sir?"

"Too right! You took the stripes, that means you share the responsibility. I will do the first session. You two can watch and then do something similar."

John Hewitt said, "You know sir, after the war, I wouldn't mind going into teaching. This might be a good start, eh? I can see if I like it. What do I need to become a teacher, sir?"

I knew it was different in the state sector. My schools had been private. All you needed was to know your subject and have the right accent. "I am not certain, John, but there will be courses, I dare say. They will need teachers after this war."

"That's what I thought sir. I thought I could teach them some of the things I have learned."

Gordy laughed, "You mean like how to break someone's neck with your hands or make a booby trap from some parachute cord and a couple of grenades?"

"No, Sarge. The major here has taught us stuff: French and German. I mean I don't say I am any good at them but I would never have even tried to speak languages before. I could teach the young 'uns that it is not hard. I have picked up a bit of medicine, too, sir. There's lots I could pass on to kids. I'd like that."

"What about training to be a doctor, John?"

"Now you are taking the Mick sir! I am not clever enough by a long chalk. Before all this started I would have just expected to get a job at the steelworks or, if I was lucky, an apprenticeship at I.C.I. For me, teaching is up there at the top of the ladder. If I hadn't met you, sir, then I wouldn't even have thought of that."

I looked out of the rain spattered window. The war had changed us all and in ways that could not be predicted. The pacifists would have said it would turn us all into ruthless killers. I didn't believe that for a moment. I had killed and would do so again but when it came to peacetime that would be put in a wardrobe along with my uniform. There were killers who would kill after the war but they already had that killer instinct in them. The S.S. and German Paratroopers sprang to mind.

Brussels was the nightmare I expected and it took two hours to negotiate its congested and damaged streets. There was still damage following its liberation and the streets were filled with servicemen on leave. The British, Canadian and American troops took advantage of the Belgian Beer and cafés. Christmas had come early and you could not blame them.

We would not reach Liège before dark. With the lighting restrictions we would be travelling with lights the size of glow worms! We reached the centre of Liège at seven o'clock at night. I could not be bothered to try to find headquarters or our billet and, as there was a small café nearby, I decided to eat there and sleep in the lorry. We were Commandos and we improvised.

"Supper is on me tonight, lads." I still had plenty of Belgian coins we had taken from the dead Germans as well as some currency Major Foster had given me. We might run out but we could always get more. As Scouse Fletcher had often said, a life in the Commandos was a great preparation for a life of crime!

We tied the tarpaulin over the back of the lorry and headed over to the café. It was still open. The owner spread his hands apologetically as we entered, "I am sorry gentlemen we have little choice left. It is late."

"What can you do for us?"

"Soup, merguez and frites and I have some cheese."

I clapped him on the back, "My friend that is a veritable feast. And we will have a couple of bottles of wine too."

He beamed from ear to ear, "I am Claude and I am the owner and the chef. It will be my pleasure to serve you." He scurried away.

John had understood our words. He smiled for he knew it would be good fare but Gordy's ear was not attuned yet. "What we eating then, sir?"

"Soup, sausage and chips and bread and cheese. All washed down with a couple of bottles of wine."

As soon as I had said, 'sausage' I had grabbed Gordy's attention. "You little beauty sir! Sausage and chips! Lovely!"

When the merguez came Gordy frowned and then grinned as he bit, tentatively, into the sausage, "A bit spicy, like. It is like they put HP sauce and Coleman's Mustard in them." He chewed and swallowed and then he smiled. "This will do for me, sir!"

It was a good evening. After a long and exhausting drive, it was good just to relax. Who knew how many more moments we might have together. Peter Crowe and Ken Shepherd had both been killed at Walcheren. We hung on to life by a thread. The war might be over tomorrow but we would make the most of such evenings for we knew not how many we had left.

Gordy could handle his beer but the wine went to his head and Hewitt and I had to carry him back to our lorry. We did not mind. Gordy was an old-fashioned soldier. If you had gone back to the battle of Hastings, or Waterloo, Blenheim, Agincourt or Rorke's Drift you would have found a soldier identical to Gordy. They were the typical Englishman. They might, as Wellington had famously said, been the 'scum of the earth' but they were belligerent, loyal and tough. I, for one, was proud to lead such men. They never knew when they were beaten and would face any odds without fear.

The next day I left Hewitt to look after a hung over Sergeant Barker and I went to find headquarters. Liège was smaller than Antwerp and Brussels. It was close to the enemy front lines. There was an edge to the town. The patrols looked at people with more suspicion and the civilians were less likely to smile than those in Antwerp. The lighter atmosphere of the previous night was soon dissipated in the morning rain shower and the scowling faces I met. I found the Headquarters by seeking the Union Flag.

When I eventually found the building the sergeant glowered at me, "Sir? Can I help you?"

I took out my orders and showed them to him. "I am to report to a Colonel Jessop. Is he here?"

He smiled. It seemed he was relieved I was not a German spy! "Yes sir. Just go in and knock on the office to the right. They will sort you out sir." As I went through the door he said, "Sorry about that, sir, but we have had all sorts trying to get in. There are a bunch of so-called refugees who would steal the coins off a dead man's eyes. I am sure some are German agents!"

It was as I headed towards the office that I realised that we were the front line. Liège had only been taken recently. Germany was less than thirty miles away as the crow flies. It was natural that they would be suspicious. There would be refugees and some could be the very Germans we had defeated. They could be hiding out. The Germans used many nationalities in their army. Our side of the lines meant that they were less likely to be shot.

Colonel Jessop was like many officers I had met. He was too old for the front line but still wished to serve his country. Running the Headquarters of a recently recaptured town was perfect for him. His neatly trimmed moustache and slightly tanned skin bespoke a career in the east. He had possibly been an Indian officer. He took in my ribbons. Major Foster had insisted that I wore my best uniform to impress our audience. Colonel Jessop stood a little straighter as he read my orders.

"Major Harsker, delighted to meet you. We did not expect you for a few days." He waved over a sergeant, "Sergeant Ganner, have we accommodation for the Major and…?"

"And two N.C.O.s. If you have nothing available, sir, don't worry. We can sleep in the lorry."

The colonel looked appalled, "Have the winner of a V.C. and an M.C. sleep in the back of a lorry? Sir, what kind of command do you think I am running here? Sergeant, sort something out!"

"Yes sir."

The Colonel smiled, "Now we have a room for you to use. Actually, it is the old cinema. Good acoustics and comfortable seating for the officers. Anything you need? Slide projector? That sort of thing?"

I shook my head. "Just the hall will be fine, sir. We just want to pass on what we have learned. Thank you for your hospitality."

He nodded, "I met your father once. I was on the Western Front with him; towards the end of the war. Well I say with him, we were on leave together. I was just a lieutenant. I didn't get to know him well, more's the pity. To tell you the truth I was in awe of him. There weren't many British Aces left by the end of the war. And yet he was so incredibly modest and didn't want to talk about the heroic acts he had performed. You come from good stock."

I smiled, "Thank you, sir."

"Well if you need anything while you are here then let me know. The Sergeant is a good chap. He will sort you out."

The sergeant waited in the doorway when the Colonel stood and waved me over. As I left I reflected that soldiers like Colonel Jessop had made the British Empire. They were a dying breed.

"This way sir. There aren't a lot of billets in the town but I got one close to the cinema and the Headquarters." When we were outside I waved over Hewitt and Barker. The sergeant took us down a side street. There was a row of small houses. They were so small that the rooms were little wider than the door itself! However, there was an outhouse and there was a bedroom. It would do and it would prove to be warmer than the back of the Bedford.

"Thanks Sergeant. We will get our gear and then, tomorrow, if you could show us where we will be giving our little talk?"

"Yes sir, do you need any grub?"

"We'll manage."

We headed back to the café we had used the previous night. The owner was pleased to see us and he rubbed his hands, "Tonight, gentlemen, I can offer you finer fare than last night's humble offering." He looked around and lowered his voice. "Today I went hunting and we have some duck. My wife has created a stew made with red wine, sausage and duck. She has thickened it with lentils." He put his finger and his thumb to his lips. "It is not on the menu it is, how do you say, a special."

"Then that will do us nicely, thank you."

Once again Gordy was suspicious but the ubiquitous sausage pleased him. "What are these things sir?"

"Lentils."

"They remind me of pease pudding. Now that is something I will have when I get home. Ham hock with pease pudding. I shall wash it down with a bottle of brown ale!"

John Hewitt then began an argument about which part of the north had the best pease pudding. That inevitably led to a debate about the various beers. I just drank my wine and enjoyed the food. After the short rations on Walcheren this was a bonus!

The next morning, we were taken to the old cinema. It had been recently used. There were still the dog ends from German cigarettes on the floor and the signs were still in German. However, it had been some time since it had been used. There was a patina of dust on everything. I would get Sergeant Ganner to have some men clean it.

Gordy grinned as he stood on the stage, "I always fancied being on the music hall stage. Perhaps I'll get my chance now, eh sir?"

"Gordy you have been to enough of these things to realise that the chaps who come here will not be happy. If they are in Liège then it means they have been pulled out of the front line. Would you want to hear three Commandos telling you how to fight a war or would you rather be in a bar having a few pints?"

"Point taken, sir. So we are on a hiding to nothing then?"

"That's the spirit, Gordy! Assume, as I do, the worst and then anything else will not seem as bad."

We spent the day working out what we would say and how to make it lively. Our orders said to talk for no more than two hours! That was an hour more than I intended. We were all nervous waiting for our first audience. No one liked to fail and this had been set up for us to fail. They were forcing men to listen to us and that was never good. We discovered that it was the 43rd Division which was based around Liège. It was the officers and sergeants who attended our little show. None was of a rank higher than Major. That was one good thing. We made it just that; a show. Gordy proved that he had missed his calling. He was a natural comedian. He got the sergeants and corporals on our side. He was funny and proved to be a good mimic. He did an hilarious impression of a German. He goose stepped around the stage with a bottle top for a monocle. It got them on our side. The officers were all keen to hear how I had got my medals and so, when we had the question and answer session at the end, I was the one on the spot. After that first lecture we knew that the rest would be less stressful and we actually started to enjoy them.

By the 10th of December we had managed to get through all the men of the 43rd Division. I was looking forward to heading back to England when Colonel Jessop broke me the bad news. "You have done rather well here, Major Harsker. The general was speaking with General Bradley and he would like you to head to St. Vith and do the same there." He was a gentleman and he smiled apologetically when he saw my smile turn to a frown. "Orders I am afraid. It seems it is to improve Anglo-American relations. As you know Monty and General Patton don't get on. General Bradley thinks that you might be just the medicine to show them a different side to the British soldier. It should only take another week or so and then you still have time to get back to England. I am sure you will be back in Blighty for Christmas. Major Foster thought it was a good idea. He sent this along for you."

He handed me a large box. When I opened it I saw that it was a new uniform. It had my medals on and the single crown of a major. "Has my promotion been confirmed then, sir?"

"Not yet but it is only a matter of time. I can't see anyone opposing the promotion of someone who has a V.C. and an M.C." I nodded but I never liked to count chickens no matter how well dressed. "Do you want a car or are you happy with your lorry? I must confess we might struggle to get a decent vehicle. We have plenty of jeeps but they would hardly accommodate your equipment."

"No sir, the lorry will be fine just so long as we have petrol."

"Thanks to your efforts at Antwerp we now have all the petrol we need. It seems the battle of the Atlantic is over too. The convoys are not getting hit as often. The newspapers might be right for once. The war might be over soon."

I shook my head, "No sir, not yet. Hitler is like a mad dog. Until he is put down then they will keep fighting."

"You are probably right. Oh, I have a driver for you. You chaps have enough to do without driving. Private Briggs is from the Royal Army Service Corps. He has been assigned to you. When you have finished at St Vith he will drive the lorry back to Antwerp where you will take ship for home."

"Thank you, sir." Of course, I had no intention of waiting for a slow ship to take us home. I would use my father's name to get a ride in a transport. In the months since D-Day the R.A.F. had been taking over airfields all over northern France. I would get Private Briggs to take us to one of them.

Albert Briggs was a dour chap. He was just over the minimum height for a soldier, five feet two, and he was almost as round as he was tall. He drove with a cigarette permanently hanging from the side of his mouth. He rarely spoke and in all the time we were with him I never saw him crack a smile once. For all that he was an excellent driver and he knew engines as well as Fred Emerson.

After we had loaded the Bedford he said, "It is fifty miles sir to St. Vith sir, but it won't be quick. The roads around here are a bugger. Pardon my French. Twisting little things through bloody great trees and the roads are covered in snow! I reckon they always have a white Christmas here. For me, they can stick it. Keep it for the Christmas cards eh sir? And the other thing is it is just twenty miles from the German lines. Sometimes they lob shells over. We will have to take it steady."

"Don't worry Private, a bit of shelling won't upset us."

As I climbed into the cab with him I wondered if he would be chatty while he was driving but that was the longest conversation I had with him. Gordy and Hewitt climbed in the back where they would play pontoon and that left me in the cab with Private Briggs and his Capstan Full Strength. It soon became apparent that I had heard the full extent of Private Briggs' conversation. He focussed on the road and his cigarettes. I looked out of the cab window at the terrain through which we travelled. He was right. It was dramatic. There were few large places. Once we had passed Verviers then we left behind signs of houses. The road twisted and turned. Forests seemed to almost touch their road and, in places the canopy was so great that it was like driving through a tunnel. Private Briggs struggled to keep us on a straight line. It was lucky that there were few other vehicles around. We passed none heading south and only a few which were heading north. Most of the troops who had been given leave were already on their way west and few replacements were being sent east.

After we had passed through the tiny hamlet of Monts we reached Malmedy. It was a relief to actually see somewhere with more than a couple of houses even though it was little more than a small town. After descending into the valley, we then climbed and slid our way up the other side of the remote little town. Snow covered forests spread out on either side of us. It was pretty country but this was war and I doubted that the Germans who had retreated just a month or so earlier, would have appreciated its beauty.

The US VIII Corps were based around this part of the front. I was aware of protocol and so I reported to the most senior officer I could find. While the others stretched their legs, I was ushered into the office of the commanding officer, Colonel Harding. The sergeant who shared the office, Sergeant Ford, asked, "Do you want a coffee sir? We don't have the tea you guys like so much."

"Coffee would be fine, sergeant. Just as it comes, black."

13

He nodded, "That is the first time I have heard of a Limey not putting in a gallon of milk and a ton of sugar. You must have American blood in you, sir."

Just then I heard a familiar voice behind me, "Oh no Sergeant Ford, Major Harsker is a Brit through and through."

I turned, "Hugo! What are you doing here?"

I shook Hugo Ferguson's hand. He had been with us in Malta. Working for Colonel Fleming of Intelligence he had been a staff liaison officer. I had no idea what he was doing here at the front.

"I am liaison officer with the Americans."

I tapped his pips, "And promoted too. Congratulations, Captain."

"And you too, Major."

"Brevet rank I am afraid."

When the coffee was brought back we chatted about soldiers Hugo had known. He was saddened to hear of the loss of so many.

"What brings you this close to the front? Are you still with Colonel Fleming?"

"You mean Brigadier General Fleming? No sir. He has flown out to the war in the Pacific. He is in Australia running a show there."

"Ah, still climbing the slippery pole, eh? And you, are you happy to be free of him?"

"To be truthful sir I missed the days in Malta. When I worked with you chaps I felt as though I was doing something useful. I asked for this."

I laughed, "You know what they say, Hugo, never volunteer."

He had the good grace to laugh. "I have improved my marksmanship sir. Still, with the war nearly over I doubt I will get the chance to fight and to lead."

The telephone rang and Sergeant Ford answered. He listened and then said, "Sorry sir, the Colonel has been held up. He asked if Captain Ferguson would show you around."

"Delighted, Sergeant. Come on Major, I'll give you and your chaps the tour. How many of you are there?"

"Barker and Hewitt. They have given us a driver too."

"Right, well your billet is just around the corner. You can leave your bus outside. It isn't far." Once outside he said, "I need to talk to you privately anyway; I should tell you about Colonel Harding."

I was intrigued but then Hugo knew army politics better than anyone and he was always discreet. He had worked with Colonel Fleming and he was the most devious of officers. While Gordy organized our billet, Hugo took me to a small bar. It looked to be the only one in the centre of the small town. There were just locals huddled around the smoky tables and we found a small table in the corner.

"The thing is sir, Colonel Harding can be a little difficult."

I put my hand up, "Hugo if this is gossip out of school then I do not want to know. If, however, it is something which might affect our efficiency then stop beating about the bush and come out with it. You know that you can trust me."

He smiled and was the young officer I had known all those years ago in Malta. "Yes sir. As you know General Patton and Field Marshal Montgomery do not get along."

"Of course. It is common knowledge but this is an American sector is it not?"

"Yes, sir but Colonel Harding served with General Patton in Tunisia and Italy. It was the general himself who promoted Colonel Harding. He is resentful of the fact that General Bradley has sent a Brit to tell him how to fight a war." He knocked back his drink. "I am just warning you, sir. Expect a little opposition."

I leaned back and smiled, "Hugo, the last thing I want is to have to talk to anyone about our exploits, let alone soldiers who do not want to listen. I am just as happy to skedaddle back to Antwerp and then back to England. I do not need this."

Hugo held up a hand, "However, sir, there are politics. Field Marshal Montgomery is the one who arranged for you to come here. It was not General Bradley. He has heard of what you have done. He knows that you went in with the Free French in Paris. He is exploiting your fame. So, you see, you have to do the work or risk running foul of the Field Marshal."

I knocked back my brandy, "A rock and a hard place come to mind! Thanks for the heads up, Hugo. I suppose in the grand scheme of things it could be worse. At least the Colonel will not be firing bullets at me. That will make a change. A few more days and then we can go home!"

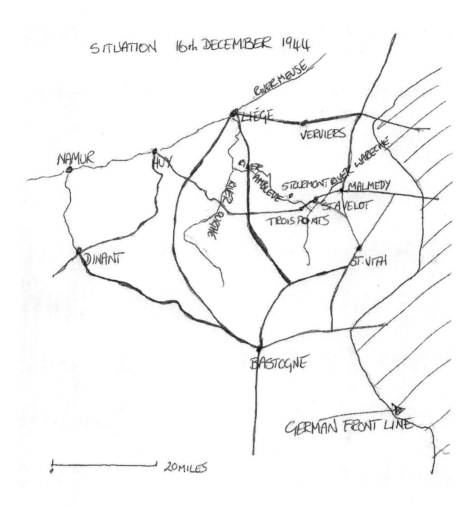

SITUATION 16th DECEMBER 1944

RIVER MEUSE

LIÈGE

VERVIERS

NAMUR

HUY

RIVER AMBLEVE

RIVER OURTHE

STOUMONT

RIVER WARECHE

MALMEDY

STAVELOT

TROIS PONTS

DINANT

ST. VITH

BASTOGNE

GERMAN FRONT LINE

20 MILES

16

Chapter 2

We were kept cooling our heels for two days. Having spoken to Hugo I now saw that politics were involved. In truth I did not mind. It gave me the chance to do some walking in the country around St. Vith. It was good hiking country and the snow made it beautiful to view. Gordy had managed to get us some decent boots from the Quartermaster rather than the flimsier rubber soled Commando shoes and I broke them in. I noticed that the trees were all pines. The soldier in me thought how useful that could be. The pine branches would make a quick mat to extract a jeep from trouble. I also saw that the roads were not the best in the world. They were narrow and they twisted, turned and climbed. It was a good job we had captured this in the autumn. In the winter it would be almost impossible.

It was the 12th of December when I was finally summoned to headquarters. Sergeant Ford greeted me. He had been most pleasant each time I had visited. He held out a mug of coffee, "Here you are sir, fresh Joe, just the way you like it!"

"You should try it the navy way, Sergeant, it is even better."

He looked intrigued, "The navy way sir? Royal Navy?"

"Yes Sergeant, they spike it with rum. Now that will warm you up on a cold day!"

He looked around conspiratorially, "Between the two of us, sir, I am quite partial to a shot of Bourbon, when we can get it." We both laughed.

Colonel Harding appeared. "Sergeant Ford, I am sure you have work to do!"

"Yes sir!" He disappeared giving an apologetic shrug of the shoulders as he did so.

Colonel Harding was a small man. He had a neatly trimmed moustache. He looked like a neat little man. His shoes were polished to within an inch of their life. His Sam Browne shone and his tie had a perfect knot. This was not a warrior. This was a career officer. He reminded me of a bird. His movements were short, staccato ones. He even cocked his head to one side when speaking; just the way I had seen blackbirds hunting. However, the thing I noticed immediately was that he affected his hero's manner. He had a Colt .45 strapped to his waist. It was pearl handled. General Patton had two! He was trying to be General Patton.

"Come in Major, although I believe it is a brevet rank?" His voice was slightly higher pitched than was comfortable. I hoped he would not talk to me for long. Dogs would appear!

We entered his office, "Yes sir. I am awaiting confirmation." If he thought to upset me with comments about rank then he was wrong. It did not bother me.

"Take a seat. I can see that you have received many decorations. Is that why you have been foisted upon us?"

I decided to pretend that I did not know this was the Field Marshal's order and I ignored the word '*foisted*'. "I thought General Bradley made the request sir or have I got that wrong?"

He waved an irritable hand before his face, "It matters not who sent you here the fact is that I do not think that we need you. We have managed to do quite well without you and your Commando tactics. We are regular soldiers here. We face the enemy and we fight him. We do not sneak around like outlaws." He pointed to the east. It was hidden by a wall and the gesture looked a little silly. "We are just a few miles from Germany! We are about to cross into Hitler's backyard! General Patton will be in Berlin by February! He will beat those Russians to the Reichstag!"

I said, calmly, "I didn't think it was a competition, sir. Aren't we all supposed to be on the same side?"

He waved a dismissive hand. "Of course, we are. I was just making the point that it is highly unlikely that any of our men will need your expertise. The war is almost over. We just dot the I's and cross the T's. However, orders are orders, no matter how unwelcome. I know how to do my duty." He gave me a thin smile. "To the letter. If we have to have a lecture from you I want it to be just the one. I have a large mess tent ready for you. You can address my sergeants and N.C.Os on the 15th. My officers are far too busy for such nonsense. How does that suit?"

"That will be fine, sir. Thank you." I did not mind that. Had he said I would not be given the opportunity to speak at all I would have been just as happy and I would have headed back to Antwerp in a shot. However, I, too, knew how to obey orders.

He seemed to be taken aback by my acceptance of what was a humiliating offer. We were not good enough to talk to officers. He didn't know that I had been a sergeant myself. This arrangement would do. This way I could obey orders and still leave the next day. I would be home for Christmas.

I told Gordy and Hewitt that our audience would just be non-coms. They both seemed happy. Hewitt said, "The officers are the ones who will be losing out, sir. Still, with the war being almost over I can see why they see it as irrelevant."

Gordy said, "But it isn't is it sir? I mean when this war here is over there are still the Nips to sort out. And we know there are always wars. They said the Great War was the war to end all wars but it wasn't was it sir? We will give these lads a good show anyway."

We were in the mess tent early. I did not want to antagonise the Colonel any more than I had to. The Americans came in noisily. I saw some scowls but most were just intrigued. They were a rowdy crew but like all soldiers they knew how to come to attention. Gordy shouted, "Ten-shun!" It worked. They all stood rigidly at attention.

"At ease. Sit down and smoke if you wish." There was a flash of lighters as they took advantage of my offer. There was a slight hubbub of conversation which I allowed to subside and then I spoke. "I am Major Harsker of the Commandos. This is Sergeant Barker and Corporal Hewitt. Today we have been asked to give a little talk to you chaps."

I saw a few smirks and giggles at my language. It was all part of the act. I played the posh officer. It had worked before. It meant that Gordy could do his part more easily. Once they were all focussed I handed over to Sergeant Barker. He stood with his feet wide apart and his hands behind his back. He flexed his knees a little. "Now I know what you lads are thinking. What the hell can a fat, ugly little Limey tell us about fighting that we don't already know?"

That brought a laugh. One sergeant shouted, "Ain't that the truth, brother!"

"And you may well be right, my friend. You are all fighting men. I can see that. You have fought in Africa, Sicily, Italy and Normandy. We were with you in all of those campaigns. You know how to attack and how to win. We have done that too but the three of us here have spent days and weeks behind enemy lines. That is something that you haven't done. There was no need was there? Lads like us had been in first so that you knew what the dangers would be. That was our job." He tapped his shoulder flash. "And you may know what this means. We are Commandos and Adolf Hitler has passed an order which applies only to us. It means that if we are caught then we are shot as spies. There are no half measures. If you are caught then it is a POW camp. For us it is a firing squad, at best."

I saw that Gordy had their attention.

"Now I have to say that, on my own, I would have no chance of surviving behind anybody's lines. I don't even speak English very well.

19

My German is... what is that American word? Ah yes, crap!" That brought a huge laugh from everyone. "Now the Major here, the one with all the fruit salad, he speaks German and French really well. He could fool old Adolf. He has got us out of scrapes you wouldn't believe. Corporal Hewitt here can speak a bit too. More than that he and the other lads in our unit are the best there is at using what the Germans have. We are like Magpies. What the Germans use, we use. Nothing goes to waste. Sir?"

Gordy was like a warm up act, "Thank you Sergeant." I held up my Colt and my Thompson. "These are our weapons of choice. You chaps use them and they are both damned fine weapons. Lots of firepower and reliable as hell. The trouble is you can run out of ammo in a battle. Especially if you are cut off." I laid my guns on the table and picked up my Luger and my Mauser sniper rifle. "Now these, on the other hand, are German. We took them from dead Germans. Germans we killed, silently. Jerry always has plenty of ammo. We are quite happy to relieve the opposition of theirs. And don't make the mistake of thinking that they are not very good. They are excellent. Jerry makes good guns. If you can get hold of an MG 42 or an MP34 then grab it. They are really reliable. Corporal."

I handed over to Hewitt who took a German grenade. "We like these potato mashers too. The Mills bombs, like your M2 grenade, are good but we use these as well." I smiled because I knew what was coming. He smashed the porcelain cap and I saw the Americans at the front duck. John smiled, "It is not armed yet." He held the cord. "You have to pull this. But don't worry. We have taken the charge out so that we can demonstrate." He then showed them how to make a booby trap.

When we came to the last fifteen minutes they were very attentive.

"You have heard plenty from us. I dare say your backsides are aching and you would like to get to the PX or perhaps a bar for a few beers. So the last part is up to you. What else do you need or even want to know? Questions?"

An enormous sergeant said, "That was damned interesting, sir, and six months ago would have been useful but it is Fritz who is running backwards right now. They have more chance of being trapped behind the enemy lines than we do. The war is almost over."

I gestured with my thumb behind me. "That, my friend is Germany. We all know how hard the average German soldier fought to hold on to France, Belgium and the Netherlands. I think I can safely say he will fight even harder for Germany. They will dispute every piece of ground. I have fought their paratroopers and their S.S. They are nasty, vicious pieces of work! They take no prisoners, quite literally. I was on the retreat to

Dunkirk and I saw them. We fought them up in Walcheren and Antwerp. They are merciless. The minute you start to think the war is over then that is when you can count your life in hours."

"You think they are going to attack?" It was a Corporal on the front row who asked the question.

"Perhaps not right away. However, I believe that they will attack for they have new tanks and new weapons. The Germans build good tanks and have excellent weapons. They don't have as far to travel to get reinforcements to the front line. They will be coming. I am not saying soon but there will be a last hurrah. Enjoy Christmas but don't stop training and if you are caught behind the lines then I hope that what we have just told you might save a life or two. We would like that. Men have died giving the three of us the chance to learn what we have. And we haven't stopped learning yet. Thank you."

To my surprise they all stood and began to clap and cheer. It was the best reaction we had had on our tour. It took almost an hour for us to get out. When we did I found Sergeant Ford waiting for us. He had a cup of coffee for me. "Inspired sir." He looked around, "I know the Colonel isn't your biggest fan but me and the guys like a straight talker and that is you. You guys are alright. I'll be sorry to see you go."

"Thank you, Sergeant. You make damned good coffee."

"When do you leave, sir?"

"In the morning, why?"

"Me and some of the guys would like to take your sergeant and corporal over to the PX for a beer tonight."

"Good. They would like that."

As they were going to be enjoying themselves I arranged to meet Hugo. It felt like Christmas. The festive season was less than nine days away and I would be able to see Mum, Mary and, hopefully, Susan. Perhaps all my ducks were being lined up.

Hugo took me to a small restaurant. There was little on the menu but when I saw game stew I knew that we would enjoy it. This was hunting country. With a rough red wine, it was perfect. I enjoyed chatting to Hugo. He was a career officer. We had little in common other than the '*Lucky Lady'* and the section. It meant we had much to talk about. When the war was over then he would continue to climb the greasy pole. I suspect that was why he yearned for action. After the war there would be others who had fought and Hugo had just talked. I had no doubt that he would end up a general. As soon as the war was over I would marry Susan and I would then think about my career. Somehow University did not seem so appealing. There had to be something I could do. I wondered how I would

21

go back to a life where people were not trying to kill me and I was not constantly looking over my shoulder. The meal provided a pleasant evening as we shared our hopes and dreams for the days when the war would be over.

It was late as we headed back to our billets. I heard the sound of aircraft in the distance and they were heading west. That, in itself was unusual. The Germans had long ago given up on heavy bombing raids. They had their rockets now with which to terrorise London. I wondered what it could be. Perhaps they were bombing Antwerp. The capture of that port had hurt the Germans. They knew that it foreshortened the war. We had had snow earlier on and it had stopped. I could see stars; the sky was clear. It would freeze later on. Perhaps that was why the Germans were flying; because they could. I was the first to return to the billet. That did not surprise me. The Americans would try to drink Gordy under the table; they would need a lot of luck to do that! He could drink at the Olympics.

I curled up in my blankets. The digs were not the warmest I had ever experienced. It was a bitterly cold night. I did not know how Private Briggs could sleep in the Bedford. He managed, somehow. Inevitably the two of them woke me when they returned. Gordy had Hewitt slung over his shoulder. Gordy was drunk and he held a finger to me and said, "Shssh. Don't wake the Major."

I took Hewitt from him and laid him on his side. The last thing we needed was for poor John to drown in his own vomit. I wrapped him in his blanket. "Are you alright, Gordy?"

"Fine, sir. Shssh!" With that he collapsed face down. I put a blanket over him. As I was awake I went to the toilet.

It was a communal one shared by a number of others. As I was coming back I met a young American Lieutenant. He was dressed and he saluted, "Good evening, Lieutenant."

"Good evening sir." He put his helmet on his head.

"You are up late, Lieutenant. Is there a problem?"

"We have had some reports of German aircraft flying to the north of us. There are unconfirmed reports of German paratroopers dropping south of Verviers; just west of Monschau along the Elsenborn Ridge."

"That's just twenty miles away isn't it?"

"Yes sir. The Colonel is sending me up there with a jeep and a couple of men to have a look see."

I felt the hairs on the back of my neck prickle. "Lieutenant, be careful. If they are paratroopers they are not to be messed with. Shoot first and ask questions later."

"It is probably nothing, sir. You know how these things get blown out of all proportion. It is probably just a downed aircraft. German aircraft were flying west not long ago. It will be one that we hit."

He was young and he was confident. I watched him go and I could not shake the thought that this was important. I could not just go back to sleep. I dressed and went to find Hugo. He was in the same building as us. I knocked on this door but I heard nothing, I went in. He was snoring away. I shook him and his eyes opened wide, "What is it?"

"I am not certain. Look could you get us in to the radio room?"

"Probably but why?"

"The Colonel has just sent a Lieutenant to investigate a possible parachute drop on the Elsenborn Ridge."

"Of course, old chap, but it's probably nothing. It's Christmas next week."

I had no idea why people thought that the Germans wouldn't attack at Christmas. The Germans had pulled surprises like this before. What I couldn't understand was why they would drop just paratroopers. We had fought some in Walcheren. They had had to fill in as infantry. If they risked dropping some then they would not be alone. Was this part of an attack to try to retake Antwerp?

When we reached the radio room there was a young lieutenant and a corporal on duty.

"What is this about paratroopers, Lieutenant?"

"The Colonel has just retired, sir. He was not concerned. He couldn't see that it was a threat to anyone. There is nothing up there to attack. He said to wake him if we had any more news."

I smiled, "Then we will sit with you, eh? Hugo, how about making us a brew, eh? Coffee will be fine."

"Right sir."

It was easy as that to gain access. I had no doubt that the young officer would be in trouble for allowing us in but if this was a major attack then the Colonel ought to have stayed longer himself. While Hugo was away I went to the map on the wall. Monschau was close to the border. If the Germans had landed in force there then they could cut the road to Liège. That would threaten Antwerp. The thought of the sacrifices men had made to capture the port made me angry. I saw pins on the map. There were almost ten thousand men between St. Vith and the German front lines. The Colonel was probably right. There were too many men here for the Germans to do anything decisive.

When Hugo returned with the coffee I noticed, through the open door, flakes of snow falling. The clear skies had not lasted long and the snow would fall on frozen ground. The weather was also on the German's side. The clear skies earlier had allowed them to drop paratroopers and now it would keep our aircraft grounded. The Germans used weather as a weapon. We had too, but the Germans were past masters at it. They had weather stations which monitored weather far to the north so that they could predict what it would do.

I saw the Corporal listening intently to his headphones, "Corporal, what do you hear?"

"It is confused sir. The Ninth are still saying that there are paratroopers in their neck of the woods but they can't confirm numbers."

I looked at my watch. It was now 0300. Dawn was a couple of hours away. The falling snow was a perfect opportunity for the Germans to attack. We would be cut off if there were ground troops racing to join the paratroopers. I said, "There is an irony to all this Hugo. Market Garden was just this plan but on a larger scale; drop paratroopers and send an armoured column to meet up with them. The difference is that the Germans don't look to have overextended themselves and there are no reports of armour yet."

The Lieutenant said, "You are making a lot of inferences, sir, from a few paratroopers."

I turned to face him. "That is what the Germans thought on D-Day, lieutenant. They didn't commit their tanks because they thought reports of isolated paratroopers was not a threat."

"Our tanks are here, sir. We have Shermans, Stuarts and the M8. They won't take us by surprise."

The corporal was the only one with headphones and he suddenly held up a hand, "Lieutenant, just getting a report in that the 106th are being bombarded." He began turning his dials. "Sir. We are being jammed. I can't hear anything anymore."

I looked at the map. The 106th were to the east of us. "Hugo, this is an attack. You had better tell General Jones that he is about to be attacked."

He nodded and I thanked God that he trusted me and my judgement. "Where are you going sir?"

"I am going to wake Barker and Hewitt. We will be in action again soon. The Germans look to have caught us with our trousers down."

The Lieutenant shook his head, "There must be another explanation, sir."

I pointed to the Corporal, "Your Corporal has told you he is being jammed. Ask yourself why would radios be jammed. By itself it is nothing but add that to paratroopers and the 106th being shelled and tell me what the answer might be" I shrugged, "It is your army, Lieutenant, but I do not intend to be put in the bag. If they want me they will have to take me!"

As I went outside I heard the muffled sound of shells to the east. The blizzard prevented me from seeing the flashes but the sound confirmed what I had suspected. Jerry was coming. The Squadron Leader's words about the new jet aeroplanes and Tiger tanks now had an ominous ring. No one had seen the new Tiger yet. I suspected that we would be the first.

Hewitt and Barker had only had three hours sleep by the time I roused them. I suspected that they were still under the influence. "Right you two, you need to sober up quickly! I think the Germans are coming. Get your gear."

"What?"

There was little point in becoming angry with them. I had told them to enjoy themselves. It was my fault just as much as theirs that they were in this condition. "Just get dressed and get your equipment. I'll wake Briggs." I had my battledress on. I strapped on my two pistols and then donned my greatcoat. I put everything else in the Bergen. I had the Mauser and the Tommy gun attached by straps. I was pleased that we had come so well equipped. If we did have to defend ourselves we had the firepower.

I banged on the side of the Bedford as I walked past it. Already it was covered in snow. The snow had fallen very quickly and was deep enough to cover my boots. "Private Briggs, up and at 'em. We need the Bedford. Get it started."

He had not been drinking but even so he put a bleary-eyed head out of the back of the lorry. "Sorry, sir, what's up?"

I threw my Bergen in the back. "Jerry is coming!"

"Bloody hell fire! Right sir!" He jumped up and donned his greatcoat which he had used as an extra blanket.

As I ran back to the billet I saw that men were already beginning to move. They were leaving billets and talking to one another. There appeared to be little urgency about their movements. Someone must have given orders for I saw some with helmets and guns. I glimpsed, to the east, the flash of a firefight. Barker and Hewitt were not entirely sobered up but they were alert enough to fight. The British Army and the Royal Navy had often gone into battle drunk. Perhaps there was something to be said for it.

"Sorry about this, sir. We never get drunk unless we are on leave."

"It's alright John. None of us were to know. Get to the lorry. I will call back in at headquarters and see what's what."

"Are we running, sir?"

I shrugged, "I am not certain, Gordy. This is the American sector. I suppose it depends upon General Jones and General Hasbrouck. They command this part of the line. I would dig in but then I am not in command, am I?"

The headquarters building looked like a disturbed wasp's nest. Soldiers were racing around. It seemed to me they were in a panic. I saw few with their helmets on or with their guns in their hands. I saw Hugo as he emerged from the building. He looked red in the face. "What is happening?"

"I have just been chewed out by Colonel Harding. He said I exceeded my authority by going directly to the general."

"I wouldn't lose any sleep about it. I mean what are they doing?"

"As far as I can see, not a lot sir. The telephone lines from the forward units have been cut and the radios are being jammed. I don't think they know what is going on just a mile or two west of here, let alone further afield. The Colonel is convinced that it is nothing serious. He keeps saying it is almost Christmas."

This was one of those moments when I had to make a decision. "Hugo, take the Bedford and head back to the British lines. Report to whoever is in charge there. If you can evade the paratroopers you should be able to get to Verviers. The telephone lines should be fine there."

"But my orders... I am liaison!"

"And as there is no radio communication you can't liaise, can you? I outrank you. I will tell Colonel Harding that I have taken over liaison and that you have been relieved. I will give you a written order if you like."

"No, sir. A verbal one is fine. The Colonel will not be happy."

I smiled, "The Colonel looks to me like he has been in a bad mood ever since he was dragged kicking and screaming into this world. We have more to worry about than a petulant colonel. Tell the lads to offload my stuff from the Bedford."

"Right sir."

I went into the Headquarters. Sergeant Ford looked to be in the same condition as Sergeant Barker. I grinned at him. He shrugged and rolled his eyes. Colonel Harding whipped his head around, "What are you doing here? I don't need you to tell me what to do. I have the situation well under control. I don't need you or Captain Ferguson panicking."

"You need to do something, Colonel. Unless I miss my guess, you will be knee deep in Tiger tanks and Panzer Grenadiers before the night is out! This is a full-scale offensive."

"We don't panic in the American army."

I sighed, "I am here to tell you that I have relieved Captain Ferguson. I will be your liaison officer from now on. I am sending him to make contact with the nearest units to the north. I think we are about to be cut off."

His face became red. Had I been an American then I would have already been on a charge but I was British and he could do nothing about that. "Major, get out of my headquarters! Do what you like so long as you are out of my sight!"

As I left I nodded to Sergeant Ford. He followed me, "Sir?"

"I need a jeep."

He glanced backwards and then nodded, "This is what you warned us about."

"It is Sergeant. The Germans are coming and in force!"

"The Colonel is out of order, sir. Hang on. I'll see what I can do."

He went back in the office and then returned a few moments later with a piece of paper. "Here is a chit for the motor pool. You stole it, right, sir?"

"Of course, Sergeant. And a word of advice. Keep a pistol, rifle, hand grenades and ammunition close to hand. You guys are going to need them. Be ready to move at a moment's notice."

"Where are you off to?"

I pointed east, "To find Jerry. Before you can fight your enemy, you need to find him."

Hugo stood by the lorry. "Well?"

"Let us just say that Colonel Harding now regards me as an enemy as bad as the Germans. Although, to be fair, I was told to get out of his sight and do as I liked. You two take off. Keep your pistol loaded, Hugo, and do not trust anyone!"

"What can you do?"

"Get information which we can use. God speed."

"And you sir. I'll tell the Major."

Chapter 3

I hefted my Bergen onto my back. I was glad that I had carefully packed and attached my two guns. It was heavy but it was filled with everything that I needed to survive in the hostile environment that was the front line. The snow was falling much faster now. It was almost a white out. It was beginning to lay. Hugo should have a good chance to reach the British lines. Private Briggs was a good driver and if he could make good time on empty roads then he might beat the storm to Verviers. The dawn was not far away. He had a good chance of reaching friendly troops in a couple of hours. The road between Malmedy and Verviers had had few houses and no soldiers at all. It all depended on the German paratroopers. They were the unknown factor. They could have dropped anywhere. I wondered what had happened to the American Lieutenant. I hoped he had not found them.

"Right lads. Which way to the motor pool?"

Hewitt pointed to the far side of the town. "Down there, sir. We passed it on our way to the party."

The Motor Pool had an office which was sheltered from the snow. Inside was a scene of high activity. There was just as much confusion in the motor pool as in the rest of St. Vith. Luckily the Master Sergeant remembered me from my talk and he grinned, "Good talk yesterday, sir. I enjoyed it. What can I do for you today?"

I handed him the chit. "A jeep please."

He did not question it. He had his paperwork and, at the end of the day, the columns would all add up. "Coming right up. Anything special in mind, sir?"

"Pardon?"

"They all have plenty of gas but we have a couple with Brownings. I could let you have one of them."

"That is perfect, Master Sergeant." As he went off to find one I said, "I will drive. You two need to sober up."

"Where are we off to then, sir?"

"We have to go to the east. That is where the firing is. There may be paratroopers but they will be well to the north. We have to find Jerry."

"And then?"

28

"That's as far as this plan goes. This little shindig means I can't see us being home for Christmas. Someone has to pay and it might as well be Jerry!"

A snow-covered Master Sergeant returned. He brushed it off with his hand. "That is a lot of snow sir." He suddenly frowned. "Are you going Fritz side?"

I nodded, "At the moment, Master Sergeant, we are operating in the dark. We need to work out who is attacking and where. I daresay that they will get aeroplanes up as soon as they can but that will not be this morning. Every piece of information will help. So, to answer your question we may well be going close to the German lines."

He nodded, "There is a map in the jeep and a radio, sir, but I hear they are jamming transmissions."

"They might be but eventually they will have to stop or they won't be able to transmit themselves. We will just find their frequency and listen in."

He grinned, "And you speak German!"

I held out my hand and shook the American's, "Thank you Master Sergeant. It has been a pleasure."

"And you sir. I can go home and tell the folks that I met a real English gentleman!"

I headed east on the road to the River Our. There were only a few bridges over the Our. If the Americans still held them then there was a chance that this offensive, if that is what it was, could be nipped in the bud. The bombardment was still going on but I knew that the Germans would have to stop soon. They were limited these days with how much ammunition they could expend. Added to that they had to stop to allow their infantry and tanks to attack. The trouble was the Germans had good mobile artillery. Their tracked guns would be with their armour.

"Gordy see if you can work that Browning. Hewitt, have a fiddle on with the radio."

"We need Scouse Fletcher sir. He would know what to do."

"Just do your best, John." The Germans would have a timetable. They would have set certain things in place and that was how they would be able to jam transmissions. Their men would be under orders to reach their objectives by precise times. Their radios would be used when the strength and depth of the opposition was evaluated by the commanders on the ground. The Germans had good leaders. They trusted them to follow orders and keep to a tight schedule.

The driving conditions were awful. We slid and slithered along the road. The Jeep was a skittish little vehicle at the best of times. We had discovered that driving to Antwerp. The snow exacerbated the problem. Ahead of me I saw the sky becoming lighter. As it did the bombardment gradually stopped. The snow laden skies promised that the day would not get much brighter than that grey and gloomy dawn. More snow was on the way. We were approaching Schoenberg, the first village at the Our, when I heard the sound of firing. A half dozen Americans suddenly burst from cover. I jammed on the brakes and we skidded to a slippery halt. I saw that none of them wore their greatcoats and only two had weapons. These were not fighting men. These were probably those who serviced the regiments based there.

A Corporal, who had a carbine in his hand, saluted, "You had better stop, sir. It looks like Fritz is going to take Schoenberg. Tanks, armoured cars and infantry are there right now! Our officer was killed when German soldiers burst into our billet. We bugged out through the back window. Can we have a ride back to St. Vith?"

"No, Corporal. I need to find out the situation further up the river. Head back to St. Vith. It is only a couple of miles across the fields and there are no Germans there yet. You should be able to go directly across the fields. Tell Colonel Harding what you told me. You should be alright. Just keep moving."

One of the others shivered, "Sir, we'll freeze to death."

"Not if you run." I had little sympathy for them. They had panicked. I wondered how many others, woken from a comfortable sleep, would have panicked? It was all in the mind. These soldiers had been preparing to enjoy Christmas. They were not prepared to fight Germans.

I looked down at the map. The next crossing was at Andler, just a couple of miles north of Schoenberg. "Gordy, keep your eyes peeled. If this crossing is in German hands too we will have to turn back."

"Sir, I have something!" Hewitt listened and then said, "The Germans are attacking along a large front but no one seems to know in what strength, sir." Then he shook his head. "Sorry sir, they are jamming it again."

"That is something anyway."

I slowed down the jeep to little more than a crawl. I had to keep us moving for if we stopped then we would struggle to move again on the slippery road surface. I saw the bridge ahead and saw, to my great relief, American uniforms.

A lieutenant stopped us in the middle of the village. I saw half-tracks and a Sherman. He looked at me quizzically. "Are the British here, sir?"

I smiled, "No, Lieutenant, just a reconnaissance from St. Vith." I pointed south. "Who are you guys?"

"18th Cavalry sir."

"You need to tell your commanding officer that Schoenberg is in German hands."

He looked south. He knew what that meant. "Shit. Sorry sir! The major is on the road to Wecheran."

I looked at the map, "That is north west of here. I will head to Auw. How many men have you here?"

"Twenty sir and the Sherman."

"I would recommend you be ready to bug out if German armour comes. You should try to keep the bridge open. Your comrades up the road may need a way out."

"Sir, the 106th Division is up there. There are thousands of men."

"And they are like you, Lieutenant. They are getting ready for Christmas. You can't do much with one Sherman against Panthers and Tigers. Just try to slow them down. The troops over the Our will need time to prepare. The Germans have caught us napping this time."

"You are right there, sir!"

The tiny village of Auw was just a couple of miles away and, when we reached it, I saw that the bombardment had obliterated it. The telephone lines had been wrecked which explained why no one had had any information. There had been a small unit there but all that we could do was cover the eight bodies we found. The houses were burned out. If there had been any civilians here then they had either fled or were dead. We found signs that troops had crossed the road. I took heart from the fact that they were footprints and not tank tracks. I could not work out if they were American or German. They were too muddled. What I knew was there were soldiers between us and St. Vith.

"Any radio transmissions, Hewitt?"

"We have lost the signal again, sir."

"Can't be helped, Hewitt. Make a note of the frequency you picked it up on and try again later."

"Where to now then, sir?"

The nearest unit was the 14th Cavalry at Kobscheid. I took the road south. This was virgin snow and I took that as a good sign. It meant that Jerry had not been down it. Up ahead I heard firing. It sounded like it was to the east of us. We slewed and slithered down the road until we came to the turn off for Kobscheid. Once again it was virgin snow.

As we approached the village I saw barbed wire. A sergeant held up his hand, "Where are you going, sir?"

"Reconnaissance from St. Vith. Where is your commanding officer?"

He seemed relieved, "Colonel Devine is at the Command Post in the centre, sir. Do you know what is going on?"

"The Germans have landed paratroopers and they are attacking on a wide front." I pointed west. "They have taken Schoenberg. There is just the crossing at Andler. They have already cut you off."

"Lift the wire out of the way, boys. Looks like you are stuck with us now, sir."

The going was easier in the village. The armoured cars of the cavalry had turned it into a slush. I jumped out of the jeep and headed into the Command Post. "Gordy, you can drive. If they ask you to, then move the jeep. Do as they say. These guys look like they know what they are doing."

"Sir."

As I entered the cosily warm house, Colonel Devine looked at me and saw the Commando flash and my crown. "What the hell are the Brits doing here, Major?" I took in the officer I would get to know well over the next few days. Jack Devine was a squat and tough looking soldier. With closely cropped hair and grizzled features he was the antithesis of Colonel Harding. This was a soldier. He looked like a bulldog. If he got his teeth into something then it would be hard to shake him. The defences he had thrown around his command showed that.

"In the wrong place at the wrong time I think, Colonel. We have driven from St. Vith. Schoenberg may well be in German hands. You are cut off."

The handful of officers suddenly found the map the most interesting thing in the room. Fingers pointed to the river crossing, highlighting their precarious position.

Colonel Devine just nodded, "That confirms what I thought. They started shelling before dawn. We heard firing further east. It sounded like tanks, big tanks. I heard 88s. That means Tiger tanks or mobile artillery. I sent a runner down to Schoenberg a couple of hours ago. I wondered why he had not returned." He banged the radio, "And this is about as much use as a one-legged man in an ass kicking contest. The Germans are jamming it!"

I pointed outside, "I have a radio sir, and my chap managed to pick something up a while ago."

"Kowalski, go and find out the frequency." He held out his hand, "Colonel Devine."

"Major Harsker. What is your plan, sir?"

"We have eight M8 armoured cars and a dozen machine guns. We have put barbed wire all the way around the perimeter. If Fritz wants this crossroads that badly they will have to eject us first."

"I saw no sign of armour on the way here but I think the Panzer Grenadiers have been going cross country. I saw signs of boot tracks. It seems obvious to me now that they are racing ahead of the armour to secure key bridges and crossroads. It is classic German strategy."

"That makes sense. Well Major, I guess you are with us now. What do you have?"

"Two men and a jeep. It has a Browning on it. And we have our own equipment: Thompsons, Colts, grenades and a sniper rifle."

He laughed, "You come packing eh, Major? Have your jeep parked up by the road. We have dug in the M8s. They have piss poor armour but the cannon on them can discourage the enemy. We are light cavalry and we are supposed to scout." He rubbed his unshaven chin and his eyes widened. "I think I will have a drive down the road and see what we can see. I hate waiting here not knowing who is coming down the road. We are scouts, let's scout. These armoured cars are nippy. If the German armour is coming down the road, then we can use the forest and see what we are likely to receive. Would you care to come with me Major? My vehicle is not dug in."

"Delighted sir."

"Jones, you stay here. Major Harsker can come in your place."

"Yes sir!"

I clambered inside the M8. "Move over Corporal Powers. Major Harsker will act as loader."

The Corporal grinned, "This will be real interesting for you sir! Welcome to our little coffin!"

"Powers!"

"Sorry sir!"

It was a good job that I was not claustrophobic. It was cosy to say the least. I could see little out of the driver's visor. Colonel Devine was half out of his turret with his field glasses. His knees were level with my head. The driver was just in front of me and Corporal Powers was next to the breech block of the 37 mm cannon. The snow was still falling and flakes fell into the tank. The driver was peering through his visor. "Right Mason, time to head into the trees. Keep the revs low. The Krauts use Panzer Grenadiers. We don't want them to hear us."

"Right sir."

One advantage of the M8 Greyhound was the quiet engine. They were known by the Americans as Patton's ghosts for the Germans rarely detected them. I was grateful for their quiet motors. We drove for another ten minutes. I could see very little. The bumpy ground meant I had to hang on to stop myself being banged into the sides. There appeared to be many objects which could cause an injury. I was grateful for the slow speed. If it was any faster then, I would be in trouble.

Suddenly Colonel Devine banged on the hatch, "Stop! Turn off the engine. Powers, do we have a shell in the breech?"

"Yes sir, armour piercing."

"Well, have the Major have another shell ready. I can hear German tanks and they sound to be big ones. Mason when I give the word get us out of here as fast as you can. I just want to see what sort of force we are facing."

"Yes sir."

He leaned down to speak to me, "We need to know what kind of armour we are up against. We are hidden behind a couple of trees. I am hoping, with the snow, that they will not see us. The armour on these babies is there to stop bullets not tank shells. If it is any consolation one hit from a tank shell will send us to our maker. You won't know a thing."

"That is good to know, sir. Thank you for the heads up." He nodded and lifted his head out of the turret once more.

Corporal Powers chuckled, "The British stiff upper lip, I love it, sir. The shells are over there. I would get another ready." He tapped the breech. "This little beauty is quick firing. It only has a small shell but you can still do some damage."

"To a Panzer?"

"All tanks are the same, sir. They don't like it up the ass!" He laughed, lewdly.

I took the shell and cradled it like a baby. At just over three pounds it seemed too light to do much damage. The waiting was awful. I could not be a tank man. The Colonel leaned down and said, "I see their tanks. There are Tigers. They look bigger than normal."

"I heard about these, sir. They are King Tigers. They have five inches of armour on their front. They weigh 70 tons. They are all brand new!"

"I will wait until the first one passes and see if we can get him at the back. No tank has thick armour at the rear. That road is narrow and the trees are too thick for them to negotiate these woods. If we damage one, then the road will be blocked and it will buy us time. Powers I want a shell putting in the middle of the rear."

"Yes sir! If the major is fast enough we might put a couple there, eh sir?"

I could now feel the vibration from the huge tanks as they trundled down the snow-covered road. It seemed impossible that it would not see us and

34

then I remembered that we were hidden in the trees. The Colonel had chosen a spot where the road twisted. The Germans would approach us obliquely. I caught a glimpse of the behemoth as it passed us. It was sixty feet from us. It was truly enormous. It dwarfed us but it would have dwarfed a Sherman too. The noise was painful. I realised that we might escape detection.

"You got him in your sights, Powers?"

"Yes sir."

"Ready Mason?"

"Yes sir!"

"Fire!"

The gun recoiled and the breech came back discarding the shell casing which clattered to the floor of the tank. Smoke filled the turret and Corporal Powers held his hands out for the next shell. I handed it to him like a scrum half with a rugby ball. "Get another one, sir!"

"Fire!"

The second shell followed the first and I handed the third shell to the Corporal. I had no idea what was happening. Automatically I turned to get a fourth. This was not my kind of war. It was obvious that we were still hidden for there was no return fire.

"Fire!"

There was an enormous explosion this time which rocked the M8. "Got the bastard! Get the hell out of here, Mason." The Colonel ducked back inside and closed the hatch above him. I replaced the shell in the rack.

The armoured car raced backwards. I cracked my head off the side. I had to brace myself with my hands. I heard the roar of an 88 and then machine guns. There was a crack as a shell hit a tree. Mason drove at high speed in reverse and then suddenly stopped and we raced forward. My head cracked off the turret. Corporal Powers tapped his tanker's helmet. grinned. "Now you see why we wear helmets, sir!"

"What happened, sir?" I was desperate to know how we had managed to hit one of these Leviathans. Was it destroyed?

"It took three shells but we got inside his armour. The turret blew off. The road will be blocked for a while. They can't get through the trees. We have bought us some time. I am just not certain how we stop them from the front. We were lucky. But at least the road is blocked, for a while at least. You were right major. The tanks are loaded with Panzer Grenadiers. I think they are S.S." We bounced through the trees as Mason drove like a maniac to escape the Germans. As the Colonel had said the huge tank had blocked the road but, eventually, they would clear it. They would follow and then we would be for it.

Once we were back at the base Colonel Devine had his men dig in the armoured cars as much as possible. Anything which could be used was packed in front of them. Some of the lucky ones were behind low walls with just their gun sticking up. "Sergeant Major we have Tiger tanks and Panzer Grenadiers coming down the road. Use anything you can as a barricade. Let's see if we can slow them down!"

"Yes sir. You guys heard the Colonel, move it!"

He waved me to the Command Post. As we entered he pointed to the Corporal on the radio, "Get on the radio and see if you can contact Headquarters. If you can get through, then tell them there are German tanks and infantry heading for St. Vith. They are in numbers and they may well be S.S. We will hold them as long as we can." His officers gathered around. They looked at us expectantly. They would have heard us firing and the resultant explosion but nothing else.

"Gentlemen, we have a new variant on the Tiger coming our way. According to the major here it is called a King Tiger. We will be outgunned and outmatched. They will drive us from here. We hold them as long as we can. I don't think, for one minute, that we can stop them but we need to slow them down and allow the men in St. Vith to prepare a reception committee. Thanks to the Major here they have some warning. We will have to sacrifice our armoured cars. We keep them dug in and we fight for every inch of real estate. Tell the men that we die hard! If we can hold out for the day we will use darkness to slip down the road."

Just then a private raced in, "Sir, Lieutenant Harrison told me to tell you, German armour is coming down the road, sir."

"Right Major, let's see if we can upset Adolf's little plan, eh?"

I was shocked by the cold as we left the cosy warmth of the command post. The snow had not stopped and the temperature had fallen even further. This weather came from the Arctic Circle! I grabbed my Mauser and Thompson. "Gordy, drive up to the edge of the village. We are back in the war."

"Right sir. Hewitt told the Yank about the frequency. We have had no signals since then."

Just then there was the sound of the 37 mm on the M8 armoured cars as they fired at the advancing Germans. "Come on Gordy! Move it!"

The infantry were dug in behind sandbags, walls and pieces of timber hewn from the forest. We had a fortress. Would it stand up to a battering by 88 mm guns? I pointed to a gap to the left of the line between an M8 and a machine gun. As Gordy turned to head to it a shell exploded in the line. The machine gun post was riddled with shrapnel and shell fragments.

We pulled in just behind where it had been. The shell had killed them all and destroyed the machine gun. We filled the gap.

"You two use the sandbags from the machine gun post and put them around the jeep."

I looked up and saw one of the young crew of the M8. He was staring down at the remains of the crew. He was being sick. I took the Mauser and hurried towards the wire. I saw the flash from the German armoured cars. They had not sent tanks yet. These were the scouts, probing for weaknesses. I saw Panzer Grenadiers moving through the snow. They were wearing white. The Germans used a camouflage cape and white breeches. They would be hard to see. I lay down in the snow and rested the Mauser on the barbed wire. When I looked through the telescopic sight I could make out faces. I moved the rifle along until I saw an officer. His pistol marked him as such as did his hand which pointed towards us. I squeezed the trigger and he fell back; his face like a burst ripe plum. I moved down the line of camouflaged grenadiers and fired at a sergeant. I hit him in the chest and he pitched backwards. The Americans had now seen the enemy and the machine guns made them keep their heads down. The M8 had a .30 Calibre and a .50 Calibre machine gun as well as the 37 mm main gun and every one of them was firing. There was a cacophony of death as every armoured car tried to stop the white robed figures. Although the snow was of blizzard proportions the red blood from their wounds showed that we were hitting them badly. The Germans hit the ground and took cover.

The German Armoured cars had a 50 mm cannon and they were more heavily armoured than the M8. I heard Colonel Devine as he shouted, "We are the US cavalry! Let's show these Krauts that we can kick their butts!"

The armoured cars switched their targets to the German armoured cars. I saw one German armoured car, less than 50 yards away, hit by a PIAT rocket. The men who fired it cheered. German shells began to fall on the village from the artillery which was supporting the scouting armoured cars. There was a sudden explosion behind us, in the centre. A wall of flame leapt into the air.

Someone shouted, "Colonel, that is the fuel dump! We have no spare gas now!"

"Just keep firing Captain, we will worry about that later on."

The Americans had the advantage at the moment for the armoured cars made smaller targets than the Germans. The M8 armoured cars were dug in and only their turrets were visible. The Germans were in the open. With one inch of armour at the front it would take a good shot to damage an M8 turret. I saw that the German armoured cars had tyres. I emptied my magazine at the front two tyres of the nearest one. They blew out as did one of the rear ones. It slewed around and the PIAT hit that one at the side. There they were very vulnerable.

"That's it boys. We are hitting them harder than they are hitting us!"

The Colonel was tempting providence for the armoured car just behind me was suddenly hit by two shells in rapid succession. One came from German mobile heavy artillery and the other was a 50 mm shell. It exploded and the concussion washed over me. I found it hard to breathe. I could hear nothing. I loaded another magazine and forced myself to find another target. I saw an officer towards the rear of the advancing Germans. He was about five hundred yards away and he stood out of the turret of the armoured car and was scanning the village with binoculars. He was not wearing white and he was the best target I had seen yet. As my hearing began to return I concentrated on the target. I aimed at his chest. The Mauser had a tendency to fire high. I squeezed the trigger twice. He slumped over the turret.

My shot attracted the attention of the infantry who were just a hundred and fifty yards from me. The air above my head was filled with flying lead. Gordy's Browning ripped back in reply and Hewitt shouted, "Sir, get back here. We have sandbags for protection not just barbed wire!"

They were right and I slithered backwards towards them. My foot struck the sandbag and I rolled around to scramble inside the safety of the machine gun emplacement.

Gordy shook his head as he reloaded the Browning. "Sir, what would your mother think?"

I laid down my Mauser and, like Hewitt, picked up my Thompson. I peered over the top of the sandbags. The machine guns had ensured that the infantry kept their heads down. The two sets of armoured cars were duelling. The Americans were getting the worst of it. They could handle the German armoured cars but not the plunging fire from artillery which found their thinly armoured tops. Their M8, nicknamed Greyhound by the British, were fast but they were thinly armoured and did not have the firepower of the Germans. Their only advantage in this situation was the other two machine guns. The German infantry were kept pinned down.

To my relief, at about 1100 hours, American shells from the west started to pepper the enemy. They were firing towards the rear of the German lines as they did not want to hit us. That suited us for it was their artillery which was the danger. I sent a short burst from the Tommy gun every time I saw a German head appear. I was acutely aware that ammunition might soon be in short supply. The barrage only lasted for thirty minutes but it drove the Germans back for a short time.

"Sir, the Colonel wants to speak with you."

"Right. Keep watch, Gordy. There is an enormous hole here. If anything happens to this Browning then we are in trouble." I nodded to Hewitt. "See if you can get any .45 ammo from the wrecked M8."

"Right sir." It would be a grisly job but Hewitt was our unit medic. He could handle it better than most.

When I reached the Colonel, I saw that he had gathered his other officers. There were just eight of them left. I was the last to arrive. "Thanks for your help today, Major. That rifle and your Browning sure made a difference. I shall be sorry to see you go."

"Go, sir?"

"Yes, we have made radio contact. We are totally isolated. HQ wants us to break out tonight. They want you back now."

I shook my head, "Sorry sir. That isn't going to happen. First of all, we have more chance of escaping if we are with you and secondly we have never run out on our comrades before and we aren't going to start now." He nodded. "Besides this is our sort of fighting. We know how to booby trap and make it hard for someone to follow. And we have other things we can do to slow them down."

Captain Jablonski asked, "Such as?"

"Sneak out before dark, at dusk, while we are preparing to leave. We can put booby traps further out and make them think that we are attacking." I took out my Colt and my silencer. "We have these. We will need to buy time to get out. If you could send someone to relieve us at 1700 hours it should be dark enough to get through the wire and do some damage to them."

"Lieutenant, see to it."

"Sir."

The Colonel pointed to the map. "We are going to be heading for Andler. They are going to make a defensive line between there and Manderfeld. We have to buy time until General Hodge can get reinforcements up to the line. We leave at 1830 hours. I will send up a flare every fifteen minutes from 1730. It should stop them getting too inquisitive. We were lucky in hitting their lead tank. It will take them some time to clear the road but they will manage to do so. I think we can expect tanks after dark. Any questions?"

"Sir," I ventured, "what about food? In my experience a man who has eaten is more alert and better suited to fighting than a hungry man. If we have to cross the snow at night, the men will use a lot of energy. Besides the alternative is to leave it for Jerry. I reckon we will all be laden down with ammo."

The Colonel said, "Captain Jablonski, see to it and Major?"

"Yes sir?"

"How do we make booby traps?"

"If we have explosives and timers…" He shook his head. "Then we use the grenades. Just disabling the armoured cars by taking out the carburettor will work and then setting fire to their petrol tanks."

"Their what?"

I smiled, "I believe, Lieutenant, that you call them gas tanks."

"That is a start. Sergeant Major O'Rourke get as many hand grenades as it takes. The Major and his men will show you how to rig them."

"Right sir."

I reached Gordy who had just reloaded his Browning. "We are leaving tonight at seven. First we need to rig booby traps."

Gordy pointed to the Germans. "Not yet sir, we still need to slow them down. They are getting quite close."

Hewitt said, "Sir, the M8 is destroyed but the 50 calibre is still operational and it has ammunition."

"Right, let's add that firepower and give the Germans a painful surprise."

We clambered through the hole the explosion had made. The twisted metal and broken hatch hid us from the Germans. The crew all lay dead. We could do nothing for them now. Hewitt loaded the heavy machine gun and I peered along its sight. The Germans were, again, creeping forward. Gordy was firing short bursts. The other guns on either side of us were also firing but the Germans were camouflaged in white and were hard to see. I saw a German armoured car begin to edge down the road. The M8s which had been there were now destroyed but there was another, two hundred yards to the right of our position and it was still firing. The Germans thought that we were all damaged and he made the cardinal error of presenting his side to us. On the front it was almost two inches of steel. On the sides less than half an inch. The .50 calibre had the chance to punch through it.

I waited until it was just a hundred and fifty yards away and then I opened fire. I fired just above the tyres. I had a bigger target that way. The barrel of the 50 mm cannon began to swing towards us. It was faster than a tank turret. I kept firing. If it fired at us and hit us then we were dead. I would fire all the ammunition we had. Luck was on our side. When the barrel was half way around the whole vehicle exploded as a shell from another M8 struck the ammunition. It was spectacular. Pieces of metal showered down on us. I had used the last of the ammunition and so we clambered out. I opened the petrol tank. It still had petrol in it.

"John, disable the .50 calibre. I am going to make a fuse for the petrol tank."

Sergeant Major O'Rourke arrived with two men and a box of grenades. "Here are the grenades, sir, what do we do with them?"

The Mark 2 was similar to the Mills bomb. I took one out of the box. "The simplest way is to tie a piece of parachute cord to the pin and jam the grenade so that the handle is held against another object. You put it at ankle height so that someone walks into it, pulls the pin, the handle flies off and five seconds later, boom! Put them on door handles and they work even better. You can use anything which is solid to attach them to. This grenade box is a good example. When they open it to see if we left any then goodbye Fritz."

"Parachute cord, sir?"

"It is what we use but baling wire, string, anything." I picked up Hewitt's Bergen and took out his parachute cord. "Here you are, Sergeant Major."

He grinned, "I like the way you think, sir. You are sneaky! Right you guys let's go make some booby traps."

"One more thing Sergeant Major, make sure you tell your men where they are. We don't want our chaps setting them off, eh?"

He tapped his nose, "Smart sir."

I had just finished rigging a cloth fuse to the petrol tank when two cooks came with hot food. They were moving like crabs, half crouched. Gordy had long since finished the ammunition for the Browning and he was now firing his Thompson.

"Gordy you and John get some food. Put some in my dixie and I will take over."

"Right sir. They are getting closer all the time."

I crept to the sandbags and peered over. He was right. They were just a hundred yards away. Even as I ducked down bullets smacked into the sandbags. I moved a foot to the right, popped my head up and fire a short burst from my Thompson in the direction of the Germans. I ducked down again and took out my Luger. The range was close enough now. I popped my head up just in time to see a coal scuttle helmet rise up behind a rifle. I whipped out the pistol and fired two bullets. There was a cry and the head disappeared. I doubted that I had killed anyone but it would make them wary of moving forward. I glanced at my watch. It was four o'clock. It would soon be getting dark.

"When you have done that disable the jeep and radio. Rig that to burn too."

Hewitt handed me my dixie and I ate between popping my head up and firing random shots at the Germans. They would now wait for dark. With their white camouflage capes, they would be invisible against the snow-covered fields. Hewitt and Barker joined me.

"In an hour we are going out there." They were not surprised and they just nodded. "We take our silenced Colts. I want to take out as many Panzer Grenadiers as we can. We have just thirty minutes to cause as much confusion as we can. If we can get a couple of white camouflage capes then so much the better. Check the bodies to see if we can identify their unit. I want to know if they are S.S. The Colonel said he thought they were. You can't tell with the white capes."

A corporal and two privates arrived, "Your relief, sir."

"We have booby trapped the M8 and jeep. We should be back in an hour. I'll say 'Yankee' and the response will be 'Doodle'."

"Right sir."

I took off my greatcoat and smeared some of the soot from the burned vehicle on the backs of my hands and my face. I took out my Colt and fitted the silencer. The other two did the same. Finally, I took out my home-made wire cutters.

The corporal looked at me and said, "Are you going out there, sir?"

Gordy nodded, "Put the wind up Jerry eh, Corporal?"

It was dark and the first of the flares was launched. The corporal and his two men opened fire. I waved my hand and the three of us crept towards the wire. We cut a hole big enough for one man and moved it to the side. We had thirteen minutes before the next flare.

I scrambled through. The snow helped for it had built up during the day into a wall three feet high. I had my Colt out and I moved over the snow. I ignored the shock of the cold as my hand touched it. The icy weather was turning the top to solid crust. I kept my hand forward. It was the best way to detect danger. The other two would flank me but I would be the first to fire. I knew we had a hundred yards before we found a German. I was not certain if they would be alive or dead.

I saw one. He was just twenty feet from me. I raised my gun to shoot and then saw the bullet hole where his right eye should have been. He was dead. I crept closer. His body was still warm. The corporal or one of his men must have shot him. I risked taking his white camouflage cape from him. There was no blood on it. I had it half way off, it was just around his shoulders when there was a movement ahead of me. I saw two Germans crawling towards our lines. They were thirty feet from me and heading for the damaged M8. They had not seen me because of the body. I slowly raised the Colt. One was ahead of the other. I squeezed the trigger. There was a phut and the second German slumped. His companion turned and saw me. I fired a second bullet. It went between his eyes. I had just taken the camouflage cape off the dead German when the second flare illuminated the night sky. I pressed my face into the snow.

It seemed an age before it was dark. By keeping my face pressed into the ground I had preserved my night vision. I donned the camouflage cape and then took the four grenades the German was carrying. Stuffing them in my battle dress, I crept forward. I was now the invisible one; at least from the waist up. I heard a soft cry from my left. That was one of my men. I heard Germans as they voiced their concerns. An officer or sergeant told them to stop being women and remain silent. Their numbers meant I could not use my silenced gun. There were too many.

I crept closer. I would soon have to turn around. I knew that there would be another flare soon and I readied a grenade. I pulled the pin. I could hear the Germans. They were thirty yards from me. One of them said, "If the Amis send up another flare now then we will know their plan."

The Colonel's flare soared into the sky. I kept my face down. As soon as it was dark again I stood and hurled my grenade. I turned and ran.

"There, someone moving!"

The white camouflage cape saved me. They did not know if I was one of their own running. The slight delay took me half way back to the wire and then the grenade went off. The night was filled with screams. The concussion washed over me. Tiny splinters of deadly shrapnel filled the air like mosquitos. I crawled through the snow. I moved along the wire until I found the gap and slipped through.

"Yankee!"

"Doodle!"

Five faces greeted me. Barker and Hewitt had returned before me. I saw that they had Germans white camouflage capes too. "I take it the grenade was you, sir."

"Yes, Sergeant." I looked at my watch. "And now we had better get ready to fire these vehicles. When the next flare goes off it will be time to run."

Just then I heard, in the distance, the sound of tanks. The ground vibrated. It was the King Tiger column. They had cleared the road. We had run out of time. The Panzers were here!

Chapter 4

I saw the flare and flash as the Colonel set fire to an M8. I put my Bergen on my back. I had already attached my rifle to its straps and I held my Tommy gun. "Right Gordy."

Gordy had his petrol lighter and he lit one end of the fuel-soaked cotton waste hanging from the petrol tank of the jeep. Hewitt and I ran as Gordy did the same to the M8. There was a crack from the direction of the German lines as the leading tank open fired. It was a Panzer Mark IV and not a Tiger or a Panther. It was still deadly but at least you could stop a Mark IV. Behind me there was a whoosh as the Jeep exploded in a fiery fireball. Sergeant Ford might be in trouble with Colonel Harding; if he still lived. All along the edge of the defences vehicles exploded. There was still some ammunition in some of the armoured cars and they began to send rounds into the air.

I saw the Colonel waiting for us, "Good job, Major. Now let's get the hell out of here!"

We had twelve miles to go across country, at night and on foot. The Germans would soon follow. Our booby traps would not delay them long. In fact, if they sent their tanks through first, then the hand grenades would not suffer much damage at all. Our grenades could not hurt a tank. As we passed the headquarters I saw the bodies of the dead cavalrymen covered in their greatcoats. The Americans had lost men and they would be angry that they couldn't bury them. We were running for we were on the road. Once we hit virgin snow the going would be even slower. The slush and wet snow would not slow us down much.

The three of us found ourselves at the back. Sergeant Major O'Rourke was with us. We had just struck the road, which ran east, when we heard the first of the grenades explode behind us. There was a ripple of explosions as others were tripped. The Sergeant Major laughed as he ran alongside me, "I sure would like to see the look on the faces of those Krauts."

"They will be more than annoyed, Sergeant Major."

"Good! I hated destroying our vehicles. We are cavalry sir! We are not infantry! No offence!"

"None taken. My dad was in the cavalry in the Great War."

"You mean he rode horses into battle?"

"He did."

"Damn! I would like to have seen that."

Just then there was a crack behind us followed almost immediately by a shell striking the field to our left. If it had not been for the wall we might have been hit by flying splinters but the snow and the wall saved us. The German armoured cars and Mark IV tanks were firing at us.

"I think we had better hurry up, Sergeant Major."

The huge American shouted to the men ahead of us, "You guys, get the lead out!"

I had been through this before and in almost the same place. When we had retreated in 1940 there had been German tanks behind us. The difference then was the Stukas which dive bombed us. At least we were spared the screaming dive bombers. This was slightly easier. And I had learned a great deal in the intervening years.

When we reached Auw the Colonel ordered a rest. The men did look tired and were out of breath. As the Sergeant Major had said, they were cavalry and not infantry. I thought it was a mistake but he was in command. I went back down the road to look for the enemy. The tanks we would hear but the Panzer Grenadiers would be invisible with their camouflaged tops. Three hundred yards from the village I knelt and listened. I could hear the tank. It appeared to be in the distance, at least a mile away. They must have struggled to get through our booby traps and burning armoured cars. There was a glow from the burning village but I could hear something else. I struggled to make sense of it and then I realised what it was. It was the sound of feet stepping through the crust of ice on top of snow. They were coming through the woods to the left and right of me. I took out a grenade. Peering into the woods I saw nothing. I was glad that I had a camouflage cape on too for I would be just as hard to see as the Germans coming towards us. If anything, I would be harder for I was not moving.

It was the movement which caught my eye. The German I saw had a camouflage cape on but his face was visible against it. When he moved I saw it. He was forty feet from me. Once I had seen him I saw the rest of his section. There were six of them. I pulled the pin and threw the grenade high into the air. I ducked down behind the wall. The grenade and shrapnel scythed through the trees and the men. The explosion lit up the night and I saw others further back. They were taking cover. I sprayed my Tommy gun and was rewarded by a cry. I turned and ran.

Hewitt and Barker were waiting for me. I waved them north. "Panzer Grenadiers! Run. They are just a couple of hundred yards away."

45

Hewitt and Barker both fired a burst and then we ran. The rest had almost cost us. I had just turned the corner when the building behind me was hit by a 75 mm shell. The tanks were closer than I had thought. We had to reach Andler as soon as possible. There would be anti-tank guns there as well as armour. I did not think we could stop the Germans, that would have to be at St. Vith but we could buy time for us to make the stronghold. I hoped that General Jones had ringed the town with tanks and wire. I knew why the armour had caught us. The German tanks had simply trundled down the empty road. Our feet had compacted it making a better surface for their tracks Their machine guns spat out as they advanced. They were firing blindly but they had a long range and I saw two of the cavalrymen fall with bullet holes in their backs.

We needed to do something. There were trees to our left and right. I knew, from our journey down, that we did not have far to run to get to Andler but the Germans would catch the Americans. We were the three back markers now. "In here!"

Barker and Hewitt followed me blindly as I plunged into the woods on the left. I knew that we could reach the river through the trees and make our escape that way but first I wanted to slow down the pursuit. I headed directly in and then turned to head back south. After ten yards I stopped by a large tree and took out my silenced Colt. The other two did the same. With our white camouflage capes we were able to hide. As I had expected four Panzer Grenadiers followed us into the wood. They looked down, trying to follow our tracks. My little loop meant that they were to the north of us. I knelt and took aim at the last in the line. My gun bucked and he fell. As he did the others turned. Five bullets later and all of them were dead. They had assumed we would head to Andler and not double back. That was the peril of fighting Commandos. They did the unexpected.

We ran to them and I grabbed one of the field caps. I jammed it on my head and headed back to the road. Barker and Hewitt each took a hat and followed me. I saw that the Germans were leaving the road for the tanks. There were three of them. It was a narrow road with trees close by. If we could stop the first tank then the pursuit would be halted, at least temporarily. We hurried up the side of the trees. I said quietly, "Stay in the trees and cover me. After we have slowed them down we head for the river."

They moved deeper into the woods. I stayed by the edge. I would not be noticed as other Panzer Grenadiers were in the woods too, taking advantage of their cover. I stayed as close to the road as I could. The tank fired its main gun again and I saw the officer with his body half out of the turret. He had binoculars. I took out a hand grenade and pulled the pin.

This would take timing. The driver on the Mark IV peered out through a visor. I intended to shoot through the visor and at the commander. Then I would disable the tank. The Mark IV makes a great deal of noise. Keeping the grenade in my left hand I hurried forward and when I saw the commander was still looking ahead I fired at him with the Colt. I guessed that the driver and commander of the next tank would see me but the noise would mean they could not raise the alarm. As the commander fell I aimed at the visor and fired four shots, blindly into it. Then I put the grenade between the driving sprocket and the track and ran as fast as I could into the safety of the snow-covered forest. I hurtled after my two comrades whom I hoped were deeper into the forest. Bullets from the second tank zipped into the trees but it had a limited traverse.

When the grenade exploded all of the power was increased by the confined space of the track and the wheel. The main force of the explosion was born by the track and the body of the tank. The track was split. The damage was compounded by the driver. I must have hit or frightened him because the tank veered to the right and the track came away. It was then that all hell broke loose. Barker and Hewitt had prepared an ambush for the men they knew would be pursuing me and they sprayed the infantry with Thompsons. The tanks behind the damaged panzer fired where I had been. The bullets tore into the trees. I ran in a zig zag fashion with Barker and Hewitt behind me. Bullets hit the trees as the infantry raced to catch us. We were wearing white in a white world and we were moving quickly. Suddenly I heard the crump of a grenade behind us and the bullets ceased. I did not stop running. I heard Gordy shout, "Sir, for the love of God stop! They aren't behind us anymore!"

I saw him bent double, "Are you hit?"

"No, sir, just buggered!" between catching his breath he said, "Nice throw, John. That grenade stopped them in their tracks."

Hewitt nodded, "Well I couldn't let the Major be the only mad one around here!"

"It worked didn't it?"

"Yes sir but you were lucky that the tanks couldn't fire for fear of hitting their own men."

I reloaded my Colt and we headed down towards the river. We made sure, when we reached the river, that no one was following us. We could have risked fording the river but it seemed too dangerous. Ice cold water could kill just as quickly as a bullet and there was little point in taking the risk. We could make Andler by following the river. I jammed the field cap in my camouflage cape and donned my beret again. It would not do to be shot by our American allies. They would be nervous of camouflaged men wearing German field caps.

The snow by the river was untouched. Nothing had passed along it. The depth of the snow sapped energy from already tired legs. We took it in turns to lead. The second and third men had an easier time of it as they stepped in the footsteps of the pathfinder. Gordy nearly came a cropper when he was leading. He slipped and began to tumble down the bank. If he fell into the water his heavy Bergen and weapons would act as an anchor and drag him beneath the icy water. Hewitt's quick thinking and strong arms grabbed him just in time.

"My turn, Gordy. You get at the back."

"Sorry, sir."

I could hear firing to the right of us. We were a little closer to the road which was heading to Andler. I took out my Colt. Then I heard a noise that sent shivers down my spine. It was the heavy rumble of huge tanks. These were not Panzer Mark IVs these were Tigers or even the new Tigers which the Squadron Leader had told me about, King Tigers. I had last heard one from inside the M8 Greyhound. Now, with the vibrations beneath my feet and the throb of their engines close by they were even more of a threat. The crack from the right confirmed it. It was an 88 mm.

"Right, chaps. We run or we will be caught and the Jerries in those tanks are S.S.! That means a bullet in the back of the head at best."

My men needed no urging and we found new energy from somewhere. The small arms fire became more intense. As we neared the edge of the trees I could see the flashes from the muzzles of rifles and machine guns. This was the Falaise Gap all over again but this time the boot was on the other foot. The Americans were surrounded by German armour and we were having to flee for our lives. Even as we emerged I saw the last of the 14th Cavalry tumbling over the bridge. Sergeant Major O'Rourke was firing his carbine as fast as he could in the middle of the bridge. Suddenly a grenade exploded thirty yards in front of him and his two men. They were knocked to the ground. As the Panzer Grenadiers raced forward the three of us burst from the road, behind them. I emptied my gun into them. Barker and Hewitt turned and threw two grenades back towards the advancing tanks and Germans.

"Run!"

As the two grenades exploded and caused confusion amongst our pursuers, an 88 mm shell smashed into the house on the far side of the bridge. I saw, in the flash of the explosion, Colonel Devine marshalling his survivors from the bridge. As we reached the end I saw that the men with Sergeant Major O'Rourke were dead but the big man was alive, albeit unconscious.

"Pick him up and I will cover you."

As they took him under the arms and carried him over the bridge to the relative safety of Andler, I reloaded my Colt and, kneeling next to the stone abutment, squeezed off targeted shots at the advancing grenadiers. I made a small target but even so chips of stone flew from the bridge close to my head. When my gun was empty I took out a German grenade, armed it and threw it high into the air. It spiralled end over end. As I ran I hoped it would explode in the air. German tank commanders liked to fight with their bodies half out of their turrets.

"Come on Major! That is a Tiger on your ass!"

The grenade went off and pieces of metal whizzed over my head. I heard Colonel Devine as he urged me forward. I saw, coming towards me, the barrel of a Sherman as it headed towards the bridge. They were brave men but they were trying to swat an eagle! They were outmatched. I saw the flash from the muzzle when I was just twenty feet from it. I was deafened. Colonel Devine took my arm and pushed me down the road. I knew he was talking to me but I heard nothing. I just ran with him. My legs were bone weary.

The defenders of Andler had erected sandbags and barbed wire. They would not stop the Tigers. Colonel Devine led me through them. It was a labyrinth. They had bazookas, PIATs and 3 pounder anti-tank guns. They would slow the armour down; that was all. Then there was an explosion as the Sherman which had advanced to the bridge was hit by an 88. A column of fire raced up into the night sky. The exploding fuel tank made the Sherman a fireball. The crew would all be dead but they had, at least, blocked the bridge. It would slow down the Germans. That was the best we could hope for; slow them down. Exhausted and with little ammunition the Colonel's unit was not going to be of much use in Andler. We reached the other side of the village. Already American trucks and half-tracks were being loaded with the wounded.

A sergeant ran up to Colonel Devine, "Sir, Colonel Descheneaux, who is in command here, orders you and your Cavalry to get to St. Vith as soon as you can. He says to tell them that there are too many tanks here for us to hold on. He intends to pull out after dark. He will need help on the road."

"Thank you, Sergeant. Tell him good luck and we will pass the message on. Captain Stewart, get the men aboard the trucks." He looked around at Barker and Hewitt. John was tending to the Sergeant Major, "How is Sergeant Major O'Rourke?"

The big man used Hewitt's arm to pull himself to his feet, "I am fine sir. I guess I owe these guys one."

The Colonel said, "After what they did we owe them more than one. Get aboard the half-tracks. We are bugging out."

We were tightly packed in the M2 but that kept us warm, at least. We left the defenders of Andler with a dozen trucks to give some of them the chance to escape. As dawn broke we all strained our necks to look east at the battle which was taking place at the river crossing. It was a cacophony of noise. The American's 76 mm battled against the deadly 88 mm of the Germans. Carbines, rifles and machine guns underscored the louder crashes. Occasional crumps of grenades could be heard in the distance. The Germans would take the crossing eventually, that was inevitable, but hopefully they would pay a price.

"Don't worry sir, the 106th has over 7,000 men. They may be scattered but they will hold."

The Sergeant Major sounded confident but I was not too sure. I hoped he was right. I rested my head against the metal of the half-track and was soon asleep.

I was awoken by Gordy, "Here sir. Back in St. Vith."

As we clambered from the back of the half-track I saw that they were preparing its defence. The peaceful town we had left a couple of days earlier was now a hive of activity. Colonel Devine turned to me, "Come on Major, let's give our bad news to the General."

"I know where the Command Post is." I led him to the familiar building. "I am not certain that Colonel Harding will be pleased to see me." As we walked I told him of my acrimonious departure.

"I know the guy. He is all West Point and Number 1s. He is a Fancy Dan! Leave him to me, Major. You are one of us now and we look after our own in the cavalry."

As we entered Sergeant Ford looked up. He grinned, "Have you got my jeep, sir?"

"Sorry Sergeant Ford, Jerry blew it up!"

Colonel Devine said, "We have news from the front. It is vital we tell the General as soon as possible."

"You had better go in, sirs, General Clarke has just arrived."

We knocked and entered. As we did I heard General Jones say, "But we have no idea what is going on five miles up the road, Bruce, and your tanks are still spread out along the road."

Colonel Harding saw me and his eyes narrowed, "What do you want?" There was aggression in every syllable.

Colonel Devine bunched his fists, "Colonel we have just spent a night fighting Germans. The Major and I have fairly short fuses. I would back off if I were you."

General Bruce Clarke, ignoring the bad feeling, said, "You have come from the Schnee Eifel?"

"Yes sir. We are about to lose the last town on the Our. Andler is going to fall. They are holding on for grim death but there are King Tigers and the S.S. attacking them. Anyone on the east will be trapped. Colonel Descheneaux told me to tell you that they are short of ammunition and he doesn't know how long he can hold out."

General Jones said, "But there are 7,000 men there!"

Colonel Devine said flatly, "There are King Tiger Tanks and Panzer Grenadiers. These guys mean business, General. I saw a Sherman hit by one shell and it blew up. We have nothing to stop these guys. It needs a tank buster and the snow means we can't get aeroplanes up."

General Jones slumped in his chair. He had been relieved but his face showed that he felt responsibility, "I've thrown in my last chips. You are in command now, General."

I could not believe that they were giving in. "Sir, there is a chance here. Those King Tigers are so big and so heavy that, while they are unstoppable they are slow and there are bridges which will not bear their weight. I don't think they can use the bridge at Andler. They will be jammed up on the road. If you call in an air strike…"

"And you are?"

"Major Harsker of Number 4 Commando."

The General smiled, "Well Major. I like your optimism but as of this moment every squadron is grounded because of the weather and my tanks are backed up on the roads here."

Colonel Harding snapped, "The Major was ordered to return to Liege. He chose to go to the east instead."

"And a damned good thing he did! This officer and his men deserve a medal." Colonel Devine sprang to my defence.

General Clarke nodded, "Thank you, Major, but perhaps you should obey your orders. Head towards Liege while you can."

I saluted, "Yes sir." I knew when I was beaten. I turned and shook Colonel Devine's hand, "Good luck, sir. You have a fine unit. It was a privilege and honour to fight alongside you."

"And you Major, and you. Who knows, our paths may cross again. I hope so. You and your men fight an interesting war."

Outside I saw that Barker and Hewitt had taken advantage of a mobile canteen to get some hot food. They were old soldiers. Gordy handed me a dixie with the ubiquitous beans and franks. The Americans seemed to enjoy it. "Well sir, what is the SP?"

"We are ordered back to Liege."

"Easier said than done, sir. This place is jammed up."

"We head for the Motor Pool. Let's see if we can bluff our way to getting a vehicle."

After we had eaten we made our way to the Motor Pool. This time there was a lieutenant in charge. "Sorry sir, I have Colonel Harding's orders. No one is allowed to take an American vehicle without a written order from him." From his words, I guessed the orders were written specifically with me in mind. The Colonel appeared to be more than a little vindictive.

The Master Sergeant, who had given us the first jeep, winked at me as he said, "How about that then sir?" He pointed to a shape covered by a piece of canvas. Like a toreador he whisked the canvas away to reveal a motorbike and side car combination. He jutted his jaw out as he faced the lieutenant, "This one ain't American, it's Kraut." He nodded to me, "It has been serviced and it is all gassed up. The boys have spent a week doing it up. To be honest we were thinking about taking it back home but if you want it, sir, then take it with our blessing" he looked at his officer. "How about it Lieutenant? You can still obey the Colonel and do the Major a favour. He is an ally after all."

I could see his dilemma. I made up his mind for him, "Thank you Master Sergeant. This German vehicle will do nicely." Turning our backs on the bemused and confused Lieutenant I said, "We will have to pack this efficiently. Get rid of everything we don't need. Pack the Bergens with ammo and food and tie them on to the sidecar."

Just then there was the sound of shells exploding. They were 120 mm guns. The Germans had arrived. They were close now.

The Master Sergeant said, "I reckon you ought to get out now, sir. While you can!"

Chapter 5

Even as we were leaving the beleaguered town of St. Vith the German assault guns were shelling it. I hoped our new friends would keep their heads down and be lucky. A soldier never discounts luck. When Napoleon was told of a good General he had asked, '*Yes but is he lucky?*' I sat in the sidecar carefully scrutinizing the map. From what I could gather the Germans had broken through at many places on a wide front. We had been badly caught out. I hated to run too but we were needed by our own army. 30 Corps was going to have to bolster up the northern flank and that was where we would be needed. Looking at the map I could see that the Germans could exploit the boundary between the British and American lines and sweep up to retake Antwerp. Once they had Antwerp then it would be the devil's own job to take it back.

I was heading for Malmedy. We had passed that on the way to St. Vith. The road passed through Wereth, a small village six and half miles from St. Vith. I saw smoke rising from the houses. It was not the smoke of a house fire, it was houses on fire. If Germans were already there then I did not want to walk into an ambush. This was the area where the paratroopers had been reported.

"Stop Gordy. Hewitt come with me." I took my Colt and we headed along the wood, keeping to the trees at the side. There had been fighting here. I saw dead Americans. When I turned over the body of a camouflage cape covered German I saw that they were S.S., the 1st SS Panzer Division Leibstandarte We had fought them at Falaise and they were vicious killers. We moved cautiously and entered the village through the back garden of a small half demolished house. As we entered the centre of the small huddle of houses I saw, against a wall, the bodies of eleven black American soldiers. They had all been shot in the back of the head but, as Hewitt examined them, he discovered that they had been tortured first.

"Bastards!" John Hewitt was quietly spoken but there was venom in his words.

"We can't do anything for these poor sods at the moment, John, but we will. Get their dog tags."

I whistled for Gordy. He shook his head in disbelief when he saw the bodies of the dead. "Who could do that, sir?"

53

"The 1st SS Panzer Division Leibstandarte. We will go steadily from now on. There are tank tracks here as well as armoured cars. Jerry is between us and home. If we have to we will have to go across country."

"We have plenty of petrol, sir, and we can always manhandle this little rig over obstacles."

"Let John drive for a little way. It will take his mind off that."

"Aye sir, you are right."

It was a grim journey. We found more bodies of Americans by the side of the road. You could not tell how they had died but if this was the S.S. ahead of us then I feared the worst. We were close to the village of Baugnez, just a mile or two from Malmedy, when we caught up with the tail end of the German column. I heard the engines of their huge tanks. We now had Germans ahead of us and behind us. I tapped John on the shoulder and he stopped. To our right was a forest and a ridge.

"Off the road." John drove along a forester's track. I spied a firebreak. "Take the motor bike up there, Hewitt, and wait for us. We will have a look see. Come on Gordy."

I took my sniper rifle and binoculars. We headed along the forester's track in the trees. It led up to a ridge. The noise of the engines told me that the Germans had stopped. They were idling and not straining. I looked through the glasses. There was a column of vehicles. Two tanks were at the front of the column. They had Panzer Grenadiers on them and there were halftracks and lorries. The road was so narrow that they would have to travel at the speed of the tanks. The tanks were still idling. As the noise grew louder I dropped to the ground and I crawled. When I reached the ridgeline I was able to look down. There were two of the King Tigers. They were enormous beasts. With them they had a couple of half-tracks. The tankers wore their black overalls but the Panzer Grenadiers had the white camouflage capes. Once I had dragged my eyes away from the enormous behemoths I saw why they had stopped. There were about a hundred to a hundred and fifty captured Americans standing in a forlorn group. The two half-tracks had their machine guns trained on them.

I moved the rifle so that I could look down the telescopic sights. The Americans had been disarmed. I saw an officer speaking on a field telephone. He then gave orders and four MG 42 machine guns were set up so that the prisoners were enfiladed. I wondered what was going on.

"Gordy, go and bring the motorbike here. We should be hidden and the noise of the German engines will disguise the sound of the bike. I want to watch what is going on."

"Sir."

I saw movement from the direction of Malmedy. I took out my binoculars. It was three American trucks. They were escorted by another two half-tracks. They stopped and more American prisoners were disgorged. Malmedy had been captured! The prisoners were herded together. As soon as the Germans moved back I knew what was going to happen. I grabbed my rifle. I was too late. The machine guns opened up. They were massacring the prisoners. I saw some, at the rear, run towards the trees. Even as I watched the rest of the Germans opened up. It was when I saw a young soldier almost reach the trees only to be pitched to the ground that I snapped. I aimed at the nearest machine gunner and shot him. There was so much firing that the other gunners did not notice. His loader looked around for the killer but did not think to look behind him. I shot another three machine gunners before someone saw the flash from my gun and attention was switched to me. The delay afforded others the chance to flee.

I did not panic. I still had more bullets. I fired at the gunner in the nearest half-track. I saw the commander of one of the Tigers swing his machine gun around. I shot him and the second Tiger's hatch clanged shut. The Panzer Grenadiers were now trying to get up the slope to reach me. It was virgin snow and they were struggling. They were firing as they ran. Their bullets were wasted for they flew high. I saw survivors from the American prisoners reach the tree line. Some had escaped. The majority lay in bloody piles where they had been murdered. I heard the motor bike behind me as I fired the last bullet from my second magazine. Drawing a German grenade from my battle dress I smashed the porcelain cap and then threw it down the slope. I rolled backwards rather than risking a bullet.

Gordy shouted, "Bloody hellfire sir! What have you done now?"

"They were shooting the prisoners. John, take us up through the trees. They are heading up the slope."

"Sir."

We were overloaded but that actually helped us as we had better grip. As John opened the throttle I pushed the back of the bike and then jumped up behind him. Gordy had his Thompson out and as the first German heads appeared at the forester's track he fired a short burst and they disappeared. Then we were among the trees. John had no choice over the direction he took. He went through the widest part of the forest. It meant we zigged and zagged. That helped us to escape for the Germans had no idea which direction we would take.

I leaned forward. "Head due North. The prisoners of war went that way. We might be able to help them."

"Sir."

I glanced around and saw that the Germans had decided we were small fry. I tapped John on the shoulder. "Stop here. Let's reload."

I put the Mauser back in the sidecar and took out my Thompson. Gordy reloaded. Hewitt turned off the engine to save fuel. Who knew when we would be able to get some more.

It was as Hewitt was stepping from the motor bike that he shouted, "There, sir, down in the gully! Germans!"

I saw a patrol of seven Germans walking along a gully. They were a hundred yards away. I took out my binoculars and saw that they were following a line of footsteps in the snow. They were chasing the escaped captives. Even as I watched I saw an American, obviously wounded, raise his hands from the snow in which he had been hiding. To my horror the officer walked up to him and shot him in the head. There must have been more hiding for at the sound of the gunshot a dozen rose from the snow and ran.

They would be massacred, "Open fire!"

I picked up my Thompson and fired at them. Gordy did the same. Hewitt hurled a grenade high into the air, "Grenade!"

We dropped to the ground. Hewitt was clever. He had used our height and his throw to enable an air shot. The grenade scythed through the air and finished off the survivors.

"John, see to the wounded Americans. Gordy, let's see what these Jerries have on them."

I saw that the Germans were, indeed, the 1st SS Panzer Division Leibstandarte. The officer was young but the sergeant looked to be the same age as Reg Dean. We stripped them of weapons, ammunition and food. I put the ammunition and food into one of the German backpacks. "Gordy, take the grenades back to the motorbike and then meet us at the Americans." I took out the ID from the men and studied them. They could be useful.

When I reached the Americans, Hewitt had just finished tending to the two wounded men. Five lay dead and there were three who were unhurt. I saw that the most senior was a sergeant.

"Major Harsker, Number 4 Commando. Are you in charge?"

Nodding, he held out a hand, "Thanks sir. You saved our bacon there. Sergeant Feldman of the 285th Field Artillery. Who were those guys?"

"S.S. If you fight them don't bother to surrender. They will shoot you anyway." I handed him the rucksack. "There is food and ammo in here. Take these weapons. There are Germans all around you. I think we saw some of your buddies up ahead. If you keep heading cross country and north by east you should be safe."

"What about you sir? Aren't you coming with us?"

I shook my head, "We have a motor bike and besides I think we could do a little sabotage."

"But there are only three of you."

Gordy climbed off the bike and said, with a grin, "We are that but we are Commandos and the Major here doesn't know when he is beaten."

Armed and ready the seven men saluted, "Thank you, sir, and good luck!" They marched off following the line of footprints in the snow.

When they had disappeared Gordy said, "What exactly are we going to do, sir? He is right. There are only three of us."

"You have seen those Tigers. Do we have anything which could stop them?" They both shook their heads. "When they are moving, they are protected by infantry so you can't get close and I am betting that one of these could take out any number of Shermans. They will have to laager up for the night. All tanks do. We do something to hurt them."

"Blow them up you mean sir?"

"We haven't got the explosives but that is the sort of thing. The fuel strikes me as their weakness. If we could cut their fuel line or drain off their fuel then they would not be able to move."

"If we had some sugar, sir, we could stick it in the petrol tank."

"This is where we need Emerson. There must be something that we could do to hurt them."

Hewitt had been pondering, "Freddie was most meticulous about keeping the carburettor clean. He also worried about the quality of the fuel. If we could put something in the fuel... oh I don't know, water, pee, something like that, and add some sand or soil then they would have to strip the whole thing down wouldn't they sir? They would have to empty the fuel tank and refuel."

"And the one thing the Germans are short of is fuel. Good man, Hewitt. Let's find some soil or something here, eh? Scrape away the snow, no better yet, collect the snow and stick it in the German water bottles. We will add the gravel and soil and then pour the whole lot in."

"Sounds easy sir but don't you think they might be guarding the tanks?"

"I am certain they will be but we have our daggers and our pistols." I pointed down the valley, "After what I have seen today I have no sympathy for these S.S. at all!"

It was dark by the time we headed through the forests and paralleled the road. I was in the side car again and I had my binoculars. I scanned the road ahead for any sign of the Leviathans and their escorts. They would have to stop sometime or risk damaging their engines. I knew we had passed Malmedy. As I looked at the map which Sergeant Ford had given me a few days ago, I noticed that north west of Malmedy was a fuel dump. That would be a strategic target for the tanks. We would head there. I doubted they would reach it before dark but so long as we had the right direction then we should be able to spot them. Two King Tigers would be easy to see. It would be like looking for two small houses. Even in the dark their bulk would give them away.

I had Hewitt stop the motorcycle every now and then. Each time he did so I could hear in the distance the rumble of the two tanks. I knew that if we were on the road then I would be able to feel the vibration beneath my feet. The snow deadened such sound. It was just after dusk when I was greeted by silence. At least the silence of Maybach engines. It was replaced by the sound of men. They were some way off but I also caught the smell of wood smoke. They had made camp.

"Hewitt, keep the revs to a minimum I just want it turning over. Head closer to the Germans so that if we are heard we will be taken for one of their own. Be ready to stop when I tap on your shoulder."

"Sir."

We had been doing this so long that there was an element of instinct about it. Ahead of us the trees seemed to be closer together and yet I knew they shouldn't be and so I tapped Hewitt on the shoulder. We stopped. I thought we were close to their camp. We used hand signals. We were at the top of a ridge. We turned the motor bike around so that it was facing downhill. When we had completed our sabotage, I intended heading towards the fuel dump. I was not happy about retreating to Liège when we could be fighting the Germans. This was our kind of war. I had a quick look at the ID I had taken. I gave one each to the other two. They nodded. They knew how to use them. Mine said that I was Feldwebel Heinrich Mannling of the 2nd Company 2nd Battalion Panzer Grenadiers. We left our rifles and machine guns but I donned my battle jerkin and attached as many grenades as I could. I had my Colt, knife and Luger. We each had two German water bottles filled with a mixture of snow, sand, soil and urine. Hewitt had also suggested we take twigs and pieces of pine to put in the petrol tank. We set off towards, what I hoped was, the German lines.

There had been a slight thaw and there was no longer a crust on the snow. It was wetter. That meant we made less noise but we sank deeper into it. I was glad we had such good boots. I could now hear the sound of the Germans. They were in good spirits. They had advanced almost forty miles and driven a huge hole between the Allies. As far as I could tell from the conversations we heard they had not lost many men and with a fuel dump almost within touching distance they were within sight of victory.

As we moved closer I was determined to avoid alerting them to our presence. That meant sneaking through their sentries rather than killing them. The reason for the slight thaw became apparent when snow began to fall again. It became a blizzard. Not only would it disguise us it would hide our tracks. I saw the glow of the German sentry's cigarette. If a sergeant found him he would be in for it. The snow was coming from behind us and so he had his head turned to get some protection from the nearby tree. It allowed us to slip past him. Getting out would be harder but we would cross that bridge when we came to it.

I saw the oil cans they were using for braziers. Their glow gave us an idea of where the Germans were. They had canvas rigged up from the trees to their half-tracks and trucks. The blizzard meant they were huddled in shelter. I saw the shape of the two King Tigers and the two armoured cars. Their crews would be close to them. We crept closer to them while keeping away from the Germans. They had a ring of sentries. We had passed one but I now saw others. The problem would come when they changed the guard.

I spied an unattended Kubelwagen and small petrol bowser. It was obviously for emergencies. This was an opportunity which was too good to miss. I signalled for the other two to keep watch and then I unscrewed the cap on the bowser. I poured the contents of one of the water bottles into it and then replaced the cap. I took out a German grenade and broke the porcelain. I put the grenade under the rear wheel but hidden from view. I tied a piece of cord to the detonator and then tied that to the nearest tree. I covered the cord with snow. The blizzard would do the rest.

I signalled for the other two to settle down with me. We would wait for the camp to go quiet. The three of us squatted beneath our camouflage capes. They were quite warm. Snow fell on us until we became just three white lumps with eyes. I saw a German approaching. I could not see my watch but I guessed it was about eleven o'clock. The camp had been quiet for some time and I was contemplating moving. He walked over to us. I thought he had seen us but he stopped six feet away and urinated on a tree. He took the cigarette out of his mouth to throw it away and then realised how close he was to the petrol bowser. He turned and threw it into the woods. When he had stared at the bowser we were in his eye line and yet he had not seen us.

I waited a while. I determined the time by counting up to five thousand. I stood. The blood rushed to my feet and the sensation was like burning. It was not pleasant. Luckily our hands had been inside our white camouflage capes. We moved through the silent camp towards the two Tigers. We had our Colts at the ready. There was no sign of life at the tanks. It took a few moments to discover where the caps for the tanks were. While Gordy and John unscrewed them I kept watch. They both poured their sabotaged liquid in and I handed over my last bottle for good measure. While they replaced the caps I took the pins from a grenade and jammed it in the driving wheel of the track of one of the Tigers. With luck they wouldn't see it.

We headed back through the camp. I thought that we had escaped unseen when a figure rose from the armoured car we were passing. "Cold, eh?"

"Freezing."

Where are you off to?"

"We are on duty."

"Ah, poor buggers."

We kept walking. Our conversation had, however, woken another German. As we approached the tree line he said, "You three, name and unit?"

I had my Colt ready beneath my camouflage cape. I smiled, "Mannling, 2nd Company 2nd Battalion Panzer Grenadiers. Don't tell me we don't have to go on duty?" I kept walking to get as close to him as I could. He had no camouflage cape on and we did. I suddenly remembered that I had not seen any of the S.S. with camouflage capes on.

I saw him frown. "Heinrich Mannling did not return from…"

He got no further. I fired twice at point blank range. The silenced gun did not wake anyone else. He fell to the ground. He would be discovered. We turned and moved quickly. We reached the tree line before he was discovered. A sentry loomed up.

"What is going on?"

Gordy's fist rammed into his chin and the back of his head cracked off a tree. He lay unconscious. We ran. The camp was now in uproar. I heard orders being shouted. It would take some minutes for them to find which way we had gone. "Hewitt go and start the bike. Gordy, booby traps."

This would not be sophisticated. I took a German grenade and, using parachute cord, tied it between two trees. Gordy did the same. If they followed our footprints, they would trigger it. I saw a torch coming up the slope. I tapped Gordy on the shoulder and we ran. It was an energy sapping climb. I heard the sound of the bike as it roared into life. If they did not know where we were before, they knew now. I grabbed my Thompson and climbed into the sidecar.

"Which way sir?"

"We can't go the way I wanted to. Go back to Malmedy."

Just then there was a double explosion as the booby traps were triggered. Hewitt took us directly down the ridge. It was a wild ride. To the right was the German camp. I heard the cough as they started the two Tigers and then the sound of the armoured cars starting. You had to run a tank's engines for a few moments. Suddenly there was a loud belch and then a second. The two Tiger's cut out. I made that assumption from the lack of noise. I could still hear the two armoured cars. Then there was another explosion and a huge column of fire leapt into the air. They had tried to move the bowser and it had exploded. Our sabotage had worked but there were now two armoured cars and they would be racing down the road to get us. The S.S. soldiers were not stupid and they had heard the motor bike. This was now a race.

As Hewitt threw the bike onto the road, we skidded. I thought for one horrible moment that we were going to crash into a tree. A huge pine loomed up at me. Mercifully Hewitt stopped us in time. The road was now covered, once more, in snow. "Hewitt use your light. The enemy are behind us. I don't fancy going off this road."

"Me neither sir."

I turned to watch the road behind. We twisted and turned but every so often I had a clear line of sight behind and I saw the dim lights of the armoured cars. The motor bike would normally have been quicker but we had laden this one. The Germans would catch us. I turned around and replaced the Tommy gun into the side car. I took out the Mauser which had a longer range. It would be hard to be accurate as we were bouncing along like a child's wood top but I might get lucky.

Of course, I had no idea who was in Malmedy but we had the advantage that we had German snow camouflage capes and we were riding a German bike. If it was the enemy it would take some time for them to realise it. I turned again. I could now see one of the German armoured cars. It was a hundred yards behind us and gaining. We had a straight stretch and the gunner opened fire with his machine gun. I rested the Mauser along the side car and tried to keep it as still as I could. I had few targets. It was armoured. As I looked through the telescopic sight I realised that the gunner was out of the turret using the top machine gun. Below him was the visor for the driver. At night it would be wide open. I aimed at the visor and emptied the magazine. I saw the bullets strike the metal turret and then, as we hit a bump one struck the gunner. He clutched his arm and I saw him slither back down. I reloaded my magazine and did the same thing. I now knew that I was firing high and so I aimed low. When the armoured car swerved briefly I knew that I had sent a bullet to rattle around inside.

Gordy shouted, "Sir, to the right, coming up. There is a track leading off to the right. We could try an ambush with a grenade."

I shouted, "Hewitt, take the track but then head parallel to the road when you find a gap big enough."

When Hewitt applied the brakes, we fishtailed. I stood and leaned over Gordy's back to keep all three wheels on the ground. He gunned the motor as we drove up the track. Gordy rolled a grenade behind us as Hewitt threw the bike left. We were so close that the tree on one side grazed my hand. The armoured car would not get through there. There was a screech and a skid as the armoured car tried the same manoeuvre. It almost stopped and then the grenade went off. I heard the shrapnel strike the metal of the car. It might not have hurt them but they lost sight of us. Hewitt drive through the trees until I was certain that they were no longer behind us.

"Hewitt, find somewhere to stop. We will listen for them. If we don't hear anything then we will get our heads down. Tired men make mistakes."

Hewitt found an open space which was flat and far enough from the road for us to be hidden. Even though it would be hard to see us I took no chances. We rigged a camouflage net over the top of us. The snow which was still falling, although nowhere near as heavily, would soon cover us. We cleared the snow from the ground and using the camouflage capes as a groundsheet sat and ate some rations. Thanks to the Americans we had plenty. I hoped we would be far enough away from the road to remain hidden. I put us in God's hands for we all slept and trusted to our instincts to wake us if danger threatened.

I woke before dawn. My in-built clock did that for me. I rolled out from under the netting. The snow had covered it and it had fallen all night. I saw no sign of our tracks. The snow had now stopped. Looking up I saw blue in patches. That meant the Allies could get aeroplanes up. After I had finished my toilet I listened. I could hear, to the south and west the sound of firing. Firing meant the enemy but it also meant that there were Americans or British nearby. I was still tempted to head north but there was just one road in that direction and we knew that the Germans were on it. More importantly they knew of us. At least heading for Malmedy we would be unknown.

I slipped back under the netting. It felt amazingly cosy with the warmth of Hewitt and Barker. "Wakey, wakey lads. John, when you have done your business how about getting a brew on, eh? We are far enough away from Jerry to risk it. I can't hear anything on the road."

"Righto sir."

When they left I took out the map. The road passed through Stavelot and Trois Points after Malmedy. There was a bridge over the Ambleve River. That would be defended.

When we left the forest to drive along the road I saw that this was not virgin snow. There were tracks and they were heading north and east. We took the road to Malmedy.

Chapter 6

Malmedy was defended. Thankfully it was by the Americans. When we arrived, there was a road block. Two Shermans were dug in on either side of the road and there was a barbed wire road block across it. We were viewed suspiciously. Guns were levelled at us.

A tough looking sergeant pointed his rifle at me. "Who are you guys and why are your riding a German rig?"

I understood their suspicion. I took off my camouflage cape, revealing my uniform. "We are three Commandos from Number 4 Commando. I am Major Harsker and we were at St. Vith. We were ordered to get to Liège but the 1st SS Panzer Division Leibstandarte up the road put an end to that idea."

I thought that would allay their suspicions but it did not. "If you are who you say you are then I will apologise, sir. But you should know that there are Germans who are dressed as Americans and speaking like Americans. They are all over the place."

Hewitt said mildly, "But we are English."

The Sergeant nodded, "Which means I can't ask you what is the state capital of Illinois can I?"

I said, "Springfield."

A corporal said, "It's Chicago isn't it, Sarge?"

"Osborne, you are a dumb ass. The Limey is right but I am still taking him to see the Major. You take charge. Watch their gear. Hands in the air and walk ahead of us."

I felt foolish but I obliged. We of all people should have understood the German ploy. We had used it often enough. We were taken into a command post.

"Sir, I have three men here. They say they are British."

The huddle of officers who were around the table looked around and a familiar voice said, "And they are. Good to see you, Tom, but I thought you would have been back with your people by now."

It was Colonel Devine, "We ran into trouble sir. Can we put our hands down now?"

"Of course. These are on our side Sergeant."

The sergeant nodded, "Sorry sir."

"Don't apologise Sergeant you were just doing your job and you did it well. Barker, could you and Hewitt go with the sergeant and retrieve the motor bike?"

"Yes sir."

Colonel Devine said, "This is Major Dunne. I arrived this morning. The situation is confused here. What can you tell us?"

They made space so that I could stand close to the map. I pointed out our route and told them what we had seen and encountered. They were not surprised by my news of the massacre. "We found some bodies when we reached here. I am glad that some escaped."

"By my reckoning sir there could be eighty or so who escaped."

"We need those. They are witnesses. Some bastard has to pay for the massacre."

"It was the 1st SS Panzer Division Leibstandarte sir and they have, had, a couple of Tigers up the road."

Colonel Devine grinned, "That was you guys, eh? A couple of Thunderbolts reported two King Tigers and they were not moving. They said that they had guys working on them. They blew them up!"

"Then the road north is clear sir?"

"I am afraid not. The weather has closed in on the airfields again. They can't get anything up. The situation is more than confused. What you see here, Major are the remains of half a dozen commands. They are sending the 82nd Airborne to help us. The 101st has been sent to a place called Bastogne, further south, but the Krauts are pulling all the strings. They have taken Stavelot. That means they hold a bridge over the river and there are reports of them driving north to Stourmont. There is a huge fuel dump there."

"Surely they can blow it?"

"There is no radio communication with them."

I shrugged, "Send a fighter bomber and blow it up, sir."

Major Dunne looked shocked, "There are Americans guarding that, Major Harsker. We do not kill our own."

"If those King Tigers get refuelled then a lot more Americans and British will die, Major. The risk comes as soon as you put on a uniform."

Colonel Devine said, "That is not our decision but we have been ordered to get to Stavelot and help retake it. General Hodges has decided to make a mark in the sand. We stop them here." He looked at me. "Are you with us?"

"Of course sir. Where do you want us?"

"In the lead vehicle, with me. You seem to have a sense of survival and you know this country. We leave in thirty minutes." As the others moved away he said, "Grab a cup of Joe first. Damned good to see you."

I nodded, "And you sir. What about St. Vith?"

"They are holding on there but only just. If we can retake Stavelot then we have a chance to relieve them."

I knew that we were short of ammunition but I also knew that the Colonel and his men would be just as desperate as we were. "Sir, are there any captured German weapons and ammunition?"

Major Dunne said, "In the next building but they don't fit our guns."

Colonel Devine laughed, "The British, it seems, are magpies. The Major here has German weapons too!"

I heard the motor bike outside. I stepped into the sunshine. Dark clouds were on the horizon but, for the moment, we could get aeroplanes up. We would have intelligence!

"Gordy, we are losing the motorbike. Get our gear. We are travelling with the Colonel and I guess that means the half-track."

"Thank God for that! I think I am getting piles!"

"There are German weapons and ammo in here. See what you can get, eh?"

"Will do sir."

I grabbed a cup of coffee. It was hot and was just what I needed. I looked up as a flight of Thunderbolts zoomed overhead. I returned to the Command Post. Colonel Devine shook his head, "The weather is closing in again. Our airfields send up fighter bombers when they can but it is a lottery. Your dad is a pilot, you know that better than anyone. It makes you wonder whose side God is on."

I finished the coffee and followed the Colonel out. Barker and Hewitt were standing there grinning. "Like an Aladdin's cave, sir. German grenades and shed loads of ammo!"

The Colonel pointed to the M3. "We will be a little crowded in the half-track. Vehicles are at a premium. We have lost all of our armoured cars. I don't want to risk losing the three Shermans we have. We will run point. Major Dunne is in command of the tanks. Most of the men are his. You and I are expendable."

When we reached the half-track, I saw that the driver was Sergeant Major O'Rourke. He was bandaged. He had a delighted expression when he saw the three of us. "Good to see you, sir. I never got to thank you guys properly for saving me back there on the road to Andler."

"Don't mention it Sarn't Major. Glad to be of help."

"Right O'Rourke. Off we go. Keep your eyes open for the Krauts."

I stood with the Colonel and the gunner at the front of the M3. He had a .50 Calibre there. Barker handed me an MP 34 German submachine gun. "We have plenty of ammo for this one, sir. The .45 bullets were as scarce as a Scotsman buying a round of drinks!"

Colonel Devine laughed, "I guess you are saying that Scotsmen are mean!"

"I thought you knew, sir. That is why they wear kilts! No pockets in kilts!" The Americans on board all laughed. They had not heard the old music hall joke before.

I put the two spare magazines in my battle jerkin and added two more grenades. I had used two. The rest we put in our Bergens. I did not think that we would need the white camouflage capes any time soon and we stored those too.

Colonel Devine pointed to my beret. "No helmet, Major?"

"In our line of work they are often a hindrance. I know they might come in handy on a day like this when Jerry is going to be lobbing shells at us but you get used to fighting a certain way."

"How long have you been fighting this way, Major?"

I noticed, idly, that the forest through which we were driving was ending. Soon we would be in more open country. The clouds had begun rolling in and the air was marginally warmer. Either snow or rain was on its way. "I first fought the Germans here in 1940. I have been in the Commandos for about four years."

He shook his head, "You guys have had a tough war."

"Yes sir but we are the survivors. The ones to feel sympathy for are the poor sods who won't be coming back. I have lost a lot of good men."

The Colonel nodded, "Until this little shindig I had lost none. I am learning."

Suddenly the road, two hundred yards from us, erupted as German shells began to lay down a barrage. Colonel Devine shouted, "Sergeant Major get us off the road."

I took out my binoculars. I could see, in the distance, Stavelot. There was a church tower of some description, and it did not take genius to work out that they had a spotter there for the field artillery which accompanied the 1st SS Panzer Division Leibstandarte. I looked down at the map. The tower would be attached to the Abbey which was at the eastern end of the town.

Colonel Devine said to the corporal on the radio, "Ask Major Dunne if his Shermans could lay down some smoke. They have spotters for their artillery." We were still edging along the soft snow by the side of the road and the barrage was creeping closer to us. The three tanks were two hundred yards behind the four half-tracks which led the column. There were three cracks from behind us and the smoke shells landed half a mile up the road. Soon a thick pall of smoke filled the road.

"Right Sergeant Major, back on the road and give it all she has got. Heads down!"

I did not need a second command and I squatted down beneath the half inch of steel. The Germans were still firing but they were firing blind now. "Sergeant Barker, pass me the Mauser."

He slid the rifle to me and I checked that it had a full magazine. A shell exploded just fifty yards to our left as we approached the smoke. Shrapnel rattled against the side. It sounded like hailstones. The acrid smoke was disgusting but it prevented their spotter from tracking us. As soon as we burst through, however, he would spot us again. The town was a mile away and so the tower was out of my range. I would, however, be ready if I got the chance.

As we burst through the smoke I risked a look over the edge of the half-track. The elevated vantage point meant that I could see further ahead than the driver. I used the telescopic sight and I saw the German ambush just three quarters of a mile up the road. They were wearing camouflage. I did not see them but I did see the Panzerfaust.

"Colonel, anti-tank guns. There are two of them and they are on either side of the road." If we carried on they would hit us and the road would be blocked.

"O'Rourke, off to the left. Sergeant, everybody off. Get the other two half-tracks unloaded. We will have to get rid of these emplacements the hard way." He turned to the radio operator. "Tell the Shermans to aim at the flashes from their artillery."

"Sergeant Barker, go with the Colonel and his men. I'll see what I can do up here."

The Colonel saw the rifle and the scope, "Good luck, Major. The range looks a little long to me."

"Even if I don't hit them I can keep their heads down."

I looked through the sight. It looked a long way off and I knew that I would have to be as still as possible. The metal rim of the half-track was ideal. I breathed slowly as I targeted the machine gunner. He was looking down the barrel. The MG 42 had the range. It might not be as accurate at three quarters of a mile but some bullets would hit. The effective range was over two thousand yards. I squeezed the trigger twice. I saw the gunner fall and clutch his shoulder. The other one opened fire, not at the Colonel and his men as they advanced, but at us. The bullets clanged off the half-track.

Sergeant Major O'Rourke laughed, "Are you trying to get us killed, sir?"

"Don't you trust American steel, Sergeant Major? Besides if they are firing at us they can't fire at the Colonel." I traversed to the other gun; it was the one which had fired at us. The angle here was a little better. I fired three bullets and one of them hit the gun. There was a flash as the Panzerfaust fired. I saw the flame and then the rocket as it headed towards us.

I saw an officer stand up to berate the rocketeer. He was too good a target and I hit him in the chest. The rocket spiralled off to the left after two hundred yards and buried itself in the snow.

"Sir, weren't you worried?"

"No, Sergeant, the effective range of those things is two hundred feet."

"How do you know that sir?"

"I have fired one."

I looked ahead and saw that the Colonel and his men were now within four hundred yards of the German front lines. The infantry there were firing back at them. The tanks had managed to hit a couple of the enemy artillery pieces. Their firing was more sporadic and sleety snow had begun to fall. The spotter would have more difficulty in accurate reports.

"Sergeant Major could you drive down this road slowly?"

"I could sir, but the Colonel said to stay here and besides they might hit us."

"If you drive slowly and stop four hundred yards from the Germans, the rockets can do us no harm and I can use the machine gun." There was silence. "Look Sergeant Major, if it gets hairy then stick it in reverse."

"It's your funeral sir. You will be a bigger target than me."

"That's the spirit."

As he put it into gear and headed back onto the road I began to fire the Mauser. With plenty of ammunition I could make life hard for them. Of course, if they had their own sniper in that tower then I was a dead man. I concentrated on the Panzerfausts. If I could make them waste more rockets then so much the better and we appeared to be immune from the machine guns, for the moment. With their officer dead the two rocketeers sent another two rockets towards us. One kept a straight line for longer than was comfortable before plunging to the ground and exploding in the road just two hundred yards from us. I shot one of the crew and the other decided to abandon the Panzerfaust and try to hit us with their rifles.

With a range of two thousand yards I decided it was time to test the firepower of the Browning against the MG 42. Of course, it meant standing up to fire it. I cocked it whilst crouching. Putting both hands on the grips and trigger I pulled myself up and I was firing even as I stood. I moved it from left to right. I managed to catch them unawares. My first bullets struck the MG 42 and as I traversed I hit the others at the road block.

"Good shooting Major!"

We were closer to their lines now and shells from their artillery began to explode before and behind us. I raised the machine gun and fired at the tower with the observer. It was within range. When I ran out of ammunition I shouted, "Stop here, Sergeant Major. I will get out. Back up if you wish."

He stopped it and then clambered up beside me. "No sir, I reckon I will have a go with this little pop gun! Let's see if I can win a little Kewpie Doll at this here country fair!"

I clambered out of the back. The German MP34 was a solid weapon. With a thirty-two cartridge magazine and a range of two hundred yards it was a handy weapon. There were half demolished houses to the left. I saw the Colonel and his men spread out. They were advancing in pairs. I saw Gordy and Hewitt act as a pair. Behind me I heard the noise of the Shermans as they moved up. I moved into the half-demolished house and headed for what had been the back garden. Just then I heard the distinctive noise of German tank. I ran to the front of the house and saw the barrel of an 88 mm as it moved from the village to the road.

"Sergeant Major O'Rourke, get the hell out of there. That is a Panther!"

The Panther was not as powerful as a Tiger but it was close. Even as the half-track backed into one of the demolished houses the Panther's gun fired. The half-track behind O'Rourke's had been abandoned. That was a mercy for the shell ploughed straight through the engine block and blew the whole vehicle into the air. The leading Sherman opened fire. They were in line and only one could fire. I saw its shell hit the glacis on the Panther. It had as much of an effect as a snowball. The German kept moving until it was in the middle of the road. The sandbags from the machine gun emplacements gave it protection for its tracks. It was, effectively, dug in. The second Sherman moved next to the first. That was their best chance. If they both fired at the same spot they had a chance of first weakening and then destroying the armour.

While Shermans distracted the Germans I left the house and ran across the open ground. The German tank was still half a mile away. I needed to be another six hundred yards closer before my little pop gun could be effective. I used the cover of the buildings and the snow to move forward. I regretted my decision not to wear my camouflage cape. The Panther fired again just as the two 76 mm Sherman guns fired. They both hit and I saw glowing metal but the Panther's armour held. In contrast the 88 mm had hit one of the Shermans and it was already on fire. Its nickname of Ronsons was well earned. It burst into flames. I saw two of the crew bale out. The rest… I hoped the shell had killed them.

The flames and smoke obscured the last two Shermans but now the German artillery was adding their firepower to the devastation caused by the Panther. When the second Sherman was hit Colonel Devine shouted, "Fall back! Fall Back!"

I clambered back through. Sergeant Major O'Rourke had managed to back the half-track behind the burning tanks. The Panther still fired, as did the artillery, but they were firing blind. I looked up at the sky. The scudding clouds would bring nightfall a little earlier. As I hurried back to the others I knew we would have to do something about the Panther or we would not take Stavelot.

Chapter 7

Colonel Devine was angry. Major Dunne had not made it. He had been one of those burned alive in the Sherman. "God Damn! I feel so helpless."

"Colonel, it is night time. We won't be helpless for much longer. Have you any PIATs?"

"Of course, but they can't stop a Panther."

"Not from this range but get close and they can."

"How do you suggest we get close Major?"

"It's night time. We sneak close. We will have snow tonight. My men will lead your PIAT crews close enough to hit the Panther." I pointed back down the road. The burning tanks were now just a glow a mile away. "Just beyond the Shermans are some demolished buildings. There is rough ground between there and the road block. If the Panther is still there then we hit it from the side. The armour there is not as thick. The glacis is five and half inches. The side is only a couple of inches. If we can get to within, say, fifty yards, then we can blow a hole in the side."

"What if they move it?"

"Unlikely. They drink petrol. They get one mile per gallon. They are short of petrol. We have them cut off. They might have Panzer Grenadiers trying to get to the fuel dump but the tanks will move as little as possible." I shrugged, "Of course they might have more tanks in the town and they will replace the Panther when we destroy it. You take it one tank at a time."

"General Hodges is keen to retake this town. He is sending in reinforcements." I saw him chewing his lip. "Volunteers?"

"Two teams; that is four men. We will go in first and make sure there are no booby traps and take out any sentries. We will keep watch while they do it."

He nodded, "We have little choice."

"Good. We'll have a bite to eat and then get our heads down and take a nap. Could you have someone wake us at ten? That should give us time to get there while Jerry is having his sleep."

"You are going to sleep?"

"Of course, sir. Tired men make mistakes. We'll use the half-track."

While we ate I went through my plan with Barker and Hewitt. "I can't see that they will have had the opportunity to plant mines. We would see them. If there is snow then that means it is safe to cross it."

"Sir, these are S.S. I don't like them but they are as good as we are. They will be ready."

"Corporal, we don't take chances. We use the Colts. Shoot to kill. One man watches the other two move. We have just over a mile and a half to cover. We take our time and we go slowly and quietly. We take grenades. If things go pear shaped then we cover the Americans with grenades."

Lowering his voice Gordy said, "That's what worries me, sir. These are damned good soldiers; they are amongst the best we have met. If they were Rangers, then I would be happy but these lads can't move as quietly as we can. I would say the same if this was the Guards or even the Rifle Brigade. There are only the Marines, the Paratroopers and us who can do this."

"Give them a chance, Gordy. Besides they will be behind us. If Jerry hears them then we have the chance to do something about it."

"I suppose so, sir."

The four men were waiting for us when we were woken. They were not young men. All looked to have experience. We discovered that Miller, Morrison, Dexter and Cooper were amongst the most experienced of the Brigade.

"The three of us will go ahead of you. We will be going through largely untouched snow. Follow our footprints."

Corporal Cooper said, "Follow sir?"

"You need to give us a five-minute head start." I tapped my Colt. "Our job is to eliminate any of the S.S. who are watching. We will get you to a position where you can have a side shot at the tank. One takes the skirt and the other the turret. You will have one shot. As soon as the night is lit up by your rockets then all hell will break loose. As soon as you have fired then turn and run. Get back here as fast as you can. No matter what you hear do not stop. We will follow."

"Have you done this before sir?"

"Exactly this, Morrison?" He nodded. "Not exactly but close enough so that we know what we are doing. We are not glory hunters. We want to survive this war and there are risks but they are acceptable ones."

Corporal Cooper was a thoughtful man. "The Sergeant Major said that if you are caught then you will be shot. Is that true, sir?"

"Yes, I am afraid it is, Corporal."

"And us?"

"Normally I would say you would be safe but yesterday we watched these chaps machine gun a hundred and fifty prisoners of war. Don't give them that chance. If you have to shoot then shoot to kill. Right. Get your gear. We leave in ten minutes. I just need to pee."

"Pee sir?"

"Yes Morrison, even the King of England has a pee now and again or so I am led to believe!"

We donned our camouflage capes and I made sure that I had two spare magazines. I would need more ammunition soon. I turned to the Corporal, "Five minutes and then follow us. Keep it as quiet as you can. If you walk in each other's footprints it should be easier. We will stop you when we are close enough for the attack."

As we set off a light flurry of snow began to fall. The night was icy and the wind swirled the snow around. Goggles would have been useful but we had none. I led the way and Gordy brought up the rear. I walked on the left of the road. The fires in the tanks had long gone. There was just the acrid smell of burning in the air. It was a mixture of petrol, cordite and human flesh. It was the smell of war. The wind came from the town and blew the smell in our faces. I would be glad when we were passed it. Ahead all was in darkness. Had the air force been able to fly they could have bombed the town and the bridge but they were still grounded.

When I reached the ruined house where I had taken cover I put my hand up to stop the others. We could shelter in the lee of the three remaining walls. I could smell something. We smelled. It had been some days since water had touched my face let alone my body. The enemy smelled too. I had noticed that the Americans smelled of cinnamon and coffee beans. What I smelled as I peered across the broken sash of the window was stale sweat and cabbage. There were Germans out there.

I made the sign for danger and the other two took cover. They hid so that the three of us had everything covered. With our white camouflage capes we were hard to see. The flaws in my plan now became apparent. We had no way of stopping the four men who were lugging their PIATs towards us and there were S.S. out there. Kneeling on the floor I held my gun in a two-handed grip and I pressed my shoulder against the wall of the building to my left. The smell was growing closer.

When the German voice said, "Shit!" It was almost in my ear and it was all I could do to stop from jumping. He was above me and had been attempting to climb through the window. He had caught his hand on a shard of glass. I raised my gun and looked up. He had his hand on the side wall and his foot on the sash. As he stepped on to the sash, he looked down and I pulled the trigger. The 'phut' seemed inordinately loud to me but no one seemed to react. He fell down and landed on me. There was no noise. My body absorbed the impact of the dying German.

I heard a hiss, "Sven what happened?"

I grunted and a face appeared in the door. He was less than three feet from me. He saw Sven's body lying on mine and began to move. My bullet took the back of his head off. There were two more silenced bullets. I pushed the German from me. I pulled the other dead German towards me. Hewitt and Barker appeared and made the sign that it was secure.

Just then the Corporal and the other three American soldiers arrived. They looked at the camouflage cape covered bodies. I held my finger to my lips and then took the camouflage cape from one of the dead Germans. I handed it to the Corporal. They cottoned on and soon they were dressed in the German's camouflage capes. I took the grenades and pistols from the dead Germans. I found some plastic explosive and detonators on them. I jammed them in my battle jerkin. They were on the same mission as we were. They were heading to our lines to blow up our tanks. I spied a chance. I knew that one was called Sven. If I needed to then I had a name. I tapped my watch and held up my hand. The Corporal nodded.

We left the cover of the demolished house. I saw the German prints in the snow. Had they gone a little further or if the wind had been in the opposite direction then the roles might have been reversed.

There would be German sentries waiting for their saboteurs. They would not expect them yet. As we neared the road block I saw that the tank was still there. I found a depression in the snow and lay down to spy out the position. It was just a hundred yards away. They had replaced the machine guns. There was no sign of the Panzerfaust. I was patient and after a moment I saw the two sentries. They were leaning against the tank. Then I saw a third. When he moved I saw the glow of the brazier and that gave him away. I crept forward knowing that my two companions were right behind me. When we were just twenty yards away I pointed to the guard on the right and then Hewitt. I pointed to the second guard and then at Gordy. I levelled my Colt and squeezed the trigger twice in quick succession. He fell into the brazier. Soon the smell of burning flesh would fill the air. It could not be helped. I saw that the other two had killed their targets.

The Americans were still three minutes behind us. I waved at my two men to cover me and I ran the twenty yards to the barbed wire. I took out the plastic explosive. I had no time for finesse. I saw that the detonator was a simple ten-minute fuse. We had used them before. I jammed it into the explosive and then placed it next to the driving wheel on the tank. I hurried back to the others pausing only to pick up the MP 34 next to the dead sentry.

The Americans were already aiming their rockets at the tank. I nodded. The flash and the noise always came as a surprise. Both rockets struck and there was a double explosion inside the tank. "Run!" As they ran away I saw by the fire in the tank that the turret had been damaged but would still function. I took out a grenade. Already the camp was coming to life as sleeping soldiers woke to the noise of the explosion. I hurled my grenade high into the air. Hewitt and Barker did the same and then we ran.

The Americans had run in a straight line, we zig zagged. Bullets zipped through the air but they were firing blind. Then the three grenades went off. We had moved far enough away to be out of the danger zone but we felt the wall of air as it washed over us. We reached the demolished house and the three of us stopped. I saw that the Germans were putting out the fire in the tank. I sprayed the MP 34. I was barely in range but I wanted their heads down. Hewitt and Barker took the pistols from the dead Germans and began firing them too. We ducked behind the wall as they returned fire. The MG 42 was a vicious weapon and I felt the bullets smash into the wall behind which we sheltered. The bullets would soon break through. Just then we heard the explosion of the plastic explosive. It destroyed the machine guns and, as looked back I saw the tank had been lifted and moved. The track lay in ruins. We ran back. One tank had been destroyed. How many more were there?

Our four companions were waiting for us by the half-track as were the Colonel and the Sergeant Major. Colonel Devine clapped me on the back. "You delivered! God Damn you said what you would do and by God you did just that!"

"They were sending men to sabotage your last tank too, sir. I would double the guards."

"In the morning we will try again. You guys get some sleep. You seem to do well after what did you call it? A nap!"

That was war. You fought. You grabbed what sleep you could, you woke and, if you were lucky, ate and started all over again.

Since we had radio communication again the picture was not quite so dark as it had been and, when I was woken and went to meet the Colonel, I heard good news and bad news. There was more bad than good. "Eighteen soldiers managed to hold up over five hundred Germans the other day! They are not having it all their own way, Major."

"If you are stubborn enough you can make life difficult for them Colonel. Just like you and your cavalry did."

"But they are still heading west. Your Field Marshal has sent some of his men south to block the northern advances. However, we know that close to us they are driving forward to the west. We have to take Stavelot today. If we get to the southern road into Stavelot then we can cut the road south. We do that by blowing the bridge over the Wareche. We can stop their reinforcements."

"If they have Tigers and Panthers then that will be difficult. You are down to one Sherman."

He nodded, "We had more men arrive in the night. Some of them were from the massacre at Malmedy. They told us what you did. You should have a medal for what you have done, Major."

"I have enough medals, Colonel. Men's lives are worth more than a piece of fruit salad on a chest." I downed the coffee I had been given, "So what is the plan?"

He gave me a wry smile, "It involves using you, Major, and your particular set of skills." We had lost many officers. There were just five of us left and I was the next senior to the Colonel. It felt strange. He went to the map. "There is a thickly wooded area close to the river. If I gave you ten men could you get to the bridge and distract them while we make our attack up the road?"

"Distract them, sir?"

"It is a tall order but if you make them think the bridge is in danger then they might have to withdraw troops from the road."

I nodded, "I take it they will be volunteers?"

"Yes, the men you took last night, Sergeant Major O'Rourke will be the officer and there are five others. They are all good men."

"I don't doubt that sir. When do we attack?"

"0900. That should give you time to get into position."

"Any news of the weather, sir?"

"It looks like the aeroplanes will still be grounded if that is what you mean. Overcast with the chance of more snow."

I saw Sergeant Major O'Rourke behind the Colonel. "Have the men by the half-track in ten minutes. They need grenades, whatever guns they have and ammo. No bags."

"Right sir."

I went back to Hewitt and Barker and found my Bergen. I took out what I would need while I told them what we would be doing. "It is up our street but I am not certain about the Americans. John, I want you as Tail End Charlie. If anything happens to Gordy and me then you pull them out."

"Right sir."

Corporal Cooper grinned when he arrived, "When I get home after this sir I'll be able to tell my kids that I went on a raid with real Commandos."

Sergeant Major O'Rourke shook his head. "What is the plan then, sir?"

"We head due south on a straight line to the river. There are woods to give us cover. Looking at the map there is a track of some sort by the river. We won't use that just in case they have it defended. Instead we will go through the woods. It is my guess that the Germans are more worried about the road. If our tanks can get down it then we can retake the bridge. They don't know that we only have the one. When we reach the German lines we use surprise. I don't know how good you are with grenades but I want all of us to throw two grenades as far as we can before we open fire. It will disorientate the Germans and confuse them as to numbers. Our aim is to make them come after us. When I tell you to fall back then do so. You do it in pairs. One runs back while the other covers. We fall back a hundred yards and form a skirmish line. We keep falling back until we reach our starting point again. Of course, if they stop following then we attack again. I want us to be like a dog worrying at a bone. Keep at it until they are forced to come for us."

They nodded.

"One more thing. These are S.S. When you shoot, shoot to kill. A wounded S.S. is dangerous."

"You don't mean kill the wounded, sir?"

"Morrison, I mean that when I shoot I will make sure that it is a lethal shot."

"Don't worry sir. We won't let you down."

I pointed to the Sergeant Major's Thompson. "If you have a machine gun then use short bursts. It's only in the movies where they never run out of bullets." I tapped my Luger, then my Colt and my MP 34 before holding up my Mauser. "When I go into action I am armed and ready. Let's go. Sergeant Barker and I will lead and Corporal Hewitt will be the rear guard."

It was virgin snow and it was deep. Gordy and I took it in turns to lead the patrol south. To the north I heard firing. A long way to the west there was the sound of tanks battling it out. The 88 mm and the 76 mm had distinctive sounds. When we reached the track down the river I saw that it too had no prints on it. That meant no one had been down the trail in the last twelve hours. I led them through the woods. Here the snow was less deep. The canopy of snow-covered branches above us made it a dimly lit world we entered. By my estimate we had a mile to go before we reached the defences of the town. There was a small lane which led from the demolished houses we had used the previous night. It headed towards the river. That would be a way point for us. Once we reached there then we would be within range of the Germans.

From the map there was a weir and an old fashioned leat which had created a defensible island. If I had been the Germans then I would have fortified that. We would be able to see it when we reached the road. I looked at my watch. It was 0830. We had time. As we approached the road I held up my hand and then, while Gordy covered me, I darted across the road. As I ran I looked north and saw no Germans. I made my way through the scrubland to the river. There was a sheen of ice on the water. Crouching behind a mound which was a snow covered bush I peered at the weir and then took out my binoculars to look at the spit of land protected on two sides by water. There were no Germans there. That told me much. They were overstretched.

I went back to Gordy and waved the men into a line. We crossed the road and headed through the trees. The map had told me that the trees ended just before the town. In fact, some of the trees appeared to be the boundary of some of the houses. I hoped we would be able to use that.

When we reached the edge of the woods I saw a snow-covered dry wall marking the boundary of the houses. This was the town. The bridge would be to our left. I pointed the ground and Sergeant O'Rourke waved his men down. Gordy and I slipped over the wall and headed towards the houses. I saw one with an open back door. We slipped over the low dividing boundary wall and headed for it. I stood on one side and Gordy on the other. I listened. I could hear nothing save the noise from the town itself. I heard an engine running. It sounded like a tank. There were distant voices but there was no noise in the house so far as I could tell.

I slipped inside, my gun at the ready. Of course if I had to use the gun then we had failed. We needed surprise. I checked the two downstairs rooms and they were both empty. Perhaps the Germans were using this as a billet. I headed up the stairs. I walked on the side of the treads to avoid making any creaking noises. There were two rooms. Gordy followed me. I nodded to one bedroom. I went into the one on the left. A German was asleep. Behind me I heard a phut. Gordy had shot someone. The noise woke the German. In two strides I was on him. I swung the butt of the gun and it smacked onto his head. His eyes rolled up and he lay unconscious.

I used his belt to bind his feet. Taking some cord from my battle jerkin I fastened his hands behind his back and to the belt. Finally, I balled his socks and pressed them into his mouth and tied his vest around his mouth as a gag. I saw that he was an officer. I grabbed his pistol and spare magazines and then went to the window. I peered through the blackout curtain. I saw the bridge. It was a hundred yards away. There was a

German machine gun just eighty yards away. I saw an anti-tank gun in a sandbagged emplacement. There were two half-tracks and the Kubelwagen. I was guessing that the Kubelwagen belonged to the officer I had incapacitated. I had seen enough.

"Gordy!"

We made our way back to the others. "We can use the houses to get close to the Germans. Cooper, go into the house with the open door. Take your three men with you. There is a German officer tied up upstairs. Keep your eye on him. You can enfilade the Germans. Pick off the officers and the gunners."

"When do we fire sir?"

"As soon as you hear the first grenade go off. Can you do this?"

"Of course sir."

I handed him the German Walther, "Here's a souvenir to show your son."

They headed over the wall and I led the others, "Follow me. We are going to become a whole regiment. Once we throw the grenades fire with everything you have and shout."

"Shout what, sir?"

"It doesn't matter, Harris, just so long as they are confused by the noise and the numbers. Then listen for my shout."

We clambered over the walls and reached the end of the houses. This time there was a high wall next to the track but there was a gate. It had not been opened for some time. I eased it open and peered down the track. There were Germans at the end but they were looking up the road. We had to get across the track and into the woods.

"I want you to get across the track without Jerry seeing you. I will go first. Then form up in the woods." I looked at my watch. We have five minutes before we are due to attack. This is the last command I give before I shout, 'fall back'!" I stood in the doorway and then darted across. I reached the trees and knelt, gun at the ready. Gordy followed me. As soon as Sergeant Major O'Rourke joined us Gordy and I made our way closer to the bridge.

I had seen, from the upstairs window, that they had sandbags and a half track on either side of the bridge. Their defences were all within thirty yards of the bridge. That suited us. I crawled forward until I could actually hear the Germans. They were laughing and joking. As the rest of the men approached to join me behind the small wooden fence I listened in. They had, it seems, found a great deal of food in the town. With Christmas approaching and the townsfolk feeling that their war was over, they had gathered in much food. The Germans were reaping the benefit. I looked at my watch as the last man joined us. There was one minute to go. I already had my grenades out. I was using German ones. The sight of them would confuse the enemy. I banged the porcelain on one of the grenades. The sound of chatter from the Germans thirty feet away drowned the slightest of cracks.

I held my right hand behind me and prepared to stand. I stood and hurled my first grenade. Even as it was in the air I was throwing my second. The Germans saw us and seemed stunned as we rose from the ground. We threw ourselves down behind the wooden fence. I cocked my MP 34 as the twelve grenades scythed through the air. Then I heard the sound of a Thompson and American carbines as Corporal Cooper began to fire.

I stood and sprayed my MP 34 in short bursts. I aimed at the machine gunners. Gordy was up with me in an instant and he aimed at the anti-tank gunners.

I began shouting, "At them! Charge!!

The American cavalrymen joined in with whoops and cheers and shouts! I heard a couple of rebel yells too. The four men in the house were having a devastating effect for they were firing down at the German defenders. In the distance I heard the sound of the Sherman tank as it belched death. I could not hear the sound of German guns firing in retaliation. I was about to tell the men to fall back when I saw that some of the German infantry were scurrying away from our deadly fire. They had no heavy machine guns to bring to bear and we had four sub machine guns. When my MP 34 clicked empty I dropped it and took out my Luger. I emptied that magazine. The aim was to keep their heads down with a veritable hailstorm of bullets. I took a Mills bomb from my battle jerkin. I stepped over the wooden fence, ignoring the bullets zipping around me and I hurled the grenade as far and as high as I could.

"Grenade!"

I dived back over the fence as the others took cover. When I stood I saw that we had the bridge. All that were left were the dead and the dying.

"Sergeant Major O'Rourke, secure the bridge."

"You two, with me. The others, stay with the Major."

"Corporal Hewitt, join Corporal Cooper and watch the top end of the street."

I stepped over the wooden fence. As I walked I reloaded the MP 34. I was watching for movement, I had just cocked it when a German S.S. sergeant, who had been playing dead, rose with a Mauser pistol in his hand. It was instinctive. I turned and fired a burst. His head disappeared.

Cooper and the others were shooting from the upper floor of the house at the Germans who were fleeing up the road in the direct of Stourmont.

"Make sure no one is playing dead. Take the guns away from them."

While the bodies were searched I headed for the bridge. Sergeant Major O'Rourke had two men watching the eastern end of the bridge. "That was easier than I thought it would be, sir."

"I was pleasantly surprised too. You had better tell your two men at the end of the bridge not to be heroes. They hear tanks and they run back to this end. We have nothing here to stop heavy German tanks. With luck we can find some explosive and blow the bridge."

"I wonder where the Colonel is?"

"I wonder too. Sergeant Major O'Rourke if you take charge here with Sergeant Barker then I will go and find him. Turn the anti-tank guns to face south and see if the machine guns can be salvaged. I'll head up into the town."

Even as I walked north I reloaded my guns and I scanned the road to identify any danger. The front was obviously very fluid. I guessed that this river formed part of the front line. That meant we were vulnerable until reinforcements could be rushed to us.

I heard firing ahead. I ran and found Corporal Cooper and Corporal Hewitt sheltering behind a wrecked German lorry. They pointed at Miller and Dexter. They lay dead. Both had been hit by a heavy machine gun.

"Where is Morrison?"

"He is over there, sir." Cooper pointed to a wrecked house. Morrison waved.

"Where is the machine gun?"

"On the other side of the square."

Stavelot was like many small Belgium towns. There was a central square with a small town hall. It was normally surrounded by cafes and shops. This one also had an enormous abbey just behind the square. I could see it, towering over the buildings of the town. That was where they had the spotter for the artillery. The Colonel would have to get beyond that tower before he would reach the square. I could see that this one had been devastated when the Germans had attacked and the rubble helped them to make it a fortress. I handed my MP 34 to Cooper and took my sniper rifle. I crawled under the truck. The snow had been turned to slush and mush by the firing and the feet. I pushed some before me to make a small wall. I was able to hide behind it. I slid the barrel of the gun slowly through the slush and hoped that it would not be noticed. When nothing happened, I looked through the sights. I scanned the buildings from left to right.

They had used the partly demolished window of a boulangerie and packed sandbags around it. They had an MG 42 and around it were the snouts of MP 34s. It looked to be a section defending that point. As I lay

82

there I could hear, to the east, the sound of the Sherman. The Germans were replying with anti-tank guns. I was thankful that it was not an 88. There had to be more Germans in the town than we had seen. Where were they? I forced myself to concentrate on one problem at a time. We had to eliminate this machine gun post before the Colonel arrived. The emplacement would be able to fire on the flank of the advancing Americans. Then I remembered the map I had studied. Trois Ponts lay to the west of us and Stourmont to the north. There was a crossroads to my left, about a hundred yards up the road. They would have that guarded. There was a fuel dump north of Stourmont and Trois Ponts also had bridges. That was where the bulk of the enemy were; they were guarding the crossroads. The soldiers fighting the Colonel were just trying to delay the Americans while they made a strongpoint even stronger.

I looked through the sight. I could not yet see the gunner. The machine gun obscured it. I could hit the loader but the gunner was the one with more skills. I did not want them to know we had a sniper. I shouted, "Morrison, fire a clip of bullets at the machine gun."

"I won't be able to hit it."

"I know. Count to five and then fire. As soon as you have fired take cover."

I aimed at the loader and as soon as I heard Morrison's bullets I fired. The loader fell. They would think that Morrison had somehow hit them. He was slightly to their left. The sub machine guns and rifles opened up. They brought another loader and moved the machine gun around. I now had a better shot.

I shouted, "Corporal Cooper, use the front tyre for protection and fire five bullets at the machine gun. You should be safe there. You are behind the engine block."

"Yes sir." He had seen what I had already done and he waited for five beats before he fired. This time I fired two bullets. One took the machine gunner and the other the loader. All hell broke loose and the already damaged lorry was riddled with bullets.

Every head disappeared as they began to work out how to deal with us. We could not rush them for the distance was too great. I kept watch. Now it did not matter if they knew there was a sniper. A head appeared and I shot at it. Then bullets were fired from my left. The petrol tank was above my head and they hit it. Fuel began to drip down on me. I was beginning to move when I saw the snout of a Panzerfaust, "Morrison! Another clip! Hewitt and Cooper, head towards Morrison!"

I wriggled backwards as Morrison's bullets bought the other two the time to reach the building. Even as I stood I heard the whoosh of the rocket. I ran. I almost made it. The rocket hit the truck and ignited the petrol. I was thrown bodily and crashed into the wall. Everything went black.

Chapter 8

"Sir! Sir!"

I heard Hewitt's voice. It seemed to be coming from a long way away. I could almost hear Colonel Devine berating me for not wearing a helmet. I forced open my eyes. I looked up into the anxious face of John Hewitt.

"You had us worried there, sir. You were spark out!" I started to rise. "You ought to rest, sir. You might have concussion."

"I am fine, Corporal. What has happened?"

"Nowt much, sir. The wall protects us here and now that they have blown up the lorry they don't seem that bothered about us."

"Morrison, do you think you could make it back to the bridge without being seen?"

"Yes sir. I can give it a try."

"Good man. Ask Sergeant Barker to join us. I am loath to weaken the bridge any more but we need more firepower if we are to dislodge those chaps across the square."

He scurried off. "You two keep watch here. I am going to see if the upstairs of this building is sound. If it is, we can enfilade the boulangerie."

The building Morrison had used for shelter had been an old building but it had been badly damaged. The back of it had been hit and there was daylight where parts had collapsed. I could see an over grown garden. I went in through the opening which had been the front door. I crawled in and then stood. The wall facing the boulangerie was still sound but there were no windows. I went into what had been the kitchen. There was a rack of wine bottles. They were empty. There was also a number of oil lamps. They had no electricity! I saw a paraffin heater. My gran had one of those. Mum thought it was a death trap. There was no food.

The stairs had been almost demolished but I managed to clamber up them and reach the next floor. Once again there was no window on to the square. Then I spied a loft. Some of these old houses had a transom in the attic. It was worth a try. I found a chest of drawers in one of the bedrooms. I dragged it out and climbed up on it. I was able to punch open the hatch and then drag myself in. There was a covering of snow. Most of the roof had been taken off. Part of it remained at the front but the gable end had been hit. I crawled along. The back half of the gable end had collapsed into the square. I peered around the end. Not only could I see the German position, I had the angle to fire down into it.

I clambered back down and returned to the others. Gordy and Hewitt were talking, "Sir, you ought to lie down. Hewitt is the medic and he is worried about concussion."

"John, you are a good man but you read too many books. I will be fine. I want all of us in the attic of this building. We can do some serious damage to the Germans from up here."

I led the way. When they emerged into the loft they were less than enthusiastic. "Sir, this is a death trap! If this was back home it would be condemned!"

"Don't worry, Gordy. We are not going to live here. As soon as we have cleared the square for the Colonel we will leave it." I glanced to the east. I could see the Sherman; it was less than half a mile from the edge of the town but the German defenders were dug in and the Americans still had only one tank. I was just grateful that the Germans had committed their tanks to their drive north and west.

"Now crawl with me to the gable end. I want us to make that a death trap for them. Don't show yourselves and keep your weapons hidden." When we reached the gable end I stood next to the remains of the wall to allow the others to lie down. They all kept far enough from the end so that the barrels of their guns would not be seen. There were twenty men in the emplacement. In the short time since they had destroyed the lorry they had added more protection. They had commandeered some tables, presumably from the nearby café. It would avail them nothing for we were above them.

"Gordy, you begin to fire from the left and Corporal Cooper from the right. Hewitt and Morrison concentrate on the middle. Keep firing until there is no one left alive down there. It will be hard for them to hit us because of the angle. We will have some protection from the bricks."

I levelled the Mauser by resting it on a brick which jutted out. I aimed at the machine gunner again. He was a replacement. "Now!"

Even as I said the word I squeezed the trigger and then worked the bolt. I fired a second at the loader. I fired a third at the gun itself. I was rewarded by sparks as my bullet knocked it over. The MP 34s and Thompsons deafened me as they hurled their bullets down on the German defenders. I saw that they had a Panzerfaust. Even as the rocketeer aimed it at me I shot him and, as he fell backwards his dying fingers squeezed the trigger and the rocket flew into the ceiling. The building collapsed on them. Any wounded would not have lasted long.

The two Americans cheered and Gordy shook his head but he was smiling. It was a good victory. Hewitt was on the end and he not only had good eyes but he knew how to be alert at all times. "Sir, trouble! There is a German tank heading along the road from Trois Ponts. It is a big 'un. It looks like a Tiger."

I risked a look around the gable end. Hewitt was right. It was a Tiger and not only that, it was a King Tiger. The Sherman was about to be demolished. I cursed. If we had brought a PIAT we would have had the simplest of shots down into the soft top of the turret. We would have to improvise. "Morrison, Cooper, Hewitt, get down into the kitchen. There is a paraffin heater, some oil lamps and some bottles. Bring the fuel from the paraffin heater, bottles, oil lamps and any spare fuel. Oh and any old cloths, tea towels and the like."

As they went down Gordy said, "Petrol bombs?"

I nodded, "These Tigers carry tons of fuel. With luck we can ignite it. You never know they may oblige us with an open turret."

Gordy nodded, "Of course, sir, you realise that once they know we are here then we are dead meat."

"That goes without saying but there are five of us. If that Tiger makes it down the road then the whole of Colonel Devine's Command will be destroyed. It is worth the gamble."

I took out the binoculars. The King Tiger had Panzer Grenadiers behind. They were not in vehicles. They were walking. That told me that the Germans were short of fuel. There were, however, more than forty of them. They were all well-armed. The Colonel would struggle to hold them unless they had been reinforced. Hewitt was the first up and he had the bottles and the cloths.

"Gordy get the wicks made and soaked."

Corporal Cooper had the oil lamps and the paraffin. He also brandished a funnel. "I found this sir. A bit rusty but it will do."

"Sergeant Barker and Corporal Hewitt will show you how to make the petrol bombs. I will keep watch on the tank. We don't have long."

As I stood next to the wall to look through my glasses I felt the building begin to vibrate. A brick tumbled from the wall. The tank might end up destroying us just by passing by! Without turning I said, "When the tank is below us we light the wicks and then throw them onto the tank. If you get it through an open hatch, you win a cigar! There are infantry behind the tank so as soon as you have thrown your bomb then head back down to the ground. We leave by the back and head for the river. With luck they won't catch us!"

"That isn't very reassuring, sir."

Gordy said, "Well Corporal Cooper, in our line of work that is as good as it gets! Ready sir."

"Right, sergeant, you do the honours with the lighter. I will use the Mauser. Wait for my command." We had eight bombs and two oil lamps. I almost laughed. The King Tiger was one of the most sophisticated weapons I had ever seen and we were going to attack it with one of the most primitive.

The vibrations were becoming alarmingly violent the closer the tank came and more bricks fell from the building. I hoped the Germans would not look up. I glanced over and saw that the tank was just forty yards away.

"Gordy, ready!"

"Sir!"

I glanced over again. The tank was now just twenty yards away. "Light 'em and throw them!"

I had a grenade ready. I did not want to throw it for the commander was leaning out of his tank. If one of my men got lucky then the tank could be destroyed. I could not resist looking at the bombs as they hit. They were spectacular. Flames shot up. I saw the S.S. commander look up and then an oil lamp hit him full in the face. He fell into the tank but his overalls, probably already oil soaked, were on fire. I dropped the hand grenade and then began to fire the Mauser. The flames leapt so high that they singed my eyebrows. Then there was an almighty explosion. I was knocked from my feet. Even worse was the gable end which teetered towards me and then, mercifully, fell into the street landing on the tank and some of the Panzer Grenadiers. I felt the whole house lurch. When I glanced around I saw that my men had obeyed me and were scurrying down the rabbit hole. I found it hard to keep my feet as the building was falling down even as I ran. Suddenly a huge hole opened up before me and I could not stop myself. I fell through. I expected a shuddering bone breaking landing but I fell onto a bed. I was winded but otherwise alright. Above me was sky. When I reached the door a surprised Corporal Cooper shook his head in disbelief.

As we ran down the stairs I took another hand grenade. As Corporal Cooper ran through the back of the house I threw the grenade towards the front door and followed him. I was half way down the garden when the grenade went off. The screams told me that I had caught Germans on their way in. When I reached the back wall I vaulted it and followed my men as we ran down the track towards the river.

There was no pursuit. We ran until we reached the bridge and a surprised Sergeant Major O'Rourke looked at us in disbelief. "We heard an explosion. What the hell happened Major?"

Corporal Cooper laughed, "We just destroyed a Tiger tank with gas and wine bottles! The Major here is like Superman. He can fly!"

"Before we get carried away, Corporal, we had better prepare for action. Those Germans will be down here soon enough. Ready to repel boarders Sergeant Major?"

"Of course sir! It's time we did our bit too!"

I sat down and drank some water. I felt a little dizzy. Perhaps Hewitt had been right. He saw my reaction and came over. "Let me take another look at your head, Major."

"I am just a little tired, Hewitt."

"Major, let him look at you, please, sir. Humour us."

Hewitt took off my cap and took the medical kit out. He washed my head again and then dabbed something on it which stung. "I am going to have to stitch this, sir. It will just be a couple but there is a flap of skin hanging loose and you keep undoing my work."

"Just do it then." I could hardly keep my eyes open. "If I have a lie down can you still do it?"

"Of course, sir. Lie on your left side."

Sergeant Major O'Rourke looked around and then took out a hip flask. "Here sir, have a nip of this. It will help."

"What is it Sergeant Major?"

"Something we make back home in West Virginia. We call it White Lightning."

I took a swallow. It felt smooth for a second and then the heat kicked in. It tasted like raw alcohol. "That has some kick."

He took the flask from me. "That's enough now sir."

Hewitt said, "Here Sergeant Major." He took the flask and poured a little on his needle and the wound. It stung!

I lay on my left side and was soon asleep. I don't know if it was the dizziness or alcohol which did it. When I awoke it was late afternoon and my head stung a little. Gordy was sat nearby talking with Sergeant Major O'Rourke. "Sleeping Beauty awakes. Alright now sir?"

"Yes Sergeant. How long was I out?"

"Forty minutes sir. Hewitt wanted you to sleep longer."

"No time for that. What is the state of play."

He pointed up the road to the square. "Jerry headed back along the Trois Ponts road. He didn't bother coming here. We sent a messenger to Colonel

Devine and there are men coming the way that we did." Even as he spoke a column of men arrived.

Lieutenant Weltzer saluted, "Colonel's compliments, Major Harsker, where do you want us?"

I struggled to my feet.

"Steady Major."

"Are you okay sir?"

"Fine, Lieutenant. I just stood too quickly. Have you a sergeant and ten men who can hold this position?"

"Yes sir."

"Then have them relieve the Sergeant Major's men. We have sat on our backsides long enough. It is time to get back into this war. You have five minutes, gentlemen." I saw Hewitt looking at me. "If that is alright with you, doctor?"

"It should be but I will be happier when the Colonel and the rest arrive. I would like a proper doctor to have a look at it too."

"Gordy, take Corporal Cooper and Morrison. Go and have a look see at the German positions. I intend to flank the men who are holding up the Colonel. Just make sure that the men on the Trois Ponts road can't attack us."

"Righto sir." He leaned forward, "John's right, sir. Don't overdo it. Your head is a right mess. Your young lady will not be pleased!"

"Thank you, Mother!"

As he headed up the road I check the German machine pistol. I would soon need some more ammunition. With luck I would get some from the Germans we were about to attack. I checked that I had grenades. I had my last two Mills bombs and two German grenades. The Americans were almost out of them too which meant we would have to get them from Jerry until the relief came.

Lieutenant Weltzer saluted, "Ready sir."

"What news of the relief, Lieutenant?"

"The 82nd Airborne are heading down from Huy but the roads are all jammed up with traffic."

"I guessed as much. I think it has hurt the Germans as much as us. Their tanks are open country tanks. There are too many trees around here. Still they have done well to advance as far as they have. The weather has helped them. There will be a window and when the air force gets up we will have a better picture of the offensive and we should be able to stop them."

"The Sergeant Major says you stopped a Tiger with petrol bombs."

I nodded, "It is the first time I have used them and we were lucky that we were able to get above them. Like I said they are not meant for streets and narrow roads."

Sergeant Major O'Rourke appeared. "Ready sir. We have thirty men. They mainly have rifles."

I pointed up the street. "We are heading up there. Sergeant Barker will have scouted out the enemy. We hit them hard and fast, make them think we are a brigade. We only have one shot at this. As soon as it is night they will counter attack. Let's go!" I suddenly remembered the German officer. "Oh by the way Lieutenant in the end house there is a German officer. He is bound. Better have your men bring him here, eh? I think he has been tied up long enough."

"Yes sir." The Lieutenant gave his orders and then followed me.

I held my MP 34 across my chest. I could still taste the alcohol on my lips. I should have had a coffee before I left but I knew that we had to strike quickly. It had been a long day. December meant that the nights were longer than the days but this one felt like it had lasted forever. We passed the bodies of Miller and Dexter. They were a stark reminder that we played for keeps here.

Corporal Cooper waved us to our feet. "Sir, Sarge says to wait here. He is finding us a way through the rubble."

A moment later he returned. "Sir, there is a way through the rubble. Jerry is five hundred yards that way. I reckon there are only a hundred or so left but they have heavy weapons and they are dug in." He pointed to the Abbey. "They have men in there too sir."

"How about the square? Any Germans?"

"Not living sir."

"Then you and Sergeant Major O'Rourke take his men and use that side of the square to enfilade the men in the Abbey. You should be able to find weapons and ammo among the dead. Take Hewitt with you. I will stay with the Lieutenant here."

I saw a frown on Sergeant Barker's face. His eyes flickered to the young Lieutenant. "With respect sir, you need either me or the Sergeant Major with you."

I lowered my voice, "We all have to learn, Gordy. I need my best men on that side. You can see that. It will be hard to winkle them out of the Abbey."

"Sir."

"Watch out for the Germans on the Trois Ponts road. The light is fading but they may still try to take pot shots at you."

I watched anxiously as the two men led the ridiculously small number of Americans across the square. "Right Lieutenant, have your men follow me. When I wave my arm clockwise they are to spread into a line and open fire."

"Sir."

I could hear sporadic gunfire. The Colonel and his men had been chipping away at the German defences all day. Ammunition would be in short supply for both sides. Ominously I could no longer hear the Sherman. I headed along the edge of the wrecked building. The rubble from the fallen gable end had covered the Tiger which was a blackened wreck. The heat had burned away any snow. When night fell it would freeze and the Tiger would become a frozen tomb of fried flesh. There were limbs peeping out of the rubble. Once we had crossed the obstacle I saw, ahead, the white camouflage capes interspersed with black S.S. uniforms. They were four hundred yards from us. It was too far for us to make an effective attack. I headed across the back yard of the wrecked house we had used and clambered over the fence at the back. Here there was still snow. I turned left and went up the track. It brought us to within two hundred yards of the Germans. Crouching I moved closer.

They were now close enough. I raised my hand and men appeared on either side of me. "Hit them and hit them hard!" I ran forward. I knew we would be seen but the closer we could be before we opened fire the more casualties we could cause. I was a hundred and twenty yards away when they saw us emerging from the gloom. As soon as I saw a face turn I fired a burst. The effect was devastating. Lieutenant Weltzer and his men did all that I had asked of them. They fired and ran. They were fearless despite the fact that the Germans ahead of us outnumbered us. I kept moving and firing. A stationary target was a dead man. I heard firing from my right Sergeant Barker was in action.

When I was forty yards from the Germans I took out a grenade and hurled it. "Grenade! Hit the deck."

Even as we all dived one of the Lieutenant's men was hit as the Germans recovered from our initial onslaught. The grenade swept through the ones who were standing to face us. I stood and emptied the MP 34 before reloading. We had hit them on their right flank. With Gordy and the Americans hitting their left flank the ones in the centre were, effectively surrounded.

I heard a German officer shout, "Fall back! Fall back!"

"Pour it into them, boys!" Lieutenant Weltzer had the joy of battle in him. As we ran forward, firing, some of his men paid the price. We were not fighting novices. These were S.S. Panzer Grenadiers. They were German elite.

I knelt and sprayed the whole magazine at the Germans who were a hundred yards from me. When that was empty I drew my Luger and emptied that magazine too. With fire on both sides we were creating a maelstrom of metal through which they had to run. It is hard to fire when you are running; even so bullets zipped over our heads and I heard another cavalryman fall. I heard the sound of American half-tracks as the Colonel led the rest of his men to batter their way through the barricades the Germans had erected.

I put another magazine in the MP 34. "Lieutenant see to your wounded."

He grinned, "Yes sir! That was some charge." Just then a German who been playing dead half rose and shot the Lieutenant in the back. I was twenty feet away and the MP 34 made the German's body jerk like a demented puppet. I ran to the Lieutenant. His glazed eyes told me he was dead.

His sergeant ran up. He kicked the dead German in the head, "Bastard!"

"Sergeant, make sure that there are no more Germans playing dead." I then shouted in German, "If you wish to surrender then put up your hands."

There was silence. I walked over to the German I had shot and picked up his MP 34. I gave it to the sergeant. "Anyone you think is playing dead, shoot them."

Just then a figure ten feet away rose and ran. The sergeant cut him down, "Sneaky eh sir?"

"And then some."

I walked over the defences. I picked up a couple of spare magazines for my gun but the Germans appeared to have been almost out of ammunition. It explained why they ran and did not fight. I saw that we had slain about fifty of them. More than that had escaped to join the defences on the Trois Ponts road.

The Colonel's half-track pulled up next to me. He looked down at Lieutenant Weltzer, "Damn! That boy had potential. What a waste."

"And he had guts, sir. He did well." I pointed to the bodies of his men who were being laid in a line by the rest of the platoon. "They all did."

"Sergeant Major O'Rourke?"

"He and Sergeant Barker are on the other flank. What happened to the Sherman, sir?"

"Panzerfaust. That is the last of our armour. More men have joined us and the road to Malmedy is in our hands but reinforcements and supplies are held up by the weather. There are German paratroopers behind the lines and they are causing all hell."

I nodded, "It is the sort of thing we do. A few determined men who can live off the land can block an entire army." I jerked my thumb behind me. "There are King Tigers that way. We stopped one. Jerry is dug in at the crossroads. We hold the bridge. If we have explosives then we can blow it and stop them sending reinforcements this way."

"We will have to leave it open, Tom. St. Vith has finally fallen. The 7th and 9th Armoured are going to be coming up that road along with the remnants of the 422nd and 433rd Regiments. We need every soldier and tank we can get."

I nodded, "Then we had better beef up the bridge defences sir. I left just a handful of Lieutenant Weltzer's men there." I pointed behind me. "A few hundred yards up there is the main square. It is far enough from the Trois Ponts crossroads to be safe from fire and we can make it defensible. It controls the road to the bridge."

I saw Sergeant Barker, Corporal Hewitt, Sergeant Major O'Rourke and Corporal Cooper heading for us. Morrison must have bought it. The Colonel said, "I want to thank you, Tom. I am not certain where we would have been without your knowledge."

"It was your men who did all this Colonel. They are fast learners. Don't forget we have been fighting Nazis for five years."

Once we had rearmed we headed for the square. We had no time to bury the dead. We covered them with their blankets and left them where they lay. We cleared the barricades so that the reinforcements we expected could reach us. The men were all exhausted. I had no idea what kept them going. They had fought all day with little food. The Colonel, however, was a bundle of energy. He organised his cooks to get a rudimentary kitchen going and he had Captain Dekker use the soldiers who had been in reserve as sentries. We reinforced the bridge with slightly fresher troops and made ourselves as comfortable as one can when you are sleeping less than a mile from German S.S.

I sat with the Colonel and his handful of officers. We had been joined by elements of the 422nd and 433rd as well as a rag tag of refugees who had managed to escape captivity. We sat around a brazier as, once again, snow fell. Sergeant Barker and Corporal Hewitt were with Sergeant Major O'Rourke and the NCO's.

Captain Dekker asked the question which was on everyone's lips. "And tomorrow sir, what then? Hold, retreat or attack?"

The Colonel smiled, "Son, we are cavalry. We attack when we can. However, unless we get tanks or artillery then we sit here and stop them reinforcing their front. The All-American Airborne division is on their way. They are tough soldiers."

I nodded, "Sadly sir, they lack armour. Unless we get a lot more armour we are in trouble. It took three Shermans to defeat one Panther."

"Technically, Major Harsker the Panther and the King Tiger were down to you and the men I loaned you."

"We were lucky. We can destroy individual tanks but not a larger number."

Captain Macmillan had recently arrived from St. Vith. "The Major is right sir. They used just six of those big German tanks to finally take St. Vith. If the roads hadn't been so crowded then they would be up our ass right now!"

"What is their weakness Major Harsker?"

"Fuel and a shot at their rear." I pointed to the burned-out King Tiger. "Go and check that one out sir. She may be burned but if Jerry started dropping bombs I would high tail it in there! It would take a helluva big bomb to hurt it. You can damage their tracks but you have to get close to them and they have Panzer Grenadiers. Hitler has sent in his very best troops. These aren't garrison troops. This is the best that the Germans have left. They have S.S. and Paratroopers; they don't come any more elite than those units. He is gambling and gambling big."

"Well one thing is for sure, Major, unless we get some more ammunition then we will be forced to defend. It is one thing taking German weapons but we need a lot more than we can pick up here."

I was awoken in the middle of the night. A runner said, "Sir, can you come to the command vehicle, the Colonel needs to see you."

When I got there the Colonel was shaking his head. "It looks like a German column of tanks broke through our lines north of Stourmont. They are heading for the fuel dump there. If they reach it then we are in big trouble. They have also managed to stop the 82nd. You were right. The Airborne don't have much heavy ordinance with them."

Just then we heard the rumble of armour coming up the Malmedy road. We were all ready for action and we grabbed weapons. It was ridiculous, of course. My MP 34 could do nothing against a German tank. I soon recognised the distinctive noise of the Ford engine. They were Shermans. The three of them were from the 7th Armoured Division. They had with them four trucks filled with the survivors of the 106th Infantry Division. The Captain who led them said, "Colonel Cavender is hot on our tails, sir. He has the rest of the 422nd and 433rd with him and a couple of tanks from the 9th Armoured."

"Where are the rest of your tanks?"

"They were sent north to the Elsenborn Ridge. If we had gone with them we would have been backed up all the way back to St. Vith."

"Don't apologise captain. Your armour is more than welcome. Point your tanks in that direction." He gestured towards the crossroads.

It was then that the Captain saw the King Tiger. He shook his head, "I thought we had seen the last of those beasts at St. Vith. How did a tank destroy this one?"

The Colonel shook his head, "It didn't. It was the Major here with petrol bombs."

The captain saluted me, "Thank you sir. I lost half of my troop to those. Not a man got out alive!"

I looked at the Colonel who nodded. He now appreciated the problem we faced.

Situation 20th December 1944

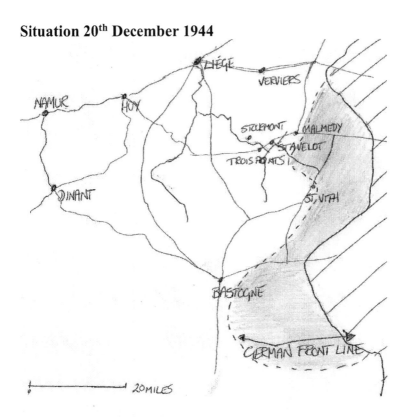

Chapter 9

"We try to take them now while we have them rattled. They won't like being driven out of here. They don't know that we have armour nor that we have been reinforced. We send the three Shermans in first. The rest of us will attack on a wide front. It worked for Major Harsker yesterday. The other tanks are still strung out on the road along with the rest of Colonel Cavender's men. They can be our reinforcements."

The captain looked worried, "Sir, what if they have Tigers or Panthers?"

"We have seen no sign of them since we destroyed this one. The last we heard they were racing up the road to the fuel dump."

As the next most senior officer I felt obliged to support the captain. "Sir, the captain has a point. What if they have Panzerfausts too? At least send a half-track or infantry in front of them."

"This is where I miss my armoured cars. They could have nipped in and out before the Krauts knew we were here." He nodded, "I hate to ask Tom but..."

"Of course, sir."

Captain Stewart asked, "Sir, a British officer leading Americans?"

"Trust me Captain, the Major here has a nose for trouble."

This time it was Corporal Cooper who drove. Sergeant Major O'Rourke was overruled. The Colonel needed him to organize the follow up. Two of the Corporal's men were on the gun and we had two privates who had volunteered. I turned to Captain Stewart, "Keep your tanks a good hundred yards behind us. They won't waste a rocket on us. If we see a tank you will be the first to know."

"Why sir?"

"Because you will see them blow us up!" I clambered on board. "Ready when you are Corporal. Still got the pistol for your son?"

"Yes sir."

"Then let's be careful so that you can deliver it to him."

I had the Mauser ready. The range for the MP 34 was too great. I saw that the Germans were hidden. They had no barricade erected. Nor was there any snow on the road. That was a worry for it could be mined. I took out my glasses and scanned the enemy positions. I saw machine guns but no tanks. Corporal Cooper was taking it as slowly as he could. Any slower and we would be stationery. I glanced behind me. The Shermans were doing as I had asked. As soon as the Germans saw the tanks then they would fire but one half-track did not constitute a real threat.

Suddenly I heard the crack of a rifle and Pfc Muldoon fell with a third eye. There was a sniper.

"Take cover! Corporal Cooper, a little faster." I looked for an elevated position. There was one but it was on a slight rise some mile away. This was a good sniper. I had no chance of hitting him. We were four hundred yards from the enemy lines. "Right lads, open fire. Let's see if we can draw their sting."

It was not the smartest decision I ever made. All hell broke loose. They had more guns than we had expected. The S.S. had enfiladed the road. They used the natural cover and the snow to hide their numbers. The two gunners on the .50 Calibre managed to clear one part of the defences but they were cut down. I heard Corporal Cooper cry out as he was hit.

"Use grenades! Cooper, get us out of here!" I hurled a German grenade high in the air. Hewitt and Barker did the same. We sheltered behind the metal of the half-track. Bullets and shrapnel rattled into it as we swung around in the road. All the time we were taking hits. The three Shermans opened fire with their main gun and their machine guns. The fire on the half-track lessened and we drove past the tanks. Colonel Devine had his men in a long skirmish line behind the tanks. They would be cut down if they advanced.

Suddenly, behind us I heard the double whoosh of two rockets being fired and a Sherman erupted in a fireball. They had anti-tank weapons. The two Shermans fired two smoke bombs and began to fall back. The Colonel realised that we had lost the initiative and he halted the advance. As we passed him I heard him shout, "Dig in! This is our new front line!"

When we reached the square Hewitt raced to the wounded Corporal. It was his leg which had been hit. I hoped that the Americans had a doctor. Hewitt fastened a tourniquet while I checked the others. They were all dead. There were just four of us left alive. The volunteers had all paid the ultimate price. The half-track looked like a sieve. The front tyre had been shredded. How the Corporal had got it back I would never know.

Sergeant Barker shouted, "Medic!" as only a British sergeant can.

I waited until the Corporal had been taken away before I went back towards the Colonel. Our new front line was less than two hundred yards from the Germans. We were lucky that there were damaged buildings to provide us with shelter. The road was clear and the two remaining tanks stopped well short of the crossroads. They could control any vehicles which attempted to use the road but they would not risk the rockets.

Captain Stewart climbed out of the turret as Colonel Devine approached. "That was a disaster and no mistake."

"Colonel, have your men watch out. They have a sniper. He is more than a mile away but he is good. He hit one of your men in the half-track."

Colonel Devine nodded, "Colonel Cavender is on the way. Perhaps when we have more men we can try something. For the present, we will just hold. Major Harsker, I would appreciate it if you would take command at the bridge. In our present position things are more than a little dangerous."

"Sir."

As we hurried down the road we heard the exchange of gunfire. Neither side was wasting ammunition. The shots were fired at clear targets. The two tanks began to fire too. What worried me was the response the Germans might make. They could not afford to leave us here. We stopped reinforcements and we, effectively, cut them off. I saw the other tanks heading up the road from Malmedy. Our two Shermans would not be isolated. I hoped that the two regiments coming to join us had anti-tank weapons.

I felt guilty to be leaving the fighting but I knew that the Colonel was right. There was just a sergeant in command at the bridge. With just twenty men guarding it the Germans could walk right in. He hadn't said so but I knew that the Colonel wanted me to make it a tougher nut to crack. As we walked down I said, "How is Cooper, John?"

"It missed the bone but it was a big bullet. I think his war is over."

"Then that is a good thing. So long as he can walk and they can get him out he can go home to his son. He will have a purple heart and, hopefully, the Colonel will put him in for another medal. He deserves it."

The sergeant at the bridge had not been idle. They had rolled some empty barrels and placed them at the far end of the bridge. I waved him over. "Sergeant."

He saluted, "Sergeant Bud Henry, sir. 18th Cavalry."

"The Colonel has put me in charge here."

"Good, sir. My guys are good but we prefer a vehicle under us."

I laughed, "Don't we all. What is in the barrels?"

"We chipped ice from the river and packed it with snow. When it melts and settles we can add more. It makes for a good road block. We can roll them out of the way if our tanks come along but they will be a little bit of an obstacle for the Krauts."

"Smart thinking. Have we any explosives?"

"No sir."

A sudden thought struck me. "Sergeant, have your men find any jerricans they can. Go back to where we lost the Shermans the other day. See if there is any petrol left in them. Syphon it off. We can use that."

"Right sir."

While Sergeant Henry found his men I said, "Barker, Hewitt, see if there are any grenades or rockets around. We can manufacture something with them." While they were busy I loaded all of my guns. I had a feeling I would soon need them.

I heard sporadic gunfire from the crossroads. The Shermans were conserving their ammunition. They were using their HE and keeping their AP for when the inevitable Panzers arrived. While I was waiting for my men to return I crossed the bridge. There was a Corporal and a Pfc guarding it. They saluted.

"Any sign of movement down the road?"

"Hard to tell sir. The trees, the snow and the bend in the road make it difficult to see too far." He chuckled, "We don't have snow in Georgia."

"Whereabouts in Georgia do you live, Corporal?"

"Corporal Powers, sir I live in Atlanta. You know, 'Gone with the Wind'?" I frowned. "The movie, sir, Clark Gable and Vivien Leigh. It was in colour."

"Well, Corporal, we can be grateful for the snow. It is holding up the enemy. I am just going to have a recce by the trees."

"Do you want Wilbur to come with you?"

"No, Corporal, I will be fine."

I had my MP 34 with me. I still had a couple of magazines for it. I also had some German grenades and the last of my parachute cord. The road was slippery. There had been a partial thaw and now that it was colder the top had frozen. It would not be an obstacle for a tank but it would make it hard for a soldier to creep up. There were some big trees. If we couldn't blow the bridge then it might be possible to chop down two of the trees and make a barricade. I walked down the road until I had turned the bend. I used my glasses to look down the road. I could see nothing. Glancing at my watch I saw that there would be about three hours of daylight before it became gloomy and then dark. That left me three hours to begin to make the bridge defensible.

I noticed that, where I had viewed the road, there was a slight slope and any tank would struggle to climb its slippery surface. There would be an increase in the engine noise. That would warn us of tanks. What about men? "They would not walk up the road. They would come through the woods. German Panzer Grenadiers keep close to the sides of their tanks. I found two trees which were really close to the road. I made sure that the snow was untouched and, kneeling on the icy road, I made a booby trap. I reached up and shook a branch so that snow fell on the cord, disguising it. I did the same on the other side. If the Americans arrived first they would come in lorries and keep to the road. However, if they tripped my traps, then, sadly that would be a hazard of war.

I walked back.

"We thought you got lost, sir."

I smiled at the nervous looks on the two soldiers' faces. "All safe and sound Corporal. I was just putting a couple of booby traps for any German infantry who try to sneak up on us. How long until your relief?"

"Another two hours sir."

"I'll be back before then."

By the time I reached the other end Sergeant Henry and Sergeant Barker had returned. "We found a dozen rockets sir."

"My guys managed to get three jerricans of gas sir."

"Good then we can use them. I need a couple of axes too."

"Axes sir?"

"Yes Sergeant Barker. I want to half cut the two trees closest to the bridge. If Jerry comes then we can chop them down and it will stop the Germans charging up the road."

"They'll be able to move them though, sir."

"You are right Sergeant Henry and while they are doing so we shoot them! This is how we are going to use the rockets. I want half taking apart. Do it carefully. Inside there will be black powder for the propellant charge and then almost two pounds of T.N.T and hexogen. We will use those if we have to blow the bridge."

"What about the other six sir?"

I picked up a rocket. "This weighs about six and half pounds. The Byzantines had an arrow with a lead weight on it. When they threw it high it always landed tip down. Now this is too big to use that method but if we tie a piece of parachute cord to the end and whirl it around our heads then when we throw it the warhead should land detonator down."

Sergeant Henry looked at me with a look of disbelief.

"When we have stripped one we will do an experiment. We should have time."

I could see that I had them all intrigued. To be truthful I had no idea if it would work but we had little choice. We had no detonators and so the T.N.T. and hexogen would have to be ignited by firing a bullet into them. That was never an easy task. Pfc Mason found a couple of axes and we put an edge on to them.

"I want you to start to cut down the two trees. Don't go all the way through. We might still have our own tanks coming across the bridge. If we have to we can use a grenade to bring them down."

"Yes sir. It will keep me good and warm!"

Soon I heard the sound of axes biting into the trees. Sergeant Henry brought me the first empty rocket casing. I immediately saw a problem. It was two pounds lighter. I unscrewed the bottom and scraped some soil into it. It felt a little heavier. I tied a short length of parachute cord around the end.

"What now sir?"

"We wait until your chaps have finished doing their lumberjack impression and then we will try it out. I have no idea how far it will go or how accurate it will be. If this doesn't work then we will tie the barrels of water and ice together and fix these in between."

When the two men came back with their axes we walked down to the end of the bridge. When Corporal Powers heard what we had he said, "Sir, do you mind if I have a go? I was an athlete and used to do the field events. This is like throwing the hammer."

"Be my guest Corporal. Accuracy is more important than length!"

He took a wide stance and whirled it around his head. When he released it, the projectile travelled fifty yards and landed just three feet from the trees. They were all cheering and clapping as soon as it landed.

I nodded. "That works. The only problem will be Jerry firing at you while you are doing it." Their balloon was punctured and I felt guilty but we had a weapon. It was not perfect but it was better than nothing.

As night fell the noise of firing diminished. I knew that the Colonel would be vigilant and protect his five tanks. The extra infantry meant he could keep a better watch. I left Sergeant Henry organize the rota for duties. He was going to put a brazier for the sentries at the end of the bridge. I persuaded him not to. "It will ruin their night vision and make them a target for any Germans who are out there. Have the fire here and surrounded by not only the men but also their equipment."

"But the guys sir! They will freeze their…"

"Have them do a duty for no more than an hour. Two men at the far end of the bridge and two at this end. We have twenty-two men. That is eleven hours of cover. That way they will be alert and they can get warm back here."

"Sir, twenty-two men means you and your guys."

"We are in this too. Don't worry, we have done a duty before. We can be trusted."

"I didn't mean that, sir."

"Don't worry, sergeant, we will be fine. Wake Hewitt and me at 0300. I rise early anyway. Sergeant Barker is a good non-com. Put him with someone you are worried about."

We sat close to the fire. It was a freezing night. The men in the section complained but I was happy and smiled. "Sir, it is as cold as a witch's tit and you are smiling, why?"

"Because we have a fire and you can bet your bottom dollar that, out there, there will be Germans who have no fire. Their tanks will either have to keep their engines going and burn valuable fuel or they will risk their engines seizing up in the cold. The ice and the snow are our friends. We have food and they, in all probability, will have none. Look on the positive side."

"Sir, I come from Florida! We never see snow."

Gordy sniffed, "Then this must be a delight for you, son, why are you complaining?"

Corporal Powers had finished his duty, "Sir, Sergeant Major O'Rourke said that you guys get shot if the Germans capture you." I nodded. "And you still go out and risk capture?"

"I have been captured, Corporal. It was in North Africa and they had the firing squad ready."

"You escaped?"

"Of course. They should have shot us straight away. Commandos are like the Vikings of old. If you fight us then make sure you kill us or we will kill you."

He looked at John Hewitt, "You too?"

"Of course."

I could see that we had set them to thinking. "Look guys, there is nothing complicated about this. Uncle Sam has trained you well. We saw that today and yesterday. You know how to fight and you have courage. That is all you need. The S.S. you are fighting are just like vicious criminals. Your Al Capone and the Mafia, they are like the S.S. They are not hard working and they have a perverted sense of values. All of you chaps want to get home to your families." I spread my arm, "We do. The S.S.? They enjoy this. As far as they are concerned Hitler can make this war last a hundred years and they will be happy. That is the difference. Never forget that. You are fighting for something worthwhile. They are fighting because they enjoy it."

Silence descended around the fire. Wilbur, Pfc Pitt, asked, "But can we win sir? Can we beat these guys and their weapons? When I went to get the gas from the Shermans I had a look at that Tiger. It had steel like the Liberty ship we came over on! How do you stop them?"

"You saw how. Use a bottle of gas and a match!" They nodded. "And a tip from an old soldier. Get as much sleep as you can. Trust that your comrades will guard you and when it is your turn to watch remember that you watch your brothers. We are family!"

Gordy said, quietly, "And that goes double for you, sir. Get your head down and that is an order. You were wounded today!"

I laughed "Yes mother!"

When we were woken for our duty, Hewitt and I left the relative warmth of our blankets for the icy reaches of the far end of the bridge. The sentries we had relieved had seen nothing save the white emptiness of the night. After checking that it was still all quiet I sent Hewitt back to the fire to put on a large dixie of water. Thanks to the snow water was not in short supply. By the time it was the time for our shift to be over it would be boiled. I had already decided that there would be little point in my going back to bed. I could go up to the Trois Ponts crossroads and view the situation there. There had been shots during the night. As the Americans were using captured weapons it was hard to tell who was doing the firing.

The secret of sentry duty on a freezing night is to keep moving. With the German camouflage cape covering my ears and upper body I was relatively warm and almost invisible. I kept my eyes on the road south. Although the night was silent I could hear, in the far distance, vehicles. I had no idea which way they were moving but it had to be along this road. It could either be towards St Vith or away from it. Towards would be German tanks closing in on the last of the defenders; the ones who could not get out. Away from it could either be Americans or, if it was truly all over, the Germans.

Corporal Hewitt returned. He looked happy. "One of the sentries searched one of the nearby houses, sir. He found a tea caddy. We can have tea this morning!"

Somehow that brightened the morning. I liked American coffee but morning wasn't morning without a mug of hot sweetened tea. I took it as a hopeful sign. "That is excellent news." I looked south again. "We won't be home for Christmas then, John."

"No sir. What is the date?"

"Today is the 22nd. I have no idea of the day of the week! Unless things change dramatically then we will be here."

"At least we will have a white Christmas. Back in the Boro it gets really cold but we rarely get snow. You see a bit on Roseberry Topping or the Eston hills but that is about it."

"Do you miss Middlesbrough then, John?"

"I didn't when I joined up but I do now. It is daft things like going to Stockton on a Wednesday for the market."

"Market?"

He grinned, "Don't get me wrong, sir, I hate shopping but the pubs are open all day on market day in Stockton. When I was a young lad me and my mates would walk to Stockton and have an all-day session in the pubs then fish and chips and walk home. I did it on my last leave. Half of the lads weren't there. Some were in action and others had died." He shook his head. "It is daft what you miss isn't it sir?"

"No John. In peacetime, we take too much for granted. I know that I will be looking at England with different eyes when I get home."

"You will be getting married won't you sir? You and your young lady."

"When the war is over, yes, but I try not to think of that."

"Brad Dexter was due to be married when he got back to Virginia, sir. He told me. He showed me a picture of her. She is a bonny lass. She will marry someone else now."

I began to recite. I had been forced to learn the poem at school and I had no idea that I still remembered it.

"What passing-bells for these who die as cattle?
Only the monstrous anger of the guns.
Only the stuttering rifles' rapid rattle
Can patter out their hasty orisons.
No mockeries now for them; no prayers nor bells;
Nor any voice of mourning save the choirs,
The shrill, demented choirs of wailing shells;
And bugles calling for them from sad shires.
What candles may be held to speed them all?
Not in the hands of boys, but in their eyes
Shall shine the holy glimmers of good-byes.
The pallor of girls' brows shall be their pall;
Their flowers the tenderness of patient minds,
And each slow dusk a drawing-down of blinds."

Hewitt nodded, "That's about right sir. Who wrote that? You?"

I laughed, "No, John, a chap who died in the Great War; Wilfred Owen. He fought all the way through it and was decorated. He was a brave soldier. He died in the last week of the war. There will be a lot of women like that. Mrs. Dean, she lost her husband in the war. It took over twenty years for her to find Reg."

"Our school didn't read poems like that. I had to learn Tennyson's Charge of the Light Brigade. I liked it though. I thought how great it would be to charge with swords flashing."

"My dad began the Great War in the cavalry. The machine guns cut down the horses. That wasn't war, that was slaughter." I pointed to the north east. "It is ironic really that he fought north of us on horseback and we fought there in a half-track. A hundred and fifty years ago, British soldiers were doing the same at Waterloo. The difference was that then we were allies of the Germans."

We finished the watch in silence. Both of us were lost in memories of a more peaceful time. That was the thing about sentry duty. You found things out about your comrades. I had no idea that Hewitt liked Tennyson.

When we were relieved I told Corporal Powers to keep an ear out for the armour. "Will it be the Krauts, sir?"

"No idea but you should be able to recognise the sound of a Sherman. If it doesn't sound like a Sherman then prepare for the worst."

I left Hewitt at the camp and headed, with my gun up to the crossroads. As I approached there was the crack of a German rifle and a muffled cry. I automatically crouched as I ran up to the brazier. It was shielded by half-tracks and Shermans. Sergeant Major O'Rourke was handing mugs of coffee to Colonel Devine and, I assumed, Colonel Cavender.

Sergeant Major O'Rourke said, "Give me a minute sir and I will get you one."

"Thanks, Sarn't Major."

Colonel Cavender stood and held out his hand, "Jack here told me what you have done. It is a pleasure to meet you. I just missed you at St. Vith. Me and my guys arrived just after you left."

"What was it like sir?"

"We did our best to hold on but we couldn't match their armour. Our soldiers were brave enough; too brave perhaps. You can't fight Panthers with rifles and machine guns." He patted the nearest Sherman. "We needed more of these."

"When we came ashore on D-Day, we had the Firefly variant. That has a 17-pounder gun. They can take a Tiger; if they are close enough."

"If they are close enough, Major, then the Krauts will have blown them up already."

I nodded as Sergeant Major O'Rourke handed me my coffee. "How are things here, sir?"

"They have kept up their sniping all night. We intend to attack this morning and see if we can retake the crossroads before they bring in more tanks. According to the radio the All-American Division is still fighting its way south. As far as we know the German advance has stopped along its northern axis but in the south…"

Colonel Cavender nodded, "We heard that Bastogne is surrounded. Thank God, they have the Screaming Eagles there. General McAuliffe is a tough soldier. It will be hard to winkle him out of there but German columns are racing towards Dinant. It won't matter what we do here if they cross the Meuse."

"Well sir, in my experience, you fight one battle at a time. Let's fight this battle and worry about the rest of the war afterwards." I pointed south. "I heard the sound of vehicles, sir. They were way to the south but they may be heading up here."

"They could be our armour. Some were still fighting when I left."

"Well I hope it is." I stood and said to Colonel Devine, "You know where I am if you need me sir. If any Germans do come up this road then you know that we are all dead. They won't get through us without a fight."

"I know, Tom, I know."

By the time I got back to the bridge the small camp was stirring. The smell of coffee had awoken those who had been on watch first. Hewitt had managed to find a jug and he was brewing the tea. He shook his head as Gordy rubbed his hands, "Don't get excited Sarge, it is only dried milk and there's precious little sugar."

"If it is tea then that will do for me. This will start the day well."

Pfc Mason approached us, "Sir, I know that looting is frowned upon but yesterday, when I was looking for the axes, I found this." He took from a sack a large joint of cured ham. Some slices had been taken but there was still plenty left.

I smiled, "Let us say that you were foraging, Private, and that shows initiative."

"What do you do with this, sir? We don't have this at home."

"You can slice it and eat it as it is but if we can find a frying pan then we can slice it up and cook it like bacon."

Gordy said, "There's some stale bread, sir. If we put that in the fat when it has finished cooking then that will be a feast fit for a king."

"Right then, John, slice it into as many pieces as you can get and don't throw away the bone. That will make some soup!"

It is amazing how such little things can lift a soldier's spirits. They were cold. We had little ammunition. Enemies lay all around us and yet the smell of ham frying over an open fire and the aroma of freshly brewed coffee brought everyone who was not on duty to gather around. I took on the duty of cook.

"Here Gordy, give me four slices of that stale bread." I laid the four pieces on top of the huge skillet I was using to cook the ham. The ham had a great deal of fat on it and that rendered down so that the ham would have been almost deep fried had the bread not soaked it up. I made up the four sandwiches and gave them to Hewitt. "Take these to the guards at the bridge. It must be torture for them to smell the ham."

"Right sir."

Twenty minutes later the ham and the bread were all gone. Sergeant Henry had just taken a bite when he stopped, "Sir, where is yours?"

The truth was there was none left. It had not quite been the loaves and fishes but it had been close. "Don't worry about me Sergeant, I ate with the Colonel." He nodded, seemingly satisfied but I saw Gordy shake his head disapprovingly.

Dawn was just breaking when I heard the sound of the Sherman's guns as the attack began. I felt guilty for we had not had a bad night all things considered. I was just contemplating going to see if we could help when Corporal Powers, who had just relieved the sentries, came running across the bridge. "Sir, tanks."

"Stand to!"

Chapter 10

Every soldier grabbed his weapon and manned his post. I went with Sergeant Henry, Barker and Hewitt and we followed Corporal Powers back to the south side of the bridge.

"You can't see it sir, but you can hear it."

I listened. "That is a Sherman. Gordy come with me. I don't want them to trip my booby traps." We did not run on the road. It was still slick after the night. If the cloud cover returned then it might thaw but the sky looked clear for the moment. That was good for it meant we might have air cover soon. When I reached the slope, where the booby traps lay, we stopped. I saw that there was a Sherman and what looked like a Kangaroo behind. The Kangaroo and the Sherman were both covered with soldiers. The trouble was I had not seen any Kangaroos at St. Vith. A line of weary looking soldiers trudged behind. I did not know if the tanks were going slowly to preserve fuel or to make life easy for the men behind. They were less than half a mile away when the men began to run and the tanks speeded up.

"Looks like trouble." I took out my binoculars. I looked down the road. I could not see anything at first and then I saw a tendril of smoke climbing into the sky. It looked to me like the exhaust of a German tank. Where there was one tank there could be others. I estimated that they were five miles or more behind the Americans. That would give us, perhaps, fifteen minutes. I looked at the sky. The clear skies of the morning had gone. There was a chill wind from the north and there were snow laden clouds scudding in.

"Gordy, go back and warn the men that we may have company soon and then go and tell Colonel Devine the bad news. Tell Sergeant Henry to move the barrels too."

"Sir."

As the tank struggled up the slope I shouted, "Keep to the centre. Turn around once you are over the bridge."

The Sergeant nodded. I saw he had a bandage on his head, "Sir, there are Kraut tanks behind. There are at least six of them and two are Panthers."

"We will stop them. Never fear."

I saw that the Kangaroo was not an armoured personnel carrier. It was a Sherman that had had its turret blown off. The men began to jump off.

"Don't go into the woods I have mined it."

"Major Harsker!"

It was Sergeant Ford, "Sergeant, you made it. Is the Colonel with you?"

"He is in the bag sir. The last I heard they captured 7,000 of us." He shook his head, "We just made it out."

"Is the tank usable?"

The driver, whose head stuck out of the broken hatch shook his head, "We barely made it here, sir. This is scrap metal but at least it saved these guys."

"When you get to the bridge I want you to turn it sideways on and block the entrance to the bridge."

"Will do, sir."

I shouted to the men who were trudging behind, "Get yourselves over the bridge." I looked south and I saw the tanks a little more clearly. They had Panzer Grenadiers clinging to the huge Panthers which led the column. As the Americans marched past me I recognized the flash of an Engineer. It was a sergeant.

"Are you an Engineer, Sergeant?"

"Yes sir, Sergeant Phil Hall, 1st Engineer Battalion."

"Do you know explosives?"

He grinned, "Does a duck quack, sir? Of course I do."

"Come with me sergeant. I have some T.N.T., black powder and hexogen. I have some detonators from German rockets. Could you make the wrecked tank into a bomb?"

"With T.N.T. you can make anything into a bomb. The question is can you make it safely and have it explode when you want."

"What I intend to do is to park the wrecked tank across the bridge and cut the fuel lines so that the engine and the ground is covered in petrol. The Germans will probably try to push the tank off the bridge. It is what I would do. Could you make it so that when they struck the tank it would blow up?"

He grinned, "I think I could do something, sir!"

"Good man."

By the time we reached the bridge the driver had managed to manoeuvre the vehicle across the bridge.

"Sergeant Henry, get the barrels back in place."

"But why sir? The tank blocks it just as effectively."

"I intend to blow it up. The barrels will give us some protection. Corporal Hewitt go and fetch the detonators, T.N.T, black powder and hexogen. Give them to Sergeant Hall here and then assist him, eh?"

"Sir."

I opened the engine compartment and, finding the fuel lines, took out my dagger and slashed them. Time was of the essence. The smell of petrol filled the air. The last of the refugees had crossed the bridge. Sergeant Hall was looking for the most efficient way of making the tank into a bomb. Hewitt hurried back across the bridge, having to squeeze between the barrels. Sergeant Henry had placed them closer together. He gave the explosives to the Sergeant who nodded, "These should do the trick. If the Panther tries to push them out of the way then it will strike it here, just above the track. I will place the explosives along the top with the detonators sticking out. Four should do it." He smiled, "You can leave this to me, sir. I know what I am doing."

"Corporal Hewitt," I handed him my glasses, "go and watch for the Germans. When they are a mile away you had better get back here and let us know."

"Sir."

Private Mason, cut down the trees!"

"Yes sir!"

It did not take many swings to bring down the snow laden trees. They blocked the road. It would only hold the tanks up temporarily but it would prevent them using wheeled vehicles. The more time we could buy the better. When they tried to move the trees then we would shoot them.

I squeezed back between the barrels and examined the bridge as I crossed. I had thought to use the explosive to blow the bridge but there was not enough. I just wanted to make a firebomb. A burning Sherman and Panther would take some shifting. Of course, when the fire died down they could simply bring up the other heavy tanks and shove the two wrecked ones into the river. We had to devise some way to stop them after that.

When I reached what I now termed, 'our side of the bridge,' I saw that the two sergeants had organised everything well. The Sherman was in the middle of the road. It would be the centre of our defence. Sergeant Barker had taken every bit of camouflage netting he could find and the front of the tank was well hidden. With branches and snow covering it the vehicle was well disguised. There was just the top of the hatch showing. They had stripped everything from the nearby buildings to give as much protection to our machine guns as possible. We could not dig trenches and so we had to make a wall in front of us. They had been clever about it. They had taken and used everything which was metal. I even saw a huge cast iron bath. When I cocked an eye at it Sergeant Barker shrugged, "If it stops a bullet or a bit of shrapnel sir, I'll be happy."

I went to the fire and retrieved my Bergen and spare weapons. If we had to fall back I would not have the time to look for them. Sergeant Ford was leading men from the houses with mattresses. "These come in useful, sir. They saved a few guys in St. Vith. They don't stop a bullet but they stop shrapnel. The Krauts used H.E. on us!"

Sergeant Hall had returned by the time I was back at the bridge. "Everything done, sir. Where do you want me?"

"Grab your gun and choose your spot." The Sergeant had a western accent and I asked, "Where are you from Sergeant?"

"Texas sir, why?"

"Then you will know all about the Alamo! This is our Alamo!"

Corporal Hewitt hurtled over the bridge, "They are on their way sir!"

I shouted, "Take cover. There is no point firing your rifles at the tanks. That will waste ammunition. Corporal Powers, have you men ready to throw the hammer?"

He grinned, "Yes sir!"

"Wait for my command. We are going to have to endure some shellfire but I think they will try to avoid damaging the bridge. It is an old one and their tanks are heavy." I looked up at the working Sherman. They had placed, beneath the camouflage netting, a mattress covered by a sheet of corrugated iron they had found. It would not stop a shell but it might slow it down. The sergeant was leaning out of the turret with the unlit stub of a cigar in his mouth. I shouted up to him. "Don't fire unless you have a target you can hit. I want you to come as a surprise to them."

"Don't worry, sir, I ain't gonna waste any shells on the front of a Panther. I might as well spit chewing tobacco at them! I will fire if they give me a flank shot. We will only get the one sir but if they are on the other side of the river then they are just a hundred yards from us. We might just punch a hole in the side of a Panther." He descended into the tank and closed the hatch. The tank was now hidden.

The first flakes of snow fell. The weather was changing. The wind was getting up. I joined Hewitt, Sergeant Barker and Sergeant Henry in the centre of the road by the bridge. The old bath was there as well as a wheelbarrow.

Corporal Hewitt said, "There are six tanks. I recognised two Panthers. The others were the Mark IV, I think although there was a bigger one at the back that could have been Tiger or King Tiger. They have some self-propelled guns, too, sir. There were three of them. I think they were Wespes."

"They can do some damage. Better batten down the hatches. I suppose now is the time a tin lid might come in handy."

Sergeant Henry reached over and pulled a mattress from in front of the bath. "Sergeant Ford reckoned this might come in handy sir. He said he owed you."

"I shall thank him later. Just keep it behind us until they actually start firing."

Five minutes later there was the sound of two explosions. They were not the 105 mm howitzers. It was the sound of the booby traps in the woods. "They are here." Then the artillery fired. It soon became obvious that they were clearing the sides of the river. Some of the shells landed short, in the river. Others peppered the bank and then they began to creep north. I saw the unmistakeable 75 mm barrel of the panzer as it turned the bend in the road. The barrel rose as it climbed over the trees. Even across the road, I heard the crack and splintering sound as they were crushed beneath the tank; there were infantry on either side of it. I was tempted to use my Mauser and hit them but that would reveal our position. I wondered if the Panther would try to blow up the damaged tank. If it did the bridge would still be blocked but the Panther would survive. The machine gun on the tank opened fire and tore into the top of the wrecked tank. It then sprayed both sides of the bridge in case we had men hiding there. Then it edged forward.

I turned. Sergeant Hall was behind me, "I think we will see if your bomb works, sergeant."

"It will work, sir. I am just not certain how much damage it will do. Those Panthers have thick armour."

The shells from the howitzer were moving north and I heard more from the east. Colonel Devine was under attack too. That did not surprise me. They would coordinate their attacks. It was a pincer movement intended to crush us. The Panzer Grenadiers were firing across the river too. They were hidden in the woods. Their bullets were wasted as my men were dug in. I heard them clang off the tank behind us. The Panther edged forward. I saw that they had elevated the barrel. It explain why it had not fired. They did not want to risk the barrel being damaged when they rammed the Sherman.

The driver used a low gear so that he would have maximum power. The tracks slipped a little on the icy surface and the slight slope which led to the bridge and then they bit when they reached the flatter section. It lurched forward and struck the Sherman. The effect was spectacular.

There might not have been much T.N.T. but there was plenty of petrol. The wrecked Sherman actually rose in the air as the bomb exploded. The petrol spurted on to the Panther and it began to burn too. The explosion must have damaged the tracks for it seemed unable to move.

"Stand by! If you have a target then fire on my command." I levelled the Mauser and aimed at the turret. "Fire!" My men had been awaiting the order and the Panzer Grenadiers in the woods bore the brunt of the firepower. I saw a figure emerge from the Panther and I fired. The commander fell backwards. The tank was going nowhere and the crew tried to bail out. Sergeant Ford shot one who came out of the rear hatch. I saw a figure push the commander from the turret and then try to climb out. He was on fire. When I shot him it was a mercy. The tank was now engulfed in flame. When the fire spread to the ammunition there was an enormous explosion and the turret flew a few feet in the air before landing in the road behind the tank.

"Cease fire!" There was little point in firing any more as thick black smoke filled the other side of the road and we had no targets. The German shells also stopped. They were conserving their ammunition. The fire burned for long time. The air was filled with the aroma of burning flesh, gasoline and oily smoke.

A runner threw himself into the mattress. "Sir, Colonel Devine asks if you can hold on. Things are pretty bad at the crossroads."

"How bad?"

"We are down to two Shermans sir. They are bringing more of our armour up. On the bright side sir we now have PIATs. A truck made it to us from Malmedy."

PIATs would not stop the kind of tanks we were fighting. We needed anti-tank weapons. "Tell the Colonel that we have managed to knock out one Panther. We are holding on."

"Right sir."

He raced off.

Sergeant Henry shook his head, "Of course you neglected to tell him that we have used our one and only weapons which might do some good."

I nodded to Corporal Powers, "Don't be so negative, Sergeant, we still have our secret weapon! That should come as a shock to them."

"You have six of those things, sir!"

"And they only have five tanks left. That means we have one to spare."

Sergeant Barker burst out laughing at Sergeant Henry's face, "Don't worry Sarge, you will get used to the Major's optimism."

I looked up at the sky. Something had caught my eye. The snow shower had been brief and I saw a patch of blue. Against it I saw a flight of aeroplanes. They were Thunderbolts. Pointing I said, "The Air Force have sent a flight up. We have a chance."

I watched them as they swooped to the south west. They were attacking something on the road. I could not see what it was but it had to be the Wespes. I saw the rockets streak and then heard the explosions. The three aeroplanes rose into the sky and then rolled to head north and low. They had another target in mind. This time they fired to the north and west of us. They used both their remaining rockets and machine guns. I heard an explosion and then a column of smoke rose into the sky.

Sergeant Ford said, "That evens up the field a little eh sir?"

"It does indeed but don't count any chickens yet, Sergeant."

After a while the sky began to darken. It was not the snow but the clouds were bringing night a little earlier. Ominously the fire on the two tanks had now gone out and I heard the rumble of more tanks as the Germans advanced.

"Now we are for it."

"Possibly, Sergeant Barker but so far we are holding on. Let's keep that attitude, eh?"

"Sir."

I glanced up at the sky. The darkness might help us. Corporal Powers and his bomb hurlers would be harder to see against the night sky. We just had to hold the Germans at bay until then. The second Panther did the same as the other one had. Its machine gun opened fire. I heard shouts and cries from my right. Some of our men were hit. The Panzer Grenadiers were not to be seen. They knew we had teeth. The tank commander turned the turret around so that it faced the rear and then it began to push its sister and the Sherman towards the river. The Sherman might have been damaged but it was not going to a watery grave without a fight. Its front jammed itself on the barrels and then the parapet of the bridge. It would not budge.

I saw a chance now. "Sergeant Powers. The barrel is facing the wrong way. Try three of your bombs."

"Yes sir. Lebowski and Hellberg, with me." They scrambled over the front of our defences. Keeping low they were well hidden by both the parapet and the skeleton of the burned-out Panther. I saw them run and then whirl around like a sort of manic Scotsmen. They hurled them high. Turning, they ran back to our lines. The tank's machine gun could still fire and chips of the bridge parapet flew into the back of Pfc Hallberg. Corporal Powers and Pfc Lebowski picked him up and hurtled back across the bridge. The three projectiles landed. Two hit the tank and one missed. Although neither projectile appeared to cause any damage we watched as the commander tried to turn the turret. It whirred and it stuck. The rockets had managed to damage the turret mechanism. The only way it could fire would be if it turned around. It pushed harder but the two burned tanks refused to slip into the water.

The Panther backed up. All the time night was falling. It moved to get a better angle and then a Mark IV joined it. It too crunched and cracked over the two logs. It turned slightly and, like the first Panther, began to raise its barrel. It reached the other tank. The two of them began to push. It was working. The Mark IV began to slip on the frozen ground and one end began to swing around. It was the chance that our Sherman's commander had been waiting for. There was a flash of flame from above our heads and a loud crack that hurt my ears. The shell hit the Mark IV squarely on the side. There was just over an inch of armour there and the shell went through as though it was paper. The tank exploded spectacularly. Flames shot out and set fire to the second Panther's tracks. It began to reverse away but the fire had caught hold. I took out my glasses and saw that it had lost one of its tracks. The second Panther was out of the battle. It could fire its machine gun but that was all.

I felt hopeful for the first time. We had, effectively, halved the German tanks. With night falling we had a chance. Then I felt the ground begin to vibrate. I had felt that sensation a few days earlier when we had been in the attic of the house. Now I felt the vibration even more. I turned and shouted, "Sergeant, get out of the tank. It is either a Tiger or King Tiger coming up the road!"

The crew did not need a second urging. Suddenly the gun flamed again and I was deafened again. A shell shot towards the 45-ton Panther. The shell hit it on the side. Although it had thicker armour than the Mark IV the fire had weakened it and it, too exploded. The sergeant threw himself next to me, his unlit cigar still in his mouth. "We might not survive this sir but at least I took out two big tanks!"

"You did well, Sergeant." I looked up and saw the barrel of the King Tiger. It belched smoke and flames from its gun. This time the concussion was so bad that it actually hurt my ears. My head seemed to vibrate and I felt as dizzy as when I had hit the brick wall. Then that was as nothing for the shell struck the Sherman. The tank seemed to jump up and then crash down before it was engulfed in flames. Four soldiers who had the misfortune to be close to the rear burst into flames. As others ran to put them out the German machine gun in the tank sprayed them and their suffering was ended. Ten men lay dead or dying. We could do nothing. We had to endure it.

The King Tiger raised its enormous barrel and began to push. This time the Sherman did move as the Panther and Mark IV were pushed against it. This was a 70-ton tank and it had power. The Mark IV was the first to tumble into the river followed by the Sherman carcass. Finally, the Panther, blackened and without a turret now, rolled into the river.

The King Tiger backed up. I knew what it would do now. It would come over the bridge and there was nothing we could do to stop it. The other two Mark IV tanks would follow and our little force would be destroyed. I wondered if I should order a retreat and then I realised that would be condemning the men to death. The German machine guns would wreak havoc. I glanced around and saw that even Hewitt and Barker were looking terrified. We had to do something.

"Everyone, open fire at the trees, let's see how many we can kill before they kill us."

Sergeant Hall shouted, "Remember the Alamo!" Men began to whoop and cheer. I had seen this before. When you knew you were going to die and there was nothing you could do about it, you embraced it. You and death became lovers!

The bridge had a slight crown on it and as it lumbered it could bring neither its main gun nor its machine gun to bear. I levelled my Mauser. Amazingly the commander of the tank was out of his turret. I would, at least, make him pay. He was only a hundred feet from me and I could not miss. My bullet threw him back and then I watched as the King Tiger's sides struck both sides of the bridge. It was too wide. The commander was dead and the noise inside must have been horrendous. The driver kept driving. He had no idea that they were stuck. As the King Tiger squeezed, bricks fell into the river and suddenly both sides of the bridge tumbled into the river. The barrel dipped as it crested the crown and the machine gunner fired. We ducked behind the cast iron bath. Then I heard a cracking. It grew louder and the machine gun stopped. I risked looking over the top of the bath. Even as I looked the bridge collapsed. The King Tiger was too heavy for the ancient bridge. It had caused its own death by damaging the side of the structure. With its integrity gone the ancient bridge died! It disappeared from sight as it fell into the water.

Sometimes soldiers do things which, if they thought about it they would never attempt. Hurling the Mauser to the ground I jumped over the barricade, oblivious to the bullets zipping over my head. Even as I ran I was pulling out a grenade. The tank lay six feet below me. I jumped and landed next to the barrel. I made the mistake of grabbing hold of it and it was hot. A hatch next to my foot opened and a head appeared. I swung my boot at it and felt bones crunch as I hit the driver. I clambered to the open

118

turret. I pulled the pin on the grenade and dropped it in. I slammed the hatch shut and then ran for the bank. I hurled myself in the air and grabbed hold of grass. Hands reached over as the grenade went off inside the tank. I heard shouts and screams and then flames began to lick out of the driver's visor.

As I was pulled up the two remaining Mark IV tanks began to drive closer to the river. They would have to negotiate the trees. "Everybody, fall back to the square, now!"

The call was taken up by the American sergeants. We knew what was coming. They would blast our lines with HE and rake the bank with machine guns. We would achieve nothing by staying. I followed Sergeant Barker and the others from the centre of the bridge; we ran towards the end house where, a few days ago Corporal Cooper and his men had helped us to take this bridge. I ran through the open door and kept going out of the back. I threw myself on the ground.

The two tanks began to fire. It seemed to me that it was as a punishment for destroying their comrades. They could not cross the river. They would have to drive along it and try to cross at Trois Ponts. They kept firing with all of their weapons. It seemed an age but I doubt that it lasted more than fifteen minutes. The house through which we had run was demolished. The front fell first and, when the walls were weakened the back fell in on itself. We were lucky. If it had fallen backwards then we would all have been killed. The air was filled with the smell of cordite and the sound of fury as the Panzers wreaked revenge on us. When it stopped the silence was almost painful.

I waited for a good five minutes before I risked standing. Sergeant Ford began to shake his head, "Well sir, I thought, twenty minutes ago that I was going to die. I was thinking of all the things I haven't done. They say when you are going to die your life flashed before your face. All that I could see was my girl, Sue Ellen. I had put off marrying her. Now all that I want to do is marry her and have kids so that I can tell them about this day. They won't believe it!"

Sergeant Hall said, "Amen to that brother, Amen."

Chapter 11

The medics and Corporal Hewitt saw to the casualties. The Germans realised the futility of shelling buildings and we heard them head towards Trois Ponts. Leaving Sergeant Henry in charge, I went with Gordy to the square. The number of American casualties there told me that they had suffered just as much as we had. There was a make shift hospital using the old hall. Half the front was missing but it had a roof and a couple of walls. In Stavelot that passed as a building. I found Sergeant Major O'Rourke amongst them. He did not look happy.

"Major, tell these guys that I need to be back with the Colonel. It is just a scratch."

The medic who was treating him shook his head, "Major, his arm is cut almost to the bone. He needs stitches or he could die!"

"Sergeant Major, just obey the orders. The Germans are going nowhere. We need you fighting fit, eh?"

"Yes sir. How is it at the bridge?"

I smiled and spread my arms, "What bridge? A King Tiger tried to cross it and found that it was too heavy. There is no bridge to defend but it means they are reinforcing Trois Ponts. I had better report to the Colonel. Get well first!"

I left the makeshift hospital and asked a Pfc, who was clutching a bleeding arm, where Colonel Devine was to be found.

"The Command Post is a hundred yards past the crossroads sir. There used to be a farmhouse on the right. It is there, sir."

"Thanks son."

"How is it going down at the bridge, sir?"

"Don't you worry about that. The bridge is not a problem anymore."

When I had last left the crossroads, and that had been some few hours earlier, there had been a few houses. Now there was rubble and the charred remains of a couple of Shermans, a half-track and a Mark IV panzer. There was a tiny gap between the German tank and the closest Sherman. It had been close fighting. I saw bodies in both grey and olive green littering the road and the remains of the buildings. Bullets zipped overhead and I zig zagged across to the Command Post. They had dug in a

Sherman next to the wall. I saw that the Sherman had thrown a track but the gun still worked.

Gordy and I dashed behind the Sherman as a German MG 42 let rip. Bullets pinged off the tank. Inside I saw the two Colonels and Captain Stewart. There was a sergeant with a clipboard. They looked up as we ducked beneath the taut canvas they were using to protect themselves from the elements.

"Has the bridge fallen, Tom?"

I smiled, "Quite literally sir. It and a King Tiger are now in the bottom of the river."

A smile spread across the Colonel's face. "That is some good news. We can use the men you have there. Things are going slowly here."

"You have made ground, sir. Yesterday you were a couple of hundred yards further east."

"The real estate is expensive here."

Colonel Cavender said, "You had better fill him in, Jack. We are running out of officers. You and I have used all of our luck up."

"Chuck is right, Tom. We'll begin with the bad news. We have no Shermans left. The last one threw a track. We have advanced as far as we can. We have tried to move forward but each time their machine guns and mortars throw us back. On the positive side they don't appear to have any Panzerfausts left so if we do get tanks we might be able to advance. They also appear to have no tanks either."

"That will change, sir. The two tanks we didn't destroy are heading with their Panzer Grenadiers up the other side of the river. I am guessing that Jerry still holds Trois Ponts. If they do, then they can cross and they will be heading down here. They will be bringing more men to the fight than those who fought with me."

"There is more good news. The British have reinforced the Elsenborn Ridge. General Hodge is sending men down the Malmedy Road. General Gavin and the All-American Division are attacking the 1st SS and we have been told that we have had the last of the snow. They will send aeroplanes up. That single flight yesterday helped us out. That Panzer you see out there was about to break through when they hit it with rockets."

I looked at my watch. It was 1010 hours. "When can we expect the reinforcements, sir?"

"Any time today. The roads, as you know are narrow and clogged. The change in weather might help but we can't change the terrain." He cocked an eye. "You have something in mind, Major?"

"Yes sir, dig in and defend. Their tanks and reinforcements will be here before ours. The burned-out tanks are obstacles. Put men behind them.

When they come the tanks will have to come down this road. They will have to negotiate the damaged tanks. We just hold on."

Colonel Cavender nodded, "My men are all in and that sounds like a good plan. It is soul destroying to keep advancing into machine guns and watching your buddies die."

"Okay, Tom, bring your men and equipment up and watch out for that machine gun. They have managed to get it in the upper floor of the last building they have standing. It is almost three quarters of a mile away but they are hard to shift."

"Right sir, Gordy, go and fetch the men and all the weapons. Set up to the left of the wrecked Mark IV."

The machine gun opened fire at our movement. The bullets missed because there were just two of us. Had there been more then we might have suffered casualties. The machine gun post needed eliminating. I returned to the command post. Captain Stewart said, "Sir, we are running out of mortar shells but we have plenty of smoke grenades. Why don't we use a smoke screen when Major Harsker's men arrive? It will minimise casualties."

"Good idea, Captain, see to it."

Colonel Cavender said, "One good thing about this disaster is that it is making my officers think a little more about how to fight. Since D-Day the Krauts have been on the back foot. This is showing what they are capable of."

"Sir, we have done well. When they came in 1940 they had passed Brussels in about seven days. We have held them up and shown them that we know how to fight. In 1940 we ran."

"To be fair to you guys the Germans had air superiority in those days. We haven't seen a German aeroplane since the offensive began."

I remembered what the Squadron Leader had said about the new aircraft they were producing. If they were as good as their new tanks then we were in trouble. Just at that moment I heard a sudden fusillade and a Corporal came running in, "Sir, they are attacking again!"

We all ran out. I only had my Colt and my Luger. They would have to do. I took shelter next to the front main drive sprocket of the Sherman. The Panzer Grenadiers were moving as we would if we were attacking. They came in pairs. One fired and the other ran. I took aim at a pair who were a hundred yards from me. I took a two-handed stance and rested the barrel on the Sherman. I squeezed three shots at the two of them. One fell clutching his middle while the other was hit in the knee. I moved to my right. An officer was urging his men on. I fired another two shots. One hit his arm and he dropped his pistol and took shelter.

The line of Americans was perilously thin. The Sherman's machine gun rattled out but I only heard two other American Brownings. We needed the weapons from the bridge. Then I remembered the Browning on the top of the turret. I holstered my pistol and went around the back. I clambered up and stood so that the turret protected most of my body. My head was exposed. I kept it down as I grabbed hold of the Browning's pistol grip and cocked it. I saw that the belt was already in the left-hand side. It looked to have already fired a quarter of the 600 rounds. I had been told that, to avoid a cook-off, I should only fire three or four rounds at a time. Taking a breath I stood and began to fire. The Germans were within a hundred feet. To my left I glimpsed the two Colonels firing their pistols. I started directly in front of the Sherman and fired four bullets then traversed a little and fired again. Bullets pinged off the turret. Below me the tank's machine gunner was firing too. The Sherman belched flame and smoke as it fired AP at the German half-track which had just emerged. Its machine gun was adding to the fire. I forced myself to ignore the steel jacketed bullets which would have torn my body to shreds had they hit me.

I kept firing as I turned the gun through 90 degrees. Then the Sherman's second shell hit the half-track and tore through the engine block. The German gun was still firing. I swung the barrel of the Browning back around and fired at the German gunner. I hit his loader and he traversed to fire at me. It was like an old-fashioned duel. I had slightly more protection from the turret and, in the end, that proved decisive. My third burst hit his head and I saw, at a hundred yard's range, it explode like a ripe plum. I switched back to the infantry. I saw a grenade being thrown.

Colonel Devine shouted, "Grenade!" and they took cover.

I gambled on the protection of the tank and, as a second Panzer Grenadier smashed the porcelain cap on his grenade I shot him. His hand was already on the cord, gravity pulled the grenade from his hand and it exploded. It scythed through the men around him. The wounded officer blew his whistle and they began to fall back.

The hatch opened and the tank commander's head popped out. I smiled, "Sorry about borrowing your gun, Sergeant."

He grinned, "You are welcome sir, but, if you don't mind me saying so sir, you are as mad as a sack full of frogs!"

I nodded. "I have been told that, Sergeant." As I was climbing down the distant machine gun fired again and the sergeant's head disappeared.

Captain Stewart shouted, "Launch the smoke bombs!"

As the mortars popped I heard feet on the road behind. It was my men from the bridge. I slid from the back of the tank. Corporal Hewitt handed me my Bergen and my weapons. "You seem to draw Germans like flies sir!"

"I know. I think I might need to change my underwear, eh? Have the men get under as much cover as they can while the smoke is there. I am going back on the tank and see if I can't do something about that machine gun."

I placed the Bergen and my MP 34 behind the tank's turret and, grabbing the Mauser and a few clips of ammunition, climbed back to the turret. The smoke obscured the distant house. I adjusted the sight and loaded a round. My worry was that the Germans still had their sniper on the hill. No one had said anything but if he was there then, as soon as I started firing, he would target me. The smoke also obscured the hill and the wind was blowing it in that direction. I glanced to my left and saw that Sergeant Henry and Sergeant Barker had organized the men well. The German and American machine guns we had brought more than doubled our fire power. The sky was clear. Our Headquarters would send air sorties. I hoped that they had rockets.

In the distanced I heard the ominous rumble of tanks. The Mark IVs were coming. The hatch of the tank was still open. I shouted, "Sergeant I would load more AP. There are a couple of Mark IVs they are heading in this direction."

"Thanks for the heads up, sir."

I knew that, unless they had bowsers with them then these two tanks would be almost out of petrol They drank it at a rate of one mile per gallon. That didn't help us that much. They still had their guns and with three inches of armour at the front the Sherman would have to be at point blank range to do any good.

As the smoke began to thin the distant machine gun began to fire. It was using short bursts. The targets were my men moving into position. I aimed at the gunner. The telescopic sight brought him into focus. I forced myself to breathe slowly and to count in my head. There was a rhythm to such things. I slowly squeezed the trigger. I was slightly off and the bullet just sent splinters of brick to shower the gunner and his loader. I loaded another round as the gunner traversed. I aimed a little lower and fired. The bullet must have hit the gun and then the gunner. It hit him in the chest. He half rose as I loaded another bullet and fired it at the gun again. The gunner and gun tumbled from the building. That threat was gone. As I looked through the sights and traversed right I saw the next threat. It was the soldiers and tanks from the bridge. Round two was about to begin.

I clambered down again, "Colonel, the Germans are sending their tanks in again."

He nodded, "Colonel Cavender is on the radio to Headquarters. He is trying to call in an air strike."

I looked at the sky. There was still time. "I will go and join my men, sir. They have Panzer Grenadiers with them."

I picked up my Bergen and guns and ran, crouching towards my men on the left. They had used the cover of the smoke to pile broken masonry and bricks into emplacements. That had been the movement the German machine gunner had seen. I noticed that Sergeant Henry was at one end of our line and Sergeant Barker at the other. Sergeant Ford and Corporal Powers were in the middle. It gave a continuity of command. These were good soldiers.

"German Tanks are coming. If we get the chance we will have to try to disable them with grenades."

The sergeants just nodded at the ridiculous suggestion. We had gone beyond sanity. We had fought for more than a week already. Men were exhausted and hungry. Most had had little sleep and there was not a soldier without an injury of some description. Yet they kept on going and the reason was simple. They were not fighting for the Army, or even America, they were fighting for their brothers in arms. This was personal.

I laid four grenades on the piece of stone before me and a spare clip for my MP 34. I reloaded my Luger. I had no ammunition left for either the Colt or the Thompson. The reinforcements and supplies could not get here quick enough. The sound of the German tanks grew louder as they approached. I heard the crack as they both fired and instinctively ducked. The Sherman fired back a heartbeat later. The Sherman erupted like a Roman candle. Two 75 mm shells had stuck it at almost the same time. The sergeant and his crew would have known very little about it. I saw that the Sherman's shell hand struck the leading Mark IV just above the driving sprocket. Although it was still moving I hoped that the AP shell had not just penetrated the skirting but also damaged the track.

Now that the armour was out of the way the two tanks could concentrate their fire on us. The two guns belched fire. They had targeted the tumble of vehicles which blocked the road. Their machine guns swept from side to side. We were hunkered down and protected but it meant that their infantry could advance without fear of fire. I raised my MP 34 above the stone and sprayed a magazine from side to side. I reloaded.

Captain Stewart commanded the mortars. They were the only weapon we could fire. They would do little against the armour but they could cause casualties amongst the infantry. At least we were hitting back. I risked a looked over our wall. The tanks were two hundred yards away and were flanked by their Panzer Grenadiers. They were too far away to accurately hit. I had wasted a whole magazine. Even as I looked the leading Panzer belched fire as it fired at the half-track which blocked its path. It was frustrating. We had nothing with which to fight the tanks. It did not matter that they were only Mark IVs. They were still too powerful for what we had left.

Machine gun bullets peppered the stone walls before us. It was now a matter of time. I saw one of Sergeant Henry's men raise his body above the parapet to fire his BAR. He had the range. He was thrown back by a mixture of machine gun fire and the rifles from the infantry. I picked up the Mauser. At least I would die fighting. I slid the gun across the stones and then raised my head to look down the sights. I saw the commander of a tank. He was looking at us through binoculars. I fired two bullets into him. At a hundred and fifty yards he was a huge target. Then I switched to the Panzer Grenadiers close by the tank. I emptied the magazine and then ducked as retribution followed.

Pfc Mason shouted, "Steady on sir!"

Reloading my rifle, I turned and grinned, "You only live once, Mason. There are three dead Germans. That is three less for us to fight!"

"Are all Limeys as crazy as you, sir?"

"Probably!"

I honestly expected to die and then, suddenly, from behind us came the whoosh of rockets. The first tank disappeared, along with the panzer grenadiers, in a fireball. A few moments later the second tank was hit by the P47 Thunderbolts which had come roaring in. The next aeroplane hit the two half-tracks which followed. All three aeroplanes strafed the German infantry before climbing high and heading north.

"Up, let's finish them!" I levelled my Mauser and fired until it was empty. The heavy machine guns operated by my men now came into play and they chopped through the S.S. The ground before us became a charnel house. The two tanks both exploded as the ammunition was ignited. It laid low all the Germans standing around them.

Colonel Cavender shouted, "Let's drive them back! Charge!"

All he needed was a horse and it would have been perfect. I slipped my Mauser over my back and grabbed my MP 34. "Come on boys! Let's follow the Colonel." Corporal Powers was next to me, "Go and tell Colonel Devine we are pursuing the enemy."

"Sir."

As I jumped over the wall two Germans rose before me just twenty feet from me. I reacted instinctively and I fired. The gun sliced them in two. I ran towards the burning tanks. My men followed and any German whose hands did not come up was shot. None surrendered but many ran. I emptied my magazine. I saw, to my left, a dead German who also had an MP 34. I quickly took his spare magazines and his hand grenades. Sergeant Henry led my men past me. He was screaming like a Sioux Indian at Little Big Horn. Gordy Barker waved forward the Americans who had attached themselves to him. There was a steely determination about all of them. We had triumphed at the river and, expecting to die, we were reborn.

I reloaded and followed. The loss of the two tanks and the reinforcements had been a body blow to the Germans. Positions were abandoned. The three Thunderbolts had broken the back of the German defence. I caught up with Sergeant Henry half a mile from the burning tanks. Suddenly he pitched forward, clutching his shoulder. I could not see any Germans. Then I realised I could see the hill. The German sniper had struck.

"Medic!" I took a dressing from his patch pocket and pressed it to his shoulder. He was awake. "Hold this tight!"

"Damn! We have our first piece of luck and I get hit!"

"Don't worry, Sarge, you will be back!"

As the Medics ran up there was the sound of a Mauser and the first medic fell clutching his ankle. Colonel Cavender caught up with us.

"Who the hell is shooting, Major?" Just then there was another bark and the Colonel fell clutching his arm.

"It is a sniper!"

I switched guns and, zig zagging, ran towards the hill. It was less than three quarters of a mile away. I saw a flash and dived to the ground sideways. I wanted the sniper to think he had hit me. I heard the bullet zip over my head. I crawled to the right where there was a wrecked German half-track. I took shelter behind it. I slowed down my breathing. I crawled behind the front wheels. I saw the hill and I saw the flash from the sniper. He was six hundred yards from me. I raised my rifle and braced it on my arm. I had to look for the flash of his muzzle. It was infuriating because it meant another of our men would, in all likelihood, die. I had a rough idea where the flash would come and I was ready. I saw him. He was well camouflaged and he was using the bole of a tree for protection Only his head and his gun were visible. I aimed at the V of the tree. I had my breathing under control and I squeezed the trigger. I saw a spark; my bullet must have struck his rifle and then he fell back. I put another bullet in the chamber and lowered my aim. I could see a leg. I fired a second shot and, through the sights, I saw blood spurt from his knee. I had damaged his gun and wounded him. He was no longer a threat.

I wriggled out from under the half-track and, slinging my Mauser hefted my MP 34. I was some four hundred yards behind my men. I saw that the Colonel was receiving medical attention and the rest of his men were moving forward.

Corporal Powers ran up behind me, "Sir, I have a message from Colonel Devine. The bridges at Trois Ponts have been blown up. The Germans can't reinforce the town."

"What does he want us to do?"

"He says to keep on going until you reach the town. He is bringing the tanks and reinforcements. He said, hold until relieved!"

"Good man. Tell him…"

"No sir, I am with you!"

"Good. Then watch my back. That may not be the only sniper around here."

We headed down the road which was now almost deserted save for the dead and the dying. We had lost the houses and the road was enclosed by trees. It forced us all closer together. I noticed that there were footprints heading into the forest. That worried me. There could be Germans there. They might be cut off but I knew that the S.S. were ruthless. We would have to track them and tend to their threat. The road twisted and turned along the river. The light was fading but, up above us, I saw another two flights of P47 Thunderbolts returning from a raid further south. Higher in the air I saw transports. Had they dropped supplies or even paratroopers?

Up ahead I heard the sound of firing. I forced myself to run faster. As I rounded a bend I saw Sergeant Barker and Sergeant Ford. They and their men were spread out across the road taking shelter behind whatever they could find.

"Sir, there are Panzer Grenadiers. They are blocking the road." He pointed and I saw them. They were just sixty yards away. Some were in the trees while others lay behind hastily dragged logs in the middle of the road.

"They are trying to buy time. We can't let them. Sergeant Barker, keep them pinned down. Sergeant Ford, take six men and go through the forest. Flank them."

"Corporal Powers find four men, we will go along the river." I handed my Mauser to Gordy, "Here Sergeant. You might find this a more useful tool."

I pumped my arm three times and plunged into the woods. The river was less than thirty feet away. I hoped that the Germans would think that flank was secure as there was a precipitous drop to the river. The water would be icy and any falling into it would not survive for long. The firing from our right told me that Gordy was keeping them occupied. The noise of firing, allied to the sound of the river made any need for stealth redundant. Speed was what we needed. I glanced to my right and saw them. I turned and waved my men forward. On the other side Sergeant Ford gave a rebel yell as he and his men fell upon them from that flank. The Sergeant's heroic charge made our life a lot easier. I waited until we were ten yards away and then yelled, "Fire!" I fired four short bursts. Corporal Powers had also picked up a gun when we had chased the Germans from the crossroads. It was the MP 35 and he sprayed along with me. The others used their rifles. There had been twenty-two Germans at the ambush. Now there were eighteen corpses and four more who would not last the night.

"Come on, the Colonel has medics. Our orders are to take the village!"

The light was fading fast as we ran along the road. The trees had stopped the snow from melting and the tanks which had driven down it had compacted it. It would be treacherous once night fell. I was anxious to reach the village. It would be more sheltered. What I did not know was what we might find. Had the ambush been to allow them to set up machine guns and wire?

Trois Ponts was just four miles from Stavelot and was a lot smaller. The bridge divided the town. On our side of the river was a tiny hamlet of, perhaps, a couple of dozen buildings. It had not suffered the same damage as the town we had just left. In fact, if it were not for the bridge destroyed in the air attack, it would have looked like a Christmas card. I held up my hand at the edge of the village and then waved Sergeant Barker and Sergeant Ford around the right side of the village. I signalled for Corporal Powers to head along the river. I took the other five men down the road. I had a fresh magazine and my eyes scanned ahead and to the sides for any danger. I saw a German half -track between two houses. I dropped to my knees and braced myself for the machine gun bullets which would end my life. Nothing happened. I ran to the vehicle and felt the engine. It was stone cold.

Corporal Hewitt put his hand underneath and tapped the petrol tank. It was hollow. "No fuel sir."

Pfc Mason clambered aboard it. "They have taken the gun sir."

"Search the buildings. John, take charge."

I ran alone into the centre of the village. It was eerie. It felt like a ghost town. When I reached the middle, I saw Sergeant Barker coming through the trees with his men while Sergeant Ford led six men down the narrow road from the north. He shook his head, "No-one sir. It is empty."

When Corporal Powers arrived he confirmed it, "The bridge is gone sir. There are two wrecked tanks on the other side."

I nodded. "They have left. Right, Sergeant Ford, set up a perimeter. All of us are on guard until the Colonel arrives."

A door creaked open and everyone turned with guns at the ready. An old man with a white flag emerged, "You are Americans?" He spoke in French.

I nodded and answered him. "Yes, we are."

"Thank God, the Germans left an hour ago. I worried they might come back."

"Hopefully they have gone for good. Where are the rest of the people?"

"They are sheltering in their basements. We feared that we would be bombed. I will fetch them!"

There were more than twenty people who emerged from their holes. They had been lucky. Their village could have been devastated like Stavelot.

The old man returned with a bottle of brandy, "And now you will have a drink with me." He handed me a glass of brandy and poured one for himself. "Merry Christmas!"

"Merry Christmas?"

"Yes! Today is Christmas Eve. In a few hours it will be Christmas Day and this is the best present we could have; freedom."

Situation on the night of 24th December 1944

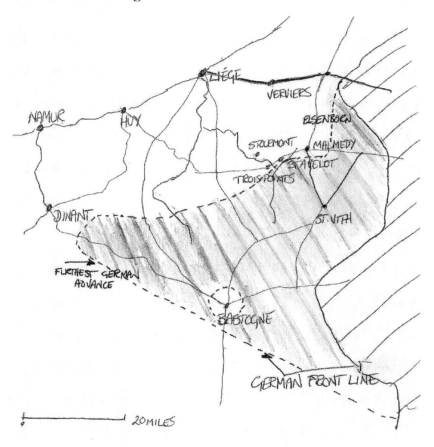

Chapter 12

"Christmas Day?"

"Yes Gordy. Not quite what we had planned eh. Still it could be worse."

"How sir?"

"We could be dead."

I had just finished the brandy when we heard the sound of Shermans. Headlights marked the column which came through the trees. Colonel Devine was standing atop the leading Sherman.

"Where are the Germans?"

"They left an hour ago." I pointed up the road. "They must have headed west."

"Then we will camp here for the night and I will see what the general has planned for us." He saw the brandy glass. "I see you are celebrating Christmas early, Major!"

"Conquering hero and all that, sir."

"You and your men have done more than enough for today. The relief troops can stand guard tonight."

The old man gestured towards the house. I am not certain how much of what we had said that he understood. "You will stay with me tonight, I think."

I shook my head, "I share the same hardships as my men."

"I can put twenty of you up if you do not mind sleeping on the floor."

There were twenty of us who had survived the road. It seemed appropriate. "Right chaps, we have accommodation tonight with Monsieur...?"

"Lagarde, Albert Lagarde! My wife, Clothilde, will be delighted to have company. It will be good to talk with you."

I felt guilty about just landing on the poor woman and so I had Corporal Powers find some coffee and ham. The Belgians love coffee and the Americans never ran out. The Belgians, like the French, are wonderfully formal. The table was covered with a cloth. Everything on the table was the best that the old couple possessed. I knew that if I took off the cloths, which were probably sheets, underneath I would find three or four tables. It didn't matter. They were trying to make us feel welcome. It told me how much they despised the Germans. Dad had told me the same. When we

132

had visited our farmhouse in France the locals always spoke glowingly of Dad and his comrades but they hated the Germans.

I was proud of the way my men, American and British, were. They were polite and they offered to help Madame Lagarde. She tried to brush their efforts away but they were all gentlemen. I suspected that the two of them reminded them of their grandparents. I sat with Albert and we drank wine. The village was too small for a mayor but we saw, over the next few days, that he was the one they all deferred to. His sons had been killed when the Germans had invaded. When he found out that I had been with the BEF he bombarded me with questions, just in case I had come across them. I had not. The fact that I could speak in French helped. He was a true gentleman.

Albert's wife, Clothilde, brought over some thin slices of cured ham for the two of us as an appetiser. She nodded to me, "Thank you Madame, my men are far from their families and you have made them feel like they are in a family again."

She smiled and a tear formed in her eye, "Thank you sir. We have lost our sons but these fine young men remind us of what our sons might have been. This is an honour for us."

I could see that she was filling up and she scurried away. The ham was beautiful. Albert looked at me, "And you have a family?"

"Not yet but I have a fiancée. When the war is over I shall marry her."

He shook his head, "I would have married her already if she is the right one. Time waits for no man, my friend."

"I know but I owe it to my men to see this through to the end."

He nodded, "I fought in the Great War. We should have learned then that the leopard does not change his spots. You say your father fought too?"

"He was an airman."

"Ah, I envied them and yet their deaths were always horrible to watch. How did they go up in such flimsy things?"

"My father still serves but he no longer flies."

We sipped our wine and enjoyed a companiable silence. "You are a gentleman and you speak truly so tell me, this new attack by the Germans, is it a threat? Should we worry that we will be invaded again?"

That was a hard question. I felt my heart sink into my boots. "They have surprised us. Not me, I did not think that they were quite beaten yet but there were others who thought that because the Rhine was within spitting distance they were finished. Those men were wrong." He nodded and drank some more wine, "However, by accident I have had to lead Americans and I can tell you this, the British and the Americans will not be beaten. Nor will the Canadians or Australians. I have fought alongside both. We might not win soon but we will win. I have seen courage which breaks my heart. I have seen sacrifices which merited medals as yet to be cast. We will win but I fear there will be more men like your sons who will die. There will be more young men who will not have children and our worlds and our countries will be the worse for that." I shrugged, "We can do nothing about that. We have a short time on this earth and we must try to make it a better place. If I have a son or a daughter, and I pray that I do, I hope that they will know what we did and why we did it."

I was suddenly aware that John Hewitt had been listening, He could speak French quite well and he said, in English, "Without doubt, sir you are right. Ours is a just cause but, like you, I mourn our dead comrades. Ken, Alan, George, Jimmy, all of them. When I go to the pub each Sunday I will raise my glass to them. I just hope that those at home remember what they have done for us."

"So do I John, so do I."

Albert hadn't understood our words but he leaned over and patted the back of my hand. "Tonight Major, forget the war. You are in my home and this is Christmas Eve. The fare might not be what we would wish but I would not change the company for anyone. Let us enjoy this night."

Poor Albert must have emptied his cellar that night. The men ate and drank as well as a five-star general in Paris. The fact that it was homecooked and served on good dinnerware helped but it was also our genial host and hostess. The men insisted on making coffee. Corporal Powers prided himself on his knowledge of beans. While he made the coffee, the others washed and dried every dish. This would be a night to remember. I knew that Sergeant Henry and Corporal Cooper would have appreciated it. They were both probably heading back to a base hospital with clean shirts and pretty nurses. I knew they would rather be with us. The house was warm and, after sleeping outdoors, no one needed a blanket. Christmas Eve 1944 was one of the best I could remember.

Every soldier shook Albert's hand and kissed his wife on both cheeks the next morning as we left before dawn had even broken. Our Christmas had been Christmas Eve and we were going back to war. We had had twelve hours of peace. It made a difference.

We had another difference. Colonel Devine now had a superior. Brigadier General Hamner of the 745th Tank Battalion. Although not at full strength it gave us more tanks than we had had since the Germans had first attacked. With 30 Sherman tanks and 10 Stuart tanks we had real armour. The 3 105 mm guns were also welcome. In addition, a company of anti-tank guns were with the column. We now had five 3 pounder guns. They were towed by M3 half-tracks.

General Hamner held an officers' meeting when he arrived at 0800 hours. He used what looked to have been a village hall before the war although it was filled with evidence of German occupation. I saw his face form into a frown when he saw a British officer but he said nothing at the time. Colonel Cavender had been sent back to Brussels with the other wounded and so I stood with Colonel Devine and Captain Stewart as the General spoke.

"I want to thank Colonel Devine for the fine job he and his men have done up to now. All things being equal we would allow the 18th Cavalry to return north and refit with armoured cars. Heaven knows they deserve it but I am afraid things are on a knife edge." He nodded. "Lieutenant Muldoon." A Lieutenant unrolled a map and pinned it to the wall. Someone had used a red pen to mark a long line, it resembled a nose, which went from the German lines almost to Dinant.

The General tapped a point half way along the line. "We are here. He tapped further west. "Here is General Gavin and the Airborne boys. We have to meet up with him and then engage the enemy. Their tanks are running out of gas. They would have run out already but they managed to capture one fuel dump up near Stourmont. The rest are already being better protected. Our aim, gentlemen is two-fold. First, we have the Engineers throw a bridge over the river here and then we will take my tanks to join up with the Airborne. Colonel Devine you and your men will wait here until transport arrives so that you can keep up with our tanks. Questions?"

There were none. All of us understood that tanks could not wait for infantry to march with them but it was disappointing. The men all had scores to settle with the S.S.

"Very well. To your tanks. The Engineers should have the bridge over by this afternoon. You have until then." As his officers began to file out he beckoned me to him. Colonel Devine came with me, "Major, what is a British commando doing here in the middle of an American battalion? Lost?"

"No sir, I was attached to the troops at St. Vith where I was delivering a lecture and I was caught up in all of this. I have been trying to get back to our lines but the Germans were always in the way."

The Brigadier smiled, "Well you can go now, Major."

"Thank you, sir, although I am guessing I will have to wait for transport to head back."

"Of course. You have men with you?"

"Two."

Then I will have my Sergeant Major give you an order authorising transport back to Brussels. In the meantime, if you would stay with the Colonel here."

Colonel Devine said, "Sir, Major Harsker here is responsible for the destruction of two King Tiger tanks as well as two Panthers and a couple of Mark IVs. If it were not for him and his men then we would not have held Stavelot."

He turned to look at me with new eyes. "Then we are in your debt, sir." He shook my hand. "And now, if you will excuse me. Time is wasting."

Once alone Colonel Devine said, "Sorry about that, Tom. It sounded a little dismissive to me."

"Don't worry about it, sir. He is right. This is an American battalion and I should be back with my own men. But I think he is wrong to think that it will be as simple as joining up with the Airborne and then driving south."

"What do you mean?"

I went to the map. "The General said that they had captured a fuel dump at Stourmont."

"Yes. So?"

I tapped the map. "That is north of here. That means there are German tanks north of the river. They can't cross the river at Stavelot and Malmedy is now being reinforced. If they are beaten then they will have to get back home." I tapped the map again. "That means through our weakest point."

I saw realisation dawn. "You mean here."

"Either here or Stavelot. This one is more likely as they will know that the bridge there is down. This one was only destroyed yesterday. They might have tried to head further west and cross at La Gleize. If so then we will be fine but, if I were you, Colonel, I would make sure that I had defences facing north as well as south."

"Perhaps the General has thought of that too."

I shrugged, "And then again, maybe not. It might be handy to have a couple of those 3 pounder anti-tank guns."

"I will go and have a word. Thanks, Tom." As we left the building a jeep pulled up and Sergeant Major O'Rourke got out. The Colonel grinned. He was pleased to see his old warhorse. "I thought you were wounded?"

"A scratch. I found this jeep just doing nothing and I followed the Engineers up." He pointed to the Engineers who were now taking their equipment from their trucks. He nodded towards the back seat. "And I found a couple of Bazookas and rockets."

The Colonel shook his head, "They will be no good at all against anything bigger than an APC."

The Sergeant Major looked hurt, "Better than we had at Stavelot, sir."

"You are right. I need to find the general. The Major here seems to think that we might have Germans trying to get back to their own lines form the north. Have the men dig pits to the north of the town in the woods and put the Bazookas there along with the .30 and .50 calibre machine guns."

"Right sir."

I pointed to Albert's house. "You will find Sergeant Barker and Sergeant Ford in there. They have had a long enough lie in."

I took my gun and headed towards the tree line. There was a small road which twisted along the small stream that fed the river. The water headed through the forest. That would be the place to put the anti-tank guns. The trees were too close together for the German heavy tanks. I was not worried about the smaller Armoured Personnel Carriers and half-tracks. We could stop those with grenades, Bazookas and machine guns. We had to do something to stop the tanks. I walked up the road. The snow was still packed. The skies might have cleared, allowing aeroplanes to fly sorties but the air was still cold enough to leave snow and ice on the ground. The tracks I saw were those of big tanks. The Germans had gone north. Now they would be hunted from the air. I looked up and saw that the canopy of trees effectively hid the road from aerial surveillance. The fighters would have to hunt these big cats.

I left the road and went into the woods. I only saw the tracks of animals. The Germans had used the road when they had headed north. When I had seen the map I noticed that this was the main road to Stourmont. Unless the Germans wanted to try and break through the Airborne Division they would have to return down this road. It confirmed what I had told the Colonel. Even if they ran out of petrol they would still have to come down this road. It was the safest route for them.

I turned and headed back. Of course, they could try to reinforce their gains and that would also mean coming across the bridge which we were now, obligingly, erecting for them. Whichever way you cut it they would be coming through Trois Ponts. I could not leave my new comrades until this threat was over. I had missed Christmas. When I was certain that the Americans had secured their lines then we would leave.

I met Sergeant Major O'Rourke talking with Sergeant Ford and Sergeant Barker. I pointed up the road. "The tanks will be coming down this road and the infantry through the trees. Did the Colonel get the 3 pounders?"

"Just two of them sir."

"Then have them dug in on either side of the road. Use sand from the river to fill bags. The Bazookas and machine guns should be in the woods."

"We have four mortars too, sir."

"Then two here and two watching the bridge."

"The bridge sir?"

"Yes Sergeant Ford, just because we have reinforced our lines doesn't mean that Jerry won't do the same. We need to watch both sides of the bridge."

Sergeant Barker said, "But you think this will be the side they will come."

"I do and it will be the best panzer general the Germans have who will be leading them. This will not be easy."

It took until the middle of the afternoon for us make the north section of our perimeter defensible. Until the Engineers had finished we could do nothing at the bridge. Colonel Devine joined me to inspect the defences. "The trouble is Colonel, that the ground is frozen. We can't put slit trenches in."

"We will just cut down some of the trees. If we take the ones behind us it will make it easier for us to fall back if we have to. Pfc Mason seems to fancy himself as Paul Bunyan. Give the job to him, Sergeant Major O'Rourke."

I was just heading back to the river when one of the Headquarters' corporals found me. "Sir, here are your travel orders from the General. He says there is a jeep which has to be returned to Malmedy. You have the authority to use that."

I smiled; Sergeant Major O'Rourke would have something to say about that. The thing about disobeying a direct order was that you could just ignore it, if you were clever enough. "Thank you Corporal." I took the envelope from him. "It is a little late in the day to travel. We will leave in the morning, Thank the general for me will you."

"Yes sir but I think he thought you and your men would leave as soon as possible."

I pointed to Albert's house. "We need to say goodbye to our hosts from last night. Tomorrow will be fine, Corporal."

I assiduously avoided the general who was fretting that the bridging was not going as smoothly as he had hoped. I was reassured by the number of aeroplanes which flew over us. They told me that the Germans would not be having it all their own way for much longer. Nothing had been said about our accommodation. I wondered if we could impose upon Albert and his wife for a second night. My fears were groundless.

Albert beckoned me over as I re-entered the hamlet. "Major, we have not seen you all day. Have you eaten? Where are your men?"

"We have imposed enough, Albert. We will get our gear and…"

"Nonsense, my wife has prepared food for you all. She will be upset if it is not eaten."

"Albert, I think the Germans will come back."

He nodded, "Down the road from Stourmont?"

"Yes, I believe so."

"It is obvious. The alternative is a long drive for their tanks. I do not think they will do that."

"When the bridge is built you should go to the other side. You need to tell all the villagers."

"But you will be staying?"

"We will stay but we are soldiers and we have an enemy to fight."

"We are not soldiers but this is our land. We lost it in 1940 along with my sons. We will not lose it a second time. We will stay. Besides I have watched you, Major. You are a soldier. You know how to fight. You do not like to lose. I do not think that the Boche will win. You and the Americans are better soldiers. Tell your men the food will be ready in an hour."

We heard the tanks heading across the bridge at 2200. I don't think that the General was pleased with the delay but the Engineers had worked manfully to get their first bridge across. The second one, the railway bridge would take longer and the third one might have to wait until peace came to this part of Belgium.

I went to the Command Post to speak with the Colonel as the last of the tanks trundled over the bridge. I saw engineers repairing their hastily erected bridge. The general had crossed it too soon and it needed attention. The Captain who was in command shook his head. "Nothing else gets over here until I have checked every nut and bolt personally. If this collapses it will be the devil's own job to get another one in place."

I gestured with my thumb behind me. "How are your guys at fighting?"

His face fell, "Fighting? Isn't it over? They said the Germans were falling back."

"They have said that before. All I am saying, Captain, is that there are still German tanks to the north of us and the best part of a German S.S. Division. This little bridge is the only way they can get back to the Fatherland. Think about it."

"Jesus! Perhaps I won't bother tightening the nuts and bolts after all."

"It doesn't really matter. Can your bridge take a 70-ton tank?" I saw him look at the structure which suddenly looked flimsy. "I have been close to one of them. The vibration demolished the gable end of a house. Just tell your men to keep their weapons handy. The river bank makes a perfect trench. They can just run across to the other side. They will be safe there."

139

"Thanks Major. I appreciate the heads up."

Before I turned in I visited the Command Post. Sergeant O'Rourke was doing the paperwork with his two corporal clerks. "Any news, Sergeant Major?"

"The Krauts have been stopped, sir. We are pushing them back. The Air Force has been pounding them all day. The general has managed to link up with the Airborne. Things are looking good."

"Don't tempt fate. So far so good. Any news of the 1st S.S. and their tanks?"

"They left Stourmont but they disappeared into the forest. They are hard to track. There is another of our tank battalions heading down from Huy. Perhaps they may have news."

I had a second night in Albert's house and a full night's sleep once more. As Sergeant Major O'Rourke pointed out, we couldn't do sentry duty as the general had ordered us out of the area. I was still awake early. Albert's wife, Clothilde, had baked fresh bread and it was the smell of it which drew me to the kitchen.

She smiled when she saw me, "You remind me of Christian, my eldest. He was like you quietly spoken. He would have been your age." I could see she was getting upset. I didn't say a word. I just put my hand on hers. I left it there and she began to smile. She leaned down and kissed my cheek. "Forgive a silly old woman. But you are a kind man. As my Albert said, you are a gentleman. I will go and fetch the coffee."

On the table was home-made butter. It reminded me of my grandmother's and there was wild blackberry jam. That too was home-made. The bread was still warm. I spread the butter on it and it melted and then smeared the wild blackberry jam on it. I was just biting into it when the coffee arrived. Everything was delicious and I left the house with a spring in my step. It had been quiet all night. Perhaps the tanks had run out of petrol. Even as the thought flickered through my mind I dismissed it. That just meant they would be coming on foot. One way or another they had to get back across the river. We would be fighting Germans and soon.

I joined the men at the forest. I looked critically at the emplacements. The two anti-tank guns had been heavily disguised. They needed all the camouflage they could get. They could damage a tank but one hit from a Panzer of any type would destroy the guns. They were not armoured. The gunners would have to hope that the tanks did not know they were anti-tank guns. The closer the range the more chance they had of scoring an effective hit. They just needed to stop the leading tank.

The gunners had a small brazier and they were gathered around it. I walked over to them. They looked young. There was a lieutenant in command. "Sir, will the Krauts be coming down this road?"

"Yes Lieutenant and the weakest tank they have with them is a Mark IV. When we fought them at Stavelot they had Panthers and King Tigers."

He shook his head. "We have to be very lucky to score a hit on one of those, sir."

I pointed down the road. "They are not cross-country tanks. They will have to come down here. If you know your ranges then you can use that to your advantage. If you stop one then you stop them all."

"And then what sir?"

"And then we take on their Panzer Grenadiers. We kill them then we can take their tanks."

"You make it sound simple sir."

"I wish it was Lieutenant, I wish it was."

Knowing that we would have to fight the Germans here I left all of my equipment by the guns. The Bergen held everything I needed except for my machine pistol and rifle. The trees had been cut down from behind us and were now a formidable barrier in front of the guns. They would give protection from shells fired with a flat trajectory. If, however, they had mobile artillery then falling shot could destroy them. I looked up at the canopy of branches. Nature might well come to our aid.

The Defences at Trois Ponts 26-27th December

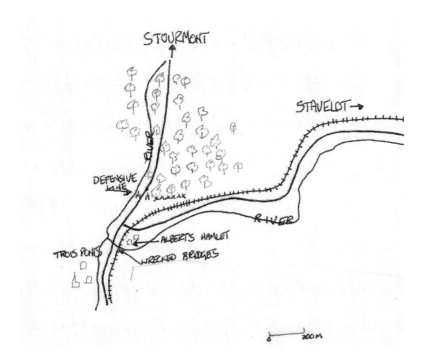

Chapter 13

Colonel Devine had skirmishers some way in the forest and it was their rifles which told us that the Germans were coming. The three survivors hurtled into our lines like March hares.

"S.S. sir, right behind us."

Captain Stewart asked, "Tanks?"

"We heard them sir but they were in the distance."

"Then these are their scouts and we have time. Go to the Command Post and tell the Colonel."

"Sir."

He turned to me, "Any suggestions, Major?"

I nodded, "Sergeant Barker, get Hewitt and Powers. Let's go and discourage their scouts."

I went to my Bergen and donned my German camouflage cape. It was no longer as white as it had been and was splattered with blood, mud and soot. I took my Mauser. If they were scouts then they would not be moving in numbers. We needed to keep them away from us for as long as possible. If they knew we had anti-tank guns then they would simply lay down a barrage and destroy them before they could even fire. My three soldiers quickly dressed in their camouflage capes and I waved them forward. I led them well to the east, away from the road. I wanted to flank the Germans. They would keep close to the road. They were finding a safe route for their precious King Tiger tanks.

As we moved into the forest I heard the sound of the German tanks to the north and west. The road was narrow and the King Tiger was over 12 feet wide. It did not manoeuvre well. It would have to drive down the very narrow road cautiously. I led the other three who fanned out behind me. I turned and headed north. I took comfort from the fact that there were no footprints in the snow. I used my sense of smell as well as my eyes and ears. The wind was from the north. I caught the distinctive whiff of petrol. The King Tiger leaked. They were also vulnerable from the rear. I wondered if we should try to get men around the rear with Bazookas. Then I dismissed the idea. They would be surrounded by Panzer Grenadiers.

I saw movement and I dived to the ground. There, just two hundred yards from us, were the German infantry. They were moving in a loose skirmish line. There were twelve of them. I waved my men to left and right and then levelled my rifle. I aimed at the officer who was leading. I squeezed the trigger and a heartbeat later my men opened up. The initial volley worked. Eight of them fell. Not all were dead but there were only four who could fire back. Their bullets shredded the trees above our heads. They were firing at the smoke. Our camouflage had fooled them. I squeezed another shot off and hit a sergeant who was firing an MP 35.

"I'll keep their heads down. Move left and right." I moved methodically across the remaining three Germans. Some were sheltering behind their dead. I fired to keep them looking down. When I reloaded they began to fire back. Then I heard Corporal Hewitt shout, "Grenade!"

There was an explosion and then Gordy shouted, "All clear sir!"

I stood and sprinted over to the Germans. Gordy was already searching them. "Sir, they only have a couple of grenades each and very little ammunition."

Just then bullets zipped from the north. I looked up and saw German half-tracks. Behind them I saw the tanks. The column was being led by Panthers. Perhaps they had no King Tigers left. We had done enough. They would be more cautious from now on. "Run!" The trees helped us. We zig zagged through them. I heard bullets striking the trees but we were hard to spot in our white camouflage capes in a white world of snow and snow covered trees.

As we neared our lines I yelled, "Friendlies coming in."

Just then there was a cry from behind and Sergeant Barker said, "Hewitt's hit sir."

I whirled around and knelt. He was still alive but hurt. "You two take him back. I will cover you." The two of them were big men and they each took an arm and half carried, half dragged him towards our lines. I saw what had shot him. A Kubelwagen with a machine gun was whizzing through the trees. The nippy little work horse was ideally suited to this type of work. I had driven one and I knew. It had been a lucky shot that had managed to hit Hewitt. The Kubelwagen had been bouncing around but that was war. Sometimes you had the luck and sometimes not. I aimed at the swerving vehicle. The bullets were zipping all around me. Due to the terrain most struck the tree above me. I fired four bullets as the Kubelwagen came across my sights. One must have struck the driver for he lurched to the side, taking the wheel with him. Ordinarily they might have all survived but the slippery surface and the trees meant that, as the wheels spun, it turned and two wheels came off the ground. The weight of the falling driver added to the momentum and the Kubelwagen crashed into the bole of a tree. Flames shot up in the air and then there was an explosion as the fuel tank ignited. I turned and hurried after the others.

One effect of our ambush appeared to be that the Germans spread out further from the road. I had not expected that. Our right flank was a little more exposed. As I hurtled through the outer defences I shouted, "Sergeant, angle the machine gun so that you are not flanked!"

Sergeant Locatelli nodded, "Yes sir! Nice shooting!"

I had to twist and turn through the labyrinth of tree stumps that Mason and his men had laid out. Covered with snow they would trip men and slow half-tracks down. As the front wheels rose up they would be a target for grenades and Bazookas. I saw that Hewitt was being attended to by two medics.

"How is he, Gordy?"

"He caught one in the shoulder." He shook his head, "He is out of this fight!"

The medics, having applied a dressing, put him on a stretcher and scurried away. At least we now had a doctor at the bridge and ambulances. Hewitt had a chance.

I looked at Gordy who shook his head, "The odds of us two surviving, sir, are getting longer by the minute."

"Just concentrate on fighting Jerry. There is no point in worrying. If a bullet has our name on it then we can do nothing about it." I turned to the artillerymen. "The column is led by Panthers. There is no point firing at their glacis. Aim for the tracks or the turret."

"They are small targets, sir."

"I know Lieutenant, just do your best." I turned to Captain Stewart. "The Bazookas might stand a chance if the Panthers give them a flank shot."

"Have you used a Bazooka sir?"

"No, Captain, just a PIAT and a Panzerfaust."

"You have to be closer than fifty yards to stand a chance. General Patton reckons thirty yards is the right range."

Colonel Devine arrived with another thirty men. I saw that some of them had Bazookas too. "You were right, Tom."

"I take no pleasure in that, sir. I wish I had been wrong! With your permission I will go to the right flank. They only have a sergeant in command there and the Germans have sent more men than I expected."

"Of course. I would say don't do anything stupid but you never do. What I really mean is don't try to be a hero all the time!"

"I never do. Come on Sergeant Barker. We will put a couple of booby traps up." I picked up my MP 34 and hurried to the right flank. The sound of the tanks was clearer now. They were less than a mile away.

Even as we ran one of them belched flames as it fired. The tree above one of the machine guns was hit. I heard a shout of, "Heads!" as branches and part of the trunk came crashing down. The bad luck Hewitt had had was now mitigated by the tree trunk landing just four feet in front of the machine gun. They had a little more protection.

I threw myself into the timber lined bunker. The sergeant said, "Are you joining us, sir?"

"I am indeed. I think it might get just a little hot here soon." Laying my gun down I ran thirty yards into the woods. Sergeant Barker went twenty feet to my left. Taking two German grenades I attached a piece of cord to the two detonators and laid it between two trees. Gordy did the same. We were both fast. We had done this many times before. I ran back and dropped behind the wood. I shouted, "Sergeant Barker, I will stay by the machine gun. You join the Bazooka team."

"Yes sir!"

The sergeant said, "Just two grenades won't stop many Krauts, sir."

"No, Sergeant, but it will make the others more cautious if they think we have booby trapped the area and it will tell us where they are. And, of course, the slower they are then the more chance we have of surviving."

"Not winning, sir?"

"Survive first and then worry about winning, Sergeant. This is the S.S. we are fighting!"

I had my German machine pistol but that would be for when it became close in fighting. Until then I would use the Mauser. I lay down behind the log and rested the barrel upon it. The dark woods and the camouflage of the S.S. meant that it was hard to see them. I heard another crack from our left as the leading tank fired again. They were still using HE. That meant they had not seen the anti-tank guns. Then I spied the half-track coming towards us.

"Sergeant Barker, have the Bazooka ready. Straight through the engine block if you please."

"Yes sir, we will do our best won't we boys?"

They chorused, "Sir, yes sir!"

I would leave the vehicle to the Bazooka. Turning to the Corporal next to me I said, "Wait until they are closer before you fire. Try to get the gunner of the half-track. Use short bursts. Keep your heads down if you can. This piece of timber should stop their bullets."

"Sir."

I levelled the Mauser and fired at the sergeant who was leading a handful of men to the left of the half-track. He fell and that brought the wrath of the machine gun on the half-track upon me. The bullets began to the right of me and so I fired a second shot at the gunner. I missed him but the bullet hit the metal and ricocheted into the interior. I saw a hand rise and fall. Then I ducked as pieces of bark showered me. The whole of our line was now engaged but each of us had our own personal battle. I only knew what was happening further down the line by the sound of the guns. When I heard the crack of the 3 pounder I knew that they were firing on the tanks and the explosion which followed told me that there had been a hit. I raised my head and saw that the infantry and half-track were now just a hundred yards from us. The half-track was still leading the men, its machine gun chattering death,

There was a cry to my right and I knew that they had managed to hit one of my men. I fired my magazine, shot by shot at every hint of a target. The half-track was just forty yards from us when the Bazooka fired. I was not certain if the range was right but I understood why Gordy had ordered it to be fired. I fired at the front tyre. The rocket hit. The operator had done as I had asked and the front of the half -track was lit up like a Christmas tree as the rocket hit the engine and ignited the fuel there. There must have been a leak too for the whole vehicle burst into flames. The S.S. who were around the vehicle were knocked to the ground but the rest rose and made a sudden rush for us.

The blast had taken some of the American soldiers by surprise. They stared at the burning vehicle and men. "Keep firing!"

I dropped the Mauser and opened fire with the MP 34. There was a double explosion as one of them set off the first booby trap. When the second one was set off I heard a German voice shout. "Fall back! Fall back!"

Gordy Barker shouted, "Keep pouring it into them!"

Then there was an explosion from our left. I looked down the line and saw that it was level with us. They had hit one of the anti-tank guns. I reloaded and saw that there were no live Germans before us.

"Sergeant Barker, take charge. I am going to see how things are by the road."

"Right sir."

I ran crouching, reloading as I did so. When I reached the road I saw that one of the anti-tank guns had been destroyed. Looking to my left I saw that the two guns had managed to destroy two Panthers before the Germans had had their revenge. There were bodies littering the cleared area behind the guns. Colonel Devine had a bloody bandage around his hand. "The boys are doing well! What I would give for a couple more of these."

I took out my glasses. The Germans were now stalled by their own tanks. The narrow road meant that they would have to clear the trees at the side. I pointed that out to the Colonel. "They will cut down the trees on either side of the wrecked tanks. All that they need to do is get around them and then they can destroy your other gun. They know where you are."

The Colonel looked at his watch. "It will be dark soon."

"And that suits them. If you have mines, sir, then I would lay them as soon as it is dark."

He shook his head, "We have none."

"Then tonight it will get messy sir. These are desperate and ruthless men."

"How are things over there?"

"We have beaten off their first attack. They will return after dark. Just let us know if you pull back eh sir? I wouldn't want to be left out on a limb."

"I will tell you; never fear."

Getting back was harder for the Germans had set up machine guns and they were firing at our lines. I ran and dived behind a snow-covered bush. It would not give me any protection but they would not be able to see me. I crawled. When I reached the machine gun my hands were frozen. Three men lay dead.

"What happened Corporal?"

"They managed to get a machine gun set up before we noticed."

That was annoying. Then I remembered their lack of experience at this sort of thing. "We have plenty of ammunition. Keep firing short bursts at anything that moves. The rest of you, your carbines have the range. Take pot shots. They have less ammo than we do. When it becomes dark then watch out. They will close with us and make it hand to hand. Find a buddy and watch each other's back."

It soon became obvious that the Germans would wait until it was dark before they attacked again. I took out my grenades and placed them before me. "Everyone keep your grenades handy. Listen for noises as soon as it gets dark. From now on no talking. Use signs."

If this was my unit then we would have a whole repertoire of signs and signals. We would have to improvise. Night seemed to come early. It became black. It was totally silent. Why could I not hear the tanks? Something was going on. I was nervous and I had done this before. I could not imagine how the young Americans were feeling.

I peered into the night. The secret was to watch for changes in the darkness. Suddenly there was an almighty explosion to my left. I thought it came from behind the German lines but I could not work out what it was. I saw a fire. Then I heard shells exploding. From the glow it had to be a mile away. What was it? The distraction almost cost me men. I forced myself to look to my front. I was certain I had seen something but I could not be sure. I pulled the pin on a grenade and hurled as high as I could.

"Grenade!"

I ducked as the explosion tore through the night and I waited until the wall of air had passed over. I grabbed my MP 34 and opened fire, spraying from left to right. I was rewarded by screams and cries. I handed the machine pistol to the Pfc next to me. I gave him a magazine. "Reload. I won't be long."

"You aren't going out there are you sir?"

"I need to see who we killed. Don't worry. I'll be back."

I took a length of parachute cord with me as I slipped over the log. I held my Luger before me as I rolled over the log and crawled through the snow. In the distance, I glimpsed the shadows of the Germans as they scurried back to the protection of their tanks. I smelled flesh. My grenade must have exploded close to someone and burned his hair before killing him. I felt the heat from their bodies as I passed. I moved to my left where I saw an unnatural shape in the snow. When I reached it, I saw the dark mark across the middle of the camouflage cape. The American machine gun had almost cut him in two. I searched him and found one grenade. I crawled another twenty feet before I found the next body. I found a second grenade on his body. I also found parachute cord. I felt his collar. This one was a German paratrooper. This was an unholy alliance: paratroopers and S.S.

When I was a hundred yards from our lines I was in ground which was devoid of the dead. I holstered my pistol and listened. To my left I could hear the crackling of the fire as it died and the occasional crack of a rifle as the Colonel and the Germans sparred. I took one grenade and primed it. I tied the cord to the detonator and around a tree. I now had more cord than before. When I reached the next tree, I did not tie a grenade to it but wrapped the cord around the tree and headed to the next one. There I placed my second grenade. We would have some warning the next time they attacked. I slipped my dagger into my boot when I had finished cutting the cord.

I turned and began to crawl back to our lines. There was a danger that I would become disorientated and lost. I looked back to where I thought our lines where. I saw the camouflage cape with the dark lines across it and headed for it. There was now silence from the battle by the river. What were the Germans planning? I had almost reached the bodies when I caught a new smell. It was human and it was close. More than that there

149

was breathing. Someone was alive. We have instincts we use and don't know why or how we use them. That night my instincts saved my life. I turned and rolled to my left. The dagger plunged into the snow where my back had been.

I reached down to grab my own knife as the German raised his hand to complete the job and stick his knife in my chest. I put up my left hand. The razor-sharp edge caught the side of my hand. I ignored the spurting blood. The unshaven German had an evil grin on his face. He thought he had me. As I brought my dagger up to slash at him he recognised it.

"Kommando!"

He fended it off but, in doing so allowed my blade to slash across his arm. He was astride me and I had to remember the moves I had been taught when we had trained in Oswestry all those years ago. I had to use his own strength against him. He had his upper body across mine but my legs were free. His left hand grabbed my wrist. I began to push up. He was strong. I just held him with my left hand. When I suddenly dropped my right hand and pushed with my left he began to overbalance. I then twisted, rolled and brought my knees up. The move took him by surprise and his weight was no longer on my chest as we turned. As we did I brought my head back and head butted him. I could smell the tobacco and sweat on him. His nose erupted. He would be temporarily blinded and, as he fell back I brought up my left knee hard between his legs. He gasped his pain. I felt his left hand weaken. I began to force the dagger towards his head. His hand was bent back. It is hard to use your full strength like that and he was wounded. Inexorably the tip began to move towards him. My weight was now on him. The wound to my hand was bloody and messy but the strength was in my arms and he could not move. The end, when it came, was quick. My dagger drove through his ear and into his brain. He became limp.

Rolling from his body I began to crawl back to our lines. As my bloody hand slid through the snow I left a trail, like a bloody snail. The cold acted as a coagulant and the bleeding slowed. I stopped when I saw the black barrels of the machine guns fifty feet from me. I hissed, "Major Harsker coming in."

I heard Gordy hiss back, "Come ahead sir. Steady as you go!"

When I climbed over the log he said, "You were out there a long time sir. We were worried."

I held up my hand. The blood dripped. "I met a paratrooper."

Sergeant Barker reached into his Bergen and brought out a field dressing. He used the powder to clean the wound and then put the dressing on. "Did you hear that explosion sir? It seemed too far away from the anti-tank gun to be a hit. What do you reckon it was?"

"A leaky fuel system and a spark? I have no idea really but things have gone quiet over there. I couldn't hear any engines."

"Do you think they have pulled out then, sir?" He finished applying the dressing.

"I would love to say yes but until it is dawn I have no idea. I laid another booby trap. We will have a little more warning the next time they come."

The American with the Bazooka asked, "Will they come again sir?"

"This is still the fastest way home and to the rest of their tanks. This offensive may not be over but unless they can regroup we can pick them off piecemeal. We take it one day at a time. Let's see what dawn brings."

When I reached the machine gun the Sergeant and the gun crew looked relieved to see me. I looked at my watch. It was almost 0300 hours. What would the dawn bring? I had been back for barely twenty minutes when we discovered what the Germans had planned. My grenades went off and then the Germans began firing as they raced towards our lines. I heard the sound of 75 mm tank guns as they opened fire at the road.

"Open fire!" My order was a little redundant as every American opened fire. I used short bursts from the MP 34. This was not a skirmish line; it was a major attack. When I emptied my MP 34 I drew my Luger and emptied that. The Corporal next to me fell to the ground, hit by the German's ferocious gunfire. I hurled a grenade, "Grenade!" It exploded just thirty feet from us. As we stood those around me took the opportunity to hurl their grenades. As I ducked below the parapet I reloaded the MP 34. I had just two magazines left.

When I rose, I sprayed the ground before me, emptying half of my magazine. To the left and right I heard the sound of guns. Smoke filled the air making it difficult to see. A German appeared before me and I fired a short burst which threw him back. I readied a grenade. I was down to my last one. A knot of men rose and ran at me, firing. Even as I threw the grenade I was aware that bullets were striking the timber below me. I dropped next to the dead Corporal. I saw that the machine gunner and his loader was also dead. The grenade ripped through the trees showering me with snow and pine. I rose with my gun, ready to fire. Before me was a line of dead Germans. There were just two privates left in our emplacement. Both were shaking.

"Reload."

"Sir!"

"Sergeant Barker?"

"We have taken casualties but we are still here."

"Sergeant Blair?"

"He is dead sir, Corporal Woods is in command. There are four of us left."

"Stand to. I will check the line. Keep a good watch." I turned to the two young soldiers, "Get the machine gun loaded and ready to fire. This may not be over."

I changed magazines and put my last one in. I headed first to Gordy. He nodded. He was dressing a wound. As I reached the last post I saw that Sergeant Locatelli and his men were all dead or wounded. Around them lay the bodies of the Germans they had killed, testament to their courage. "Medic!" I saw the signs of footprints. I followed them briefly and saw that they had continued south. They were heading for the river and Trois Ponts. The Germans had broken through and were behind us. I went to the Germans and kicked over a couple of bodies. Some were S.S. and some were Paratroopers. Bizarrely one was dressed in an American uniform. When I reached in and took out his dog tags I saw that he was a German Paratrooper. He must have been one of the men they had warned us of. American speaking Germans. I picked up three or four magazines. None of them had spares. They were running out of ammunition.

I ran back to Gordy, "Watch the rear. They are behind us."

He was applying a dressing to a corporal's head. "Sir, they nearly had us. One more attack and we are done for."

"I know. I will head to the anti-tank guns and see how the Colonel has fared. I just can't work out why it was just men and not the tanks too."

Corporal Woods was also acting as a medic. I saw that there were signs here that the Germans had broken through. What I could not understand was why they had not turned and attacked from the rear. I saw that they had bulldozed their way through the men next to Corporal Woods. None were left unwounded.

When I reached the guns, I was greeted by the Colonel. I pointed behind me, "They have broken through sir. We need medics."

He nodded, "Sergeant, see to them."

"Did they attack here, sir?"

"They just used their tank guns. I think it was to cover." He pointed to the river on the left. They killed the men who were there. I think they are in Trois Ponts."

I suddenly thought about Albert and his wife. "Then we are surrounded."

He nodded, "They will have the bridge now. We just have to wait for their tanks. You had better bring your men here. We have to stop them. This will be our last stand."

Chapter 14

As I ran back I told each group of men to take their equipment and head for the road. When I reached Sergeant Locatelli I took the dog tags from the three men who had died with him. The medics had already taken the wounded. I repeated it along the line. When I finally returned to the Colonel it was dawn and he had made a circle of the survivors. More had survived than I had expected. We had lost twenty men killed. I was desperate to see how Albert and the villagers had fared but we still had tanks along the road and goodness knew how many Germans left.

By 0900 hours no attack had materialized. I turned to the Colonel. "Let me take Barker and Powers and go and have a recce, sir."

"Too risky, Tom."

"We can't sit on our backsides all day, sir."

"Our job is to stop the armour."

"They may have pulled out. Let me have a look sir and then we will know. From the tracks, there are a couple of hundred S.S. and paratroopers behind us."

"I have been on the radio. The General already knows. He says to leave well alone for the moment."

"A quick look sir. If we see any danger, we will be back here instantly."

He nodded. He could see the sense. "And when this is over, Major, you and Sergeant Barker get back to your own unit! You have done enough here."

"Barker, Powers, with me." I had spare magazines now and I reloaded. We kept to the tree line. We passed the bodies of the Germans killed in the attack. Their bodies were already stiffening. The road twisted along the river. When we turned I saw, ahead of us, two Panthers. I ducked behind a tree expecting gun fire. The other two did the same.

Corporal Powers said, "Why aren't they firing sir?"

"I have no idea. Let's move through the woods. Use all the cover you can."

We sprinted from tree to tree. I kept peering out at the tanks but there appeared to be no sign of life. When we were twenty feet from the leading Panther and it had not fired, I risked running towards it. I sheltered in front of it. Powers and Barker joined me.

"I think it is empty sir."

"You might be right, Gordy. Cover me." I jumped up and used the driving wheel to climb on to the chassis. The hatch was open. I was going to drop a grenade in but when I peered down I saw that it was empty. "It is empty. Check the other one. I will cover you."

I swung the machine gun around and then saw that it only had four bullets left in it. Beyond the second one I saw a burned-out King Tiger and, beyond that three half-tracks. Here was a mystery. I saw Gordy and Corporal Powers climb up and peer into the hatch. "It is empty!"

I climbed down inside. The dials were in German but I could see, straightaway, that the fuel gauge was on 0. They had run out of fuel. Everything that could have been used as a weapon was gone. There were just six shells left and there was no ammunition for the machine gun. I climbed out. I joined the other two and we headed towards the King Tiger. "No gas, sir. I banged the tank. Empty and no ammo either. That is why they stopped here and why they didn't attack with them."

I tapped the blackened and still warm hull of the King Tiger. "They burned this one so that it wouldn't fall into our hands. I am betting that the half-tracks are the same. Corporal, go and tell the Colonel that the Germans have gone. He might want to check out the village."

"Sir." He turned and sped off.

I was right. There was neither fuel nor ammo in the vehicles. They had taken the machine guns from the half-tracks. We found a dozen bodies. They were all covered with their camouflage capes.

As we went back Gordy said, "Where do you reckon they went, sir?"

"Back to their own lines to join up with the rest of their army. It is what we would have done. I did it in 1940."

"Then that is it sir, it is over."

"Not necessarily. This was one regiment. What about all the others? This country can hide thousands of men. They will have to be found and captured or killed."

"No, sir, I meant for us. It is over for us."

"I reckon so."

We headed back towards the hamlet. Bodies lay where they had fallen. There were more Germans than Americans. It could have been worse. The Colonel had left the last anti-tank gun and a dozen men to guard the road. The Lieutenant said, "Is that it sir? Will any more tanks be coming down the road?"

"I doubt it and, if they do then they will have to clear the road. We should be safe for a while." We crossed the railway line and then the road. I saw the Colonel and Sergeant Major O'Rourke. They were deep in conversation outside Albert's house. When they saw me they began to walk towards me. I saw their faces were filled with sorrow.

"What is it sir?"

"Don't go in Tom. It is the old man and his wife. They have both been shot. It looks like the old guy put up a fight. There are two paratroopers he hit with his shotgun. He almost cut them in two."

"But why? They couldn't hurt them! They just wanted to be left alone."

"All the villagers who stayed have been killed and their homes ransacked for food. The Krauts are starving." He pointed to the bridge. "They have gone that way. The bridge guards were also killed. I am going after them as soon as the armoured cars and half-tracks arrive. I will leave some men to see that they are buried properly."

"We are coming with you."

He shook his head, "No, you are not. Corporal Hewitt and the other wounded were evacuated last night. They are all safely on the road to Verviers. I am not disobeying the General. He gave you the jeep and told you to get back to your own unit."

"But sir, it is not finished. This is an old-fashioned blood feud. I have to have vengeance for Albert and his wife."

"This is not a private war, mister! I don't want to do it but I will have the pair of you put in irons if I think you are going to disobey me." His harsh voice softened, "Look, Tom, you have done more than anyone could have expected and you have survived. The last thing the General needs is for you to be killed fighting for us. Monty would never forgive us. Go home. Enjoy your leave." He held out a hand. "Go on, son." He pointed north, "That is your road."

Sergeant Major O'Rourke saluted, "And can I say, Major, that you have earned the respect of every man in this regiment!"

I knew when I was beaten. "Well good luck to you chaps. Hunt the bastards down! They are like mad dogs and the only way you deal with a mad dog is to put it down."

"And we will."

The Sergeant Major pointed, "Your bags and Corporal Hewitt's are in the jeep." He lowered his voice, "And a bottle of brandy we found."

"Thank you, Sergeant Major."

"And a full jerrycan of gas sir. You don't want to run out, eh sir?"

It took some time to pack the jeep properly and stow all of our equipment. Then we had to wait for the road to clear as the relief column arrived with the new vehicles for the Colonel as well as another armoured brigade. It was afternoon by the time we headed down the road. All morning we had watched flights of Allied aeroplanes heading to what was now termed the Bulge. They were hitting the Germans before they could dig in and consolidate their gains.

Gordy drove and I sat back to contemplate the unfairness of war. Albert and his wife had lost everything in this war; their family, their home and their lives. I closed my eyes as I pictured what had gone on. The first attack had been to draw our attention to the forest. While that was going on the majority had slipped down the river and escaped. Blowing up the tank and the subsequent attack had been to keep our attention on the forest. The last attack would have been by the fanatics. The hard-core killers who were determined to get glory in a last charge. The Colonel and his regiment would have a hard job to track them. They would have disappeared off the road into the forests which led all the way to Germany. That was why they had taken the food. They could evade the Americans but not hunger.

I must have dozed off for Sergeant Barker woke me. "Sir, Stavelot."

I opened my eyes and saw that it was almost dusk and we had reached the town which was still a graveyard of armour. "We might as well stay the night here. We have missed Christmas and I don't fancy risking the roads."

There was a roadblock at the edge of the town. I did not recognise the unit but our papers allowed us to be admitted. "Is there a canteen, Corporal?"

"Yes sir there are three messes in the main square."

"Thank you."

We drove down to the main square. It looked different now. The burned-out Tiger was still there. The wall of the house had given it a brick shroud. The rest, however, was filled with large tents. "Park it by the King Tiger, eh?"

Gordy laughed, "Yes sir."

We carried our side arms with us but left the rest of our gear in the jeep. I had no idea where we were going to sleep. I said, "I will try and get something to eat in the officer's mess. See you at the jeep afterwards."

"Yes sir."

There was one thing about the American army; they knew how to recover. They might have been caught napping but like a bear woken from winter hibernation, once awake there was no stopping them. The tent was filled with uniforms and the smell of the food told me that they had meat! I could smell roast pork and chicken. A sergeant stopped me at the entrance, "Which unit sir? I don't recognise it."

Just then a voice from behind me said, "That, Sergeant Hofstadter, is a British Commando and this one is a real tiger!"

156

I turned and saw Colonel Cavender. His arm was in a sling. Not wearing my hat I came to attention without saluting. "Colonel, good to see you."

"And you. We were listening to the reports of the battle at Trois Ponts like it was a ball game. We were battening down the hatches here in case they came this way."

I shook my head, "No sir, they ran out of gas and ammunition. They headed across the bridges we had repaired."

"Damned inconsiderate of them. Come with me, let's get some food. After what you have been through you must be starving."

In truth I was not. The last decent meal I had eaten had been cooked by Albert's wife, Clothilde, but I could not be rude, "Starving sir."

The cooks, seeing me with the Colonel, loaded my tray with food. A space was cleared for us and then the Colonel plied me with questions. The officers around all listened in. I was one of the first officers to return from the most recent battle and they were all anxious to know the details.

"If they had had fuel, Colonel, then they would have kept their gains. We would have lost too many tanks trying to defeat them."

A Captain said, "Sir, there is a King Tiger across the square. They can't be that hard to destroy."

The Colonel shook his head, "Captain Taylor that tank was destroyed by men led by the major here and it was not easy was it?"

I shook my head. "We were in the building which has now fallen on top of the King Tiger. We were lucky. We used petrol bombs. When I was with Colonel Devine in his Greyhound we managed to destroy a King Tiger but we were twenty yards away and it took three shells into his rear. That was lucky too. Their Achilles heel is their fuel consumption. Your tanks drink as much fuel but we have plenty of supplies. The Germans do not."

The Colonel waggled a finger at the officers around the table. "Do not underestimate the Germans. As we found out to our cost they are hard to remove from dug in positions."

I nodded, "And the ones we are fighting are the fanatics. They think that Hitler can still win."

The officers were all suitably subdued after we had finished speaking. It was not their fault. They had all been in reserve. The German blow had not fallen on them. They saw the results of the labours of the brave Americans who had stopped their advance. I now knew that our defence of the river and the Elsenborn ridge had been the decisive moments. I was not naïve enough to think that the battle was over but, with air power, I could not see how they could finish what they had started.

As I walked back to the jeep with the Colonel I said, "What they have done, sir, is to extend the war. I know your country has the ability to produce hundreds, nay thousands of tanks and guns but we have to get them across the Atlantic. With a smaller frontier the Germans will defend every inch."

He nodded. "You are right Major and these Germans seem to enjoy war. I don't understand them. I will have my Sergeant get you a couple of tents. I take it you are leaving in the morning?"

"Yes sir. Your general made it quite clear that I was to head on home. Colonel Devine also made that point quite clear too."

"Well you have made an impression Major." He pointed north. "Your chaps hold the country north of Malmedy. Montgomery sent 30 Corps to bolster the line. That is why we have so many of our troops here. They had been held in reserve. We can't afford to lose Antwerp."

"No sir." He saluted and left me. As I picked up my Bergen I thought of Alan Crowe and Ken Shepherd. They had lost their lives taking Antwerp. We owed it to them and others like them to hold on to it.

The sergeant came over with two tents over his shoulders. "Here you are sir. I don't know where you are going to camp though. It is cold as a witch's tit tonight, sir!"

"Don't worry sergeant, we had endured worse. I think we will camp by the river and the damaged bridge. The trees there will give us some shelter and make it a little warmer."

"The Engineers have a camp there, sir. They have a brazier!"

"Even better."

"Oh by the way, Major, keep the tents. We have plenty and you might need shelter before you get home."

"Thank you, Sergeant."

Sergeant Barker came along with someone in tow. "Sergeant Henry!"

"Hello sir. Good to see you still alive. Gordy here has been telling me about the S.S. Bastards."

I nodded, "The guys we fought alongside at the river are mostly still alive though, sergeant. When you come through something like that it makes you stronger."

"Ain't that the truth." He nodded. "Anyway, I am glad I saw you. They are shipping me Stateside tomorrow. First to Antwerp and then on a ship to England. Then home. I am sorry I won't be here at the end."

"What will you do now, Sergeant?"

"I was a regular sir. The life of a soldier was my life. I am not certain anymore. I have another two years before my enlistment is up. The Chaplain said that they are going to have me training new recruits for a while. I think I would enjoy that. If someone had taken me to one side before this offensive and given me a few tips then I might have saved some of the boys who died on my watch."

"Never look back, Bud. Hindsight is always perfect. We do the best we can at the moment. If it is wrong then so be it. The only time you should regret is if you don't do what you know is right."

"Anyway, I have Gordy's address. We are going to keep in touch. If I ever marry then I might bring the wife to England. I like it. Gordy has said he will show me some decent pubs,"

"And if you do come then look me up. I shall be delighted to see you too."

"Really sir? I would get a kick out of that. You being a hero an' all."

I shook my head, "Bud we fought together. All of you and your men were heroes and never let anyone tell you otherwise."

Gordy said, "Told you what he was like."

"Come on Sergeant Barker, we have tents to erect. See you, Sergeant Henry, and enjoy the sea voyage!"

The Engineers made us feel welcome especially when Gordy told them the story of how the bridge had been destroyed. They had the job of removing the tank before they could build a new bridge. The Lieutenant thought that the war would be over long before they had finished.

"Do not be too sure, Lieutenant. There are many twists and turns in this war yet."

After a hearty breakfast, the Americans had bacon, Gordy and I set off towards Malmedy. I drove. Gordy was in reflective mood. I think he and Sergeant Henry had become sentimental about the campaign. He was still in that mood as we headed north.

"You know sir it feels like we are the last two at a party. You know what I mean? Everyone else has sloped off during the night and there are just two of you left with the smell of stale beer and tobacco. That's what this feels like. When Hewitt was with us it wasn't so bad but he will be back in some hospital now and the other lads will be enjoying a leave. There are just the two of us left here fighting the Germans."

"Very maudlin, Gordy. They will give us a two week leave; if we are lucky. Then it will be back to Falmouth to get the section up to speed and then they will send us somewhere else."

"Germany?"

"Probably. That is where our expertise lies."

"Bud was saying that the Americans will be sent to the Far East. They have the Japanese to fight."

"I know. My Dad is there too. We could be sent there."

"Jungle warfare? I wouldn't fancy that. The cold is bad enough but at least they don't have bugs and snakes and the like."

I laughed, "I think that the Japs might be more of a problem than the bugs and snakes."

We met our first British soldiers in Malmedy. They were Highlanders. Once again, our papers were scrutinised. The sergeant said, "We have had those German paratroopers pretending to be Yanks." He shook his head. "Sneaky, very sneaky. He pointed to the north east. "The only road open is the one through Mont. Although I am not sure how long it will stay open. We have had more snow in this sector. I should watch out, sir. There are still pockets of Germans there."

"Thank you, Sergeant. If the snow stays away then we should be in Liège before dark."

"Aye, mebbes but my bones tell me there will be snow. We have had a couple of days of blue skies. It canna last!"

As we drove off Gordy shook his head, "Why are the Scots such miserable buggers sir?"

"I think, to be fair to him, that he is right. There is snow in the air. Let us push on, eh? I will give it a couple of hours and then we swap over."

"Whatever you like, sir."

The dour Scotsman had been right and snow began to fall. We had been driving without the canvas cover. We stopped to fit it when the snow began to become uncomfortable. I was annoyed with the delay because it was our fault. We should have put it on before we had started to drive. The road became extremely slippery and the going was hard for there were inclines, hills, dips and hollows. A couple of times Gordy had to get out and push. We had to cut pine branches to make the road passable. It took us forever and I began to despair of reaching anywhere. We might have to spend the night in the jeep and that was not an attractive prospect.

Gordy was driving and I checked the map. "It looks like there is a village up ahead; Monts. We will see if we can find shelter for the night. I can't see us getting to Liège. Perhaps we might make it to Verviers."

When we neared Monts we were stopped by a pair of M.Ps. "Papers sir." I handed them over. He seemed satisfied. "I am afraid you can't get any further north at the moment sir. There are Germans. They have cut it."

"Cut it? I thought this sector had been secured?"

"It was sir. 30 Corps drove the Germans out of Celles."

"Celles? That is over eighty miles behind our lines."

"I know, sir. It was a mixture of the paratroopers who were dropped some time ago along with S.S. and Volksgrenadier. They have armour too. Caused absolute confusion and mayhem, sir. From what we heard Monty was none too happy. The Guards Division and the Royal Horse Artillery sent them packing and now they are driving them east. The captain said there is no order to their movements. They are just trying to get home but that makes them even more dangerous. There are reports of whole regiments of Germans wandering through Belgium. The captain has us on high alert."

"Captain?"

"Yes sir. Captain Ferguson is in command of the troops in the village. They are a hotch potch of soldiers he has collected." He laughed, "He is like a pirate, sir. He makes use of anything. He is going after them."

I smiled at Gordy, "I think we both know the Captain. Where is he?"

"In the centre of the village, sir. He will be glad to see another officer."

Chapter 15

As we drove through the village Gordy said, "It can't be our Captain Ferguson, can it sir?"

"I am taking a guess that it is Gordy. He told me that he was keen to do some fighting and leading before the end of the war."

The centre of the village was filled with soldiers. The majority were British but I saw a few Americans too. They also had a couple of lorries. I was intrigued. What was the Intelligence officer doing here leading such a disparate group of men?

We had to stop some way away from the house which had a Union Flag nailed to it. There were just too many men gathered around. We climbed out and made our way through the throng. I could hear Hugo's voice. It confirmed his identity. "Sergeant Armstrong will organize your duties. Remember that we don't know exactly where Jerry is and so we will need to cover a wide area."

A Corporal tugged at his sleeve. "Sir, a senior officer."

I almost looked round to see who he was talking about and then I realised he meant me. Hugo turned and his face broke into a grin, "Major! You made it! Excellent!"

"Do you mind telling me what is going on, Hugo?"

He nodded, "Carry on Sergeant Armstrong. I shall talk to Major Harsker in the headquarters' building."

"Yes sir."

"Headquarters'?"

Hugo looked sheepish. "Just the old hall here. There was no one using it and it is comfortable."

We went into the hall which looked both ancient and decrepit. There was an oil lamp which gave off a smoky orange light. I took off my greatcoat. There was a log fire in the house which made it warm. Hugo poured wine for the three of us. "Right Hugo. What is going on?"

"After I left you I drove to Verviers. I met Lieutenant-General Galloway. He is now commander of 30 Corps. But then he was just on a fact-finding mission prior to taking over from Lieutenant-General Horrocks." I nodded, wishing that he would get to the point. "Anyway when I told him what we had discovered he acted immediately and ordered the units there to begin to prepare defences. He had me help him and in three days we had managed to make the perimeter secure. He was then whisked off to take over the Corps but, before he left he gave me the job of finding all those soldiers who had become separated from their units. He gave me Sergeant Armstrong. He is an absolute genius at organising, by the way, and we headed south to find and organize the lost men as I call them."

"Now it makes sense." I sipped the wine.

"What date is it now? Ah yes the 29th, well we left Verviers on Christmas Eve and found this place on Christmas Day. Just driving down here we found about twenty men. Since we established headquarters here more than sixty others have turned up. Most were half starved, especially the Americans. By the way some mentioned you, sir. They said they escaped the Malmedy massacre and you gave them food and weapons. Good show, sir."

"But the M.P. said something about going after the Germans."

"Yes sir. We have radio contact with HQ and we have been ordered to round up as many Germans as we can. When the roads are clear we will have tanks but, for the moment we have to make do with small arms, machine guns, mortars and PIATs."

I swallowed the wine in one. "No offence, Hugo, but Headquarters are mad if they think you can take on S.S. and paratroopers with these orphans."

"Sir, I have my orders. We have had a couple of run ins with some of those who escaped from the west. We killed some and we captured some. They were sent back to Namur before the bad weather returned and the snow closed the road."

I shook my head. Gordy said, "I'll just go and have a word with Sergeant Armstrong, sir. I'll leave you two gentlemen to chat."

Gordy was becoming a diplomat. After the door had closed I said, "Hugo, you are out of your depth. You will get yourself and these men killed. They can't do much damage east of here. It is forest and then Germany."

Hugo shook his head, "Not true sir. When we arrived here we found the villagers slaughtered. We chased the Germans from the village. We buried the villagers. The road east of here leads to the Elsenborn Ridge. There was hard fighting there, sir. The last thing we need is for them to be attacked in the rear. Besides these orders come directly from Monty. You may be right, I might not be a hero like you sir, but I can obey an order and this is not one you can countermand. I am sorry sir, I thought that you would be pleased for me."

I could see that I had hurt his feelings, "Hugo, I want to see you survive this war. I have lost too many good friends already. If it is orders then you must obey and I shall stay with you. I will give you the benefit of my knowledge."

He grinned, "Good show sir!"

"Now tell me what you know."

Hugo took out a map. He knew his way around a map even if he didn't know his way around a battlefield. "They have been coming across the road north and south of us here." He shook his head, "To be truthful, sir, I tried to place men to stop them but it didn't work. We lost ten that way."

"Tank tracks? Vehicles?"

"We have seen a couple of tracks but they were on the road." He jabbed a finger at a place on the map just half a mile from the village. "This is the only track that we have seen which could accommodate a tank. There are tracks heading east. The track ends up in Germany but there is a river to ford."

"Until the snow melts then they can use a ford. They will use that track. Right, it is too late to do anything tonight. I might take Commandos out to tackle Jerry but not this disparate group of soldiers. Too many would get hurt. I want all of your men pulled back to the village."

"But what about watching the track sir?"

"Hugo, we are quite remote here. If a tank heads down the track then we will hear it. I want every one of your soldiers to be within shouting distance of this Command Post."

"Command Post?"

"This hall. From now on that is what it becomes. I want your radio man in here, as well as your Sergeant Armstrong and Sergeant Barker." I had a sudden thought. "The ones you drove from the village; what unit were they?"

"Volksgrenadiers sir. There were just ten of them. We killed five and the others fled east."

That explained why and how Hugo had managed to find the village intact. Had it been S.S. it would have been a different story. "Now you go and tell the two sergeants what we have planned and I will walk the perimeter. Oh and pull back the M.Ps. We don't need them there. We need every man who can fire a gun, close."

"Sir." He smiled, "Thanks sir."

"Thank me after the war... if we survive."

I went back to the map. The roads were typical of this part of the Ardennes. They were very narrow. In winter people normally stayed close to their houses. The roads would stay closed if it snowed and people

164

would hunker down. I knew that if we searched the cellars we would find food stored for such times. The Germans would also know that. It explained their choice of route. To the east were forests, a lake, streams, rivers and hills. It was not tank country. If the Germans took tanks over it then they would be desperate. That was what Hugo did not understand. If these were desperate S.S. and paratroopers then his hotch potch of soldiers would stand no chance. It would not be a level playing field. Gordy Barker and I would have to make it level.

I put on my greatcoat and stepped outside. It was still snowing. That meant no air force and no relief column. Malmedy might be only a few miles away but the roads were impassable. We had seen that on the way here. Men saluted as I went passed. The two sergeants had set them to work. I could see Gordy organizing men to make barricades across the road. They would wonder why. In a perfect world I would explain but I did not have time.

I walked up the road to the edge of the hamlet. There were just a dozen houses here. The memory of Albert's little huddle of houses brought back a painful memory. The poor people of Belgium were paying the price for our lack of vigilance. There were four soldiers there manning a Lewis gun. I saw that they were from the East Lancashire regiment. They had a nervous expression on their faces. They were staring up a road which was like an abyss.

"Where are you lads from?"

"Corporal Parr, sir, Wigan, sir!" He pronounced it '*Wiggin*'. I knew the accent. My grandparents had lived not far away.

"Missing the pies, eh lads?"

The Corporal grinned, "Aye sir. I could go a nice meat and potato one right now!"

"Nah Corp, steak pie, full of gravy, dripping down your chin."

I nodded amiably, "Me too. Well we will have to get out of this little mess first won't we? You need to make your defences higher."

"Higher sir?"

I pointed to the last house, just behind us. There was a block of wood with an axe in it and, next to it, a pile of firewood. "Take the axe and cut down some of the larger branches or smaller trees. Make yourself a dugout. You want it four logs high and with a roof. Cover the roof with branches and then snow. Disguise it. Trust me the wood will stop a bullet better than anything and if a tank comes down and tries to climb over it then a grenade underneath can do some damage."

"A tank sir?"

"It could happen but, hopefully, it won't. The other thing is that the wood will keep you a little warmer. Cut the branches and I will come back and help you make a dugout."

"Right lads you heard the Major!"

They had something to occupy their minds now other than the thought of Germans coming down the road. I walked back. There was another road coming from the west. Gordy had already been there and was helping them to make it more defensible. At the southern end of the hamlet they were giving their Browning .30 Calibre a thorough check. I approved.

"Where are you chaps from?"

"Virginia sir. Most of us are from Winchester in the Shenandoah Valley."

"Stonewall Jackson, eh?"

"Yes sir!"

"I hope you have all of his qualities then for we shall need them here."

"We just want the chance to kill a few Krauts sir. They killed our buddies. We want payback!"

"How did you chaps end up here?"

The sergeant said, "Bad luck I guess, sir. We were heading towards Stavelot with more bridging equipment. We were ambushed close to Spa. The Lieutenant and the rest of the guys were killed. We took to the woods. The Krauts took our trucks and headed south. We came east. If the Captain hadn't found us." He shrugged, "They would have found our bodies in the Spring, I guess."

"Well you are Engineers and I think you can make this into a little fort. Use wood, stones, anything to protect you. Put a roof on it if you like. When Jerry comes make it hard for him. This becomes your home. Defend it."

"But the road south of here leads to Malmedy sir. That is in our hands."

"Your Airborne and the 30 Corps, along with the Air Force, have stopped the offensive. The Germans want to get home. We are in their way. None of us chose to be here but we are and that means that we have to endure whatever they throw at us. Remember that they have less ammo than we do and they are hungry. No matter how tough it gets, remember that."

"Yes sir. Right guys. Let's show these guys how to build!"

By the time I got back to the men from Wigan they had assembled logs and branches. I showed them how to lay them so that they interlocked and formed a three-sided dugout with a couple of small logs and branches for a roof. "This will keep the snow off you but, more importantly it will keep shrapnel off you. I'll leave you to it, Corporal Parr. You will be relieved in a couple of hours."

"Right sir."

The camp was now more compact and there were no isolated men any more. Corporal Parr and his section were flanked by two houses which had men in them. It was the same with the American point at the southern end. The last road was the most heavily defended as it was close to what I had termed the Command Post.

Sergeant Barker had organized some food for me. He ladled me a plate of stew. I knew what it was. It was standard fare in the field. He had chopped up a tin of bully beef and added water to the soup powder from our rations before thickening it all with oatmeal. It was not the tastiest of fares but it had the right number of calories and the oats kept us going for longer. A Commando ate to survive and not for the taste.

The Corporal with the radio was sat by the window with his headphones on. Hugo and Sergeant Armstrong were going over the duty rotas. Gordy sat by me as I ate, "What do you reckon, Gordy?"

"The lads have guts, sir, but there are clerks and engineers amongst the fighting men. Most weren't even at D-Day. If Jerry comes then survival will be the best we can hope for."

I nodded and wiped my mouth, "Good stew!"

He laughed, "Lost your taste buds then sir?"

"As my granddad might have said, '*I was hungry enough to eat a horse... with the skin on*'!"

"Jerry might not come."

I gestured with my spoon at the map on the wall. Hugo had marked the extent of the German gains. "They reached almost as far as Dinant. There are perilous few roads here and if we know how to survive in this country then you can bet that the best German soldiers can too. They won't surrender and they will come. It is that road north of us that will draw them. They can use that to get back to Germany. We are less than twenty miles from the border. Well the border before the Offensive. We could be just ten miles or so from German troops. I would not like to be on the Elsenborn Ridge. From what I heard yesterday in Stavelot it was those lads there that saved Antwerp. It was why we had so many to fight around Stavelot and Trois Ponts. They couldn't follow their original plan and headed through that gap."

"They might not come here and this snow can't last forever, sir!"

"In this part of the world it can. I daresay that they will move heaven and earth to reach us but my bet is that the Germans reach us before reinforcements or supplies." Gordy nodded, "How are supplies?"

167

"Better than for some time. All the men have a week of rations. You can live off it, I suppose."

"Hugo, would you and the sergeant join us? Gordy go and fetch the brandy from the jeep."

"Sir!"

The two joined me. The Sergeant stood rigidly to attention. "We don't bother with such things at the front, Sergeant. At ease. Sit down, both of you."

"Sorry, sir, force of habit."

Gordy returned with the brandy. I put four mugs there and I poured a generous measure into each one. "Gentlemen, the King!"

We all touched mugs and they said, "The King!" We drank."

Sergeant Armstrong and Gordy swallowed theirs in one. Gordy wiped his mouth with the back of his hand. "That was nice sir. Reminded me of the rum on the '*Lucky Lady*'."

"Well we shall keep the rest for after this battle. Now listen there are just the four of us here to command Fred Karno's army. Here we have to be of one mind. Now I may be wrong and Jerry might not come. I hope I am wrong but we I might not be." I took a piece of paper from the sergeant's clipboard and began to sketch. "Now we are here. From now on this Command Post is Buckingham Palace. Here is the southern end where the Americans are. That is Fort Shenandoah. The Engineers and the M.P.s can man that one. Up here at the north are the East Lancashires. That is Blackpool Tower. I have a feeling that is where the hardest fighting will be. Finally, here, at the crossroads," I looked at Sergeant Armstrong, "That will be Alnwick Castle. The rest of the men will be there. Now I want all the emplacements improving. Pile the firewood in front of them. Cover the tops with branches. We need forts. What we lack in firepower we will make up for in the strength of our defences."

"Right sir."

"Gordy, go and have a look for food."

"Will there be any sir?"

"Check for cellars. They normally keep things like ham and preserved foods there. If the cellar has an earth floor see if they have buried apples and carrots in straw. You might be lucky and find some potatoes."

"Now don't get my hopes up sir! Tatties would make a lovely corned beef hash!" He stood and wandered off to find a cellar. I noticed that he took his sidearm. We were always careful. Hugo sipped his brandy as did I. I poured another shot into the Sergeant's mug.

"Thanks sir. I'll sip this one eh sir? Like you two gentlemen."

I looked at his shoulder patch. "Royal Tank Corps? What brings you here?"

"I was in the Eighth Army sir. I was wounded in Sicily." He tapped his leg. "This is a bit gammy for action but I was given a job at Field Marshal Montgomery's Headquarters. He liked to have me around." He smiled. "I think it was a reminder of when he was in Africa. He knew that I had been yearning for a bit of action and when the Captain arrived he saw it as an opportunity to reward me." He grinned, "I am loving it sir."

I saw now that he was about the same age as Daddy Grant and Reg Deane. I suspected that he had been a regular before the war. But for the wound he might have ended up as a Sergeant Major or Warrant Officer. "So you don't know the men then?"

"No sir. Right little rag bag but they seem a good set of lads, even the Yanks."

"Don't knock the Yanks, Sergeant. I have a great deal of respect for them. Gordy and I have just spent more than two weeks fighting with them and believe me they are as tough as any soldier I have met."

"Sorry sir. The Field Marshal is not very keen on them."

"I know. Anyway, there are four of us. I want us to do four hours on and four hours off. These lads will need us to be around. When Gordy comes back I will send him for a sleep. Hugo, get your head down. The Sergeant and I will have the first watch. Gordy will relieve the sergeant in four hours and you can relieve me in eight."

Sergeant Armstrong said, "But, sir. that means you have a longer watch!"

"Sergeant, what is your first name?"

"Alun sir."

"Well Alun, I am the commanding officer here. That means you lot are my responsibility until this is over. I can sleep after the war. Don't worry, Alun, I have done this before as has Sergeant Barker. You two, with due respect, have been behind the lines for a long time. If we are still here in three days' time then you can do the eight-hour stag. Fair enough?"

"Fair enough sir."

Hugo stood, "I shall get my head down then. Don't worry sir. I shan't let you down."

"Have the Corporal here relieved too." I turned to the Corporal who was still staring at the radio. "Anything Corporal?"

"Not much sir. Certainly nothing for us. The Germans are being pushed back but the snow is keeping the air force grounded. They reckon the 1st will see a break in the weather, perhaps even New Year's Eve."

"Right, well keep me informed. If I am not in here then find me and if I am asleep then wake me!"

"Yes sir."

When Gordy returned, laden with all manner of goodies and eating an apple, I told him of the arrangement. "No problem sir! All of this is from here! I shall try the other houses while we do our rounds." He laid down hams, cheese and three bottles of wine.

I nodded, "I shall wear my camouflage cape."

Gordy paused mid bite, "You aren't thinking of doing anything stupid are you sir?"

"No, Sergeant Barker. However, I want to go into the woods to check for sign and this might be a good opportunity to test the sentries. I doubt they have come across camouflage capes much."

"Just be careful, sir."

"I will. I intend to check the northern area first and then the west."

"Righto. I will take south and then meet you at the west road. To be honest sir, that is where I think they will come. It is a wider road and has a direct line here."

"We'll see."

I took my Luger and Colt. I also took the German grenades we had collected. There were four of them left. I put on my comforter rather than my beret and I pulled it down over my ears.

I stepped out of the hall. The cold shocked my system. The temperature had plummeted. I was glad that the men all had braziers. The Germans would be freezing out in the cold. As I turned north I realised that did not bode well for us. It would make them even more desperate to take what we had. I reached Blackpool Tower and saw that Corporal Parr had been relieved and it was a section from the Royal Engineers who were on guard duty.

I checked that they knew what they were doing and noticed, idly, that they had improved their little fort with more pine branches. It not only helped to disguise the position it also added to the strength. The skies were clear but I saw clouds. There would be snow before morning and that would, probably, help to disguise the emplacement even more.

"I am heading north, lads. When I come back I will say 'steak' and your reply is 'pie'."

The Sergeant laughed, "That sounds like the Lancashire lads we relieved. They were going on about pies!"

"Well from now on this is Blackpool Tower. Keep a sharp lookout. If you hear an engine then send a runner to wake the Captain and Sergeant Armstrong."

I headed up the road. By the time I had gone twenty yards there were no more tracks. A great deal of snow had fallen in the last twenty-four hours. I headed up to the track. Hugo had said that there had been tracks there. Now there were none. No one had passed east since we had arrived. I was not certain if that was a good thing or a bad thing. I looked at the forest which was opposite the track. There had been no track there but a tank must have come down for there were young trees at an angle and their bark had been scraped by something big. I went deeper into the forest. Here the canopy had stopped some of the snow. It had not completely obliterated the German boots which had crossed it. I saw something black in the snow. I picked it up. It was a German field cap. They had come this way.

I went a little deeper and then rigged up an elaborate booby trap. I attached the four German grenades to four trees. I then tied the parachute cord to two further trees. I spent some time putting snow down to disguise both my foot prints and the cords. Anyone coming along would think that the wind had drifted the snow. I then walked back to the road. I listened. The night was so silent that I could hear the murmur of the Royal Engineers as they talked. I decided to test them. I crept down the side of the woods. There was a gap of thirty yards between the trees and the first house. I crawled the last thirty. There were sentries in the windows of the house. I expected them to raise the alarm but they did not. I paused for I saw one of the Engineer's cigarettes glowing in the night. That meant he was facing me.

"I wonder where the Major is. He has been gone some time. Do you think owt has happened to him?"

"Nah, he is a Commando. Killers they are. He'll be alright."

The glowing cigarette disappeared and I continued my crawl. I passed by the side of the emplacement and drew my Luger. I stood and clicked off the safety. I rose at the rear of the dugout.

I said, "Bang! Bang! Bang! Bang! You are all dead."

"Bloody hell sir! Where did you come from?"

I pointed up the road. "One of you was smoking and looking up the road. He should have seen me. I was lying there just thirty yards away. You were talking about Commandos being killers."

"Sorry sir we didn't…"

"I am not bothered about your opinion but I am concerned that you cannot watch for an enemy."

"Sir you had the camouflage cape on!"

I shook my head and said, as I left, "I took this from a German I killed! They wear them too!"

To be fair to them I was not surprised they had not seen me. I was good at what I did. The lesson would not be wasted. They would be on their toes and the story would be passed around the fires as they drank their tea in the morning.

When I reached the west guard post, Alnwick Castle, a Corporal was in command there. "Quiet as sir and as cold as I can remember."

I pointed to the skies. "And by dawn we will have snow. Eyes peeled."

"Sir, Sergeant Barker was just here. He said he would meet you at Buckingham Palace."

Once back in Buckingham Palace I told Gordy what I had done. He chuckled. "They must have filled their pants when you appeared with a Luger, sir!"

"If it had been Germans...."

"Then we would have heard the gun shots, sir and known there was bother. These might be S.S. and paratroopers but they won't have silencers."

"I hope not, Gordy, I hope not."

I woke Sergeant Armstrong so that he could relieve Gordy. Gordy was reluctant to go to bed while I was still on duty but I ordered him.

"Anything on the radio?"

The radio operator shook his head. "Just a bit of traffic further south sir. The Airborne and the armour have joined up and are driving towards Bastogne."

"Good. Keep me informed." After explaining to Sergeant Armstrong what I had done I took him on a tour of the men. As we stepped outside I saw that the snow had begun to fall.

As he spoke I noticed a distinctive accent. The Sergeant came from the North East of England. "You know sir, at home we would be delighted by this. Nothing like a bit of snow in the middle of winter. When I was a bairn we would go sledging."

We had reached the Engineers and they pointedly spoke to us to show that they had heard us. We turned back and trudged through the snow.

"And where is home, Sergeant Armstrong?"

"Gateshead sir. Just south of Newcastle."

"You appear to have lost most of your Geordie accent."

He nodded, "I have lived away from Newcastle and Gateshead for most of me life. The Field Marshal had me speaking proper, like. I joined the army as soon as I could. The choice was the pits or the shipyards and I fancied neither. Mind, I still miss home. I am a Northern lad. I miss a decent pint of ale. The Crown Posada, now that is a proper pub. I always enjoy going back for a few pints there. And fish and chips from North

Shields or Seahouses. The fish is so fresh a good vet could coax it back to life!"

"Will you go back there after the war then, Sergeant?"

He gave me a rueful smile. "I was talking to Gordy before, like, and he told me about you, sir. We both know that the odds on coming out of this war whole or alive drop every day. I'll think about that when the war is over and I am walking down the Haymarket with no uniform and a bonny lass on me arm. Until then I take each day as it comes. When I wake up in a morning I say, 'well thank God I'm still alive.'"

"You are a wise man, Sergeant Armstrong."

"Aye well me dad didna raise any divvies that's for sure!"

"Divvies?"

"Folk who aren't very clever, Major. You know, from Sunderland!" He laughed and I guessed it was a local joke. I smiled. I had heard jokes like this for years. They were in every society.

"Well Sergeant, if we can get through the next few days then you might well survive and get home."

"Sir, Gordy, Sergeant Barker tells me that you have a bonny lass waiting for you at home and your family are well to do."

"I suppose so. Lots of men do."

"But he tells me that you are always the first over the top and you go places you aren't ordered to. Do you mind telling me why? I mean I go where I am ordered but you are an officer."

"Not quite, Sergeant Armstrong You could have stayed at Headquarters and been Field Marshal Montgomery's lucky mascot until the war was over but you asked for this." He nodded. "We come from the same stock. Did your mum, sorry, mam and dad, both work?" Again he nodded, "And live in a little house?"

"Aye sir, a canny little thing."

"Well my dad came from the same background. He joined up in 1914 and worked his way up to sergeant and then pilot. He was like me or, more likely, I am like him. It is in my bones and my blood. I have to fight for England. I bet your dad fought in the Great War."

"Aye sir, Northumberland Fusiliers."

"Then you know why I go where there is danger. I can't ask another to go where I fear to, can I?"

"I suppose not, sir, but at the end of the day what difference will it make? My dad said that all the lads who died in the Great War were just wasted. He might be right. Here we are fighting the Germans again. I daresay when this is over our sons will fight another war and for what?"

We had reached the hall. I opened the door and the warmth flooded over me. "I suppose because we are English and have been doing this for almost a thousand years. We are an island people but we feel we owe the world the benefit of our life. Canada, Australia, India, they are all reflections of England. Why even America, although they had a revolution, still speak the same language and have the same values." I pointed east and south. "The Americans with whom I fought the other day were just like you, Sergeant. But I will agree on one thing; I will be glad when this is over and I can go home and enjoy England, the country I have fought for since 1940."

"Amen to that sir."

"One thing, Sergeant Armstrong."

"Sir?"

"Captain Ferguson is a brave officer and one of the cleverest men I know. However, he does not have a great deal of combat experience. Keep your eye on him, eh? Don't let him make reckless decisions."

"You can rely on me, sir. I like him. He is a nice bloke and, present company excepted, some of the officers I have met have been right bastards. Sorry sir." He stood. "I'll go and put the kettle on. You'll be due a brew, eh?"

"That would be perfect Sergeant."

By the time I woke Hugo and went to bed I was ready for sleep. I had said I would stay awake because I was convinced that the Germans would use the cover of the blizzard to break through. I was wrong.

Chapter 16

I was awake when a runner came racing from Blackpool Tower. "Sir, Sergeant Baxter says he can hear German armour sir. It is to the north of us and moving east."

"Stand to. Corporal, get on the radio. We have German armour heading east." I put on my camouflage cape and picked up my MP 34. I had more ammunition for that than my Tommy gun. I slipped my Mauser over my arm. I had no German grenades but when I had donned my battle jerkin I saw that I had three grenades left. They were American M2s. "Gordy, go and tell Alnwick Castle and Shenandoah that they have to hold. Sergeant Armstrong, get every other man and take them to the north. I want a PIAT crew to stand by."

"Sir."

Hugo strapped on his pistol. I smiled. "You will find a rifle or a machine gun will be more use than your six shot Webley. When he comes back ask Sergeant Barker to get you something with more firepower."

"I am out of my depth aren't I sir?"

"No, Hugo, let us just say that this is my line of work. Stay close to me. We are the only officers here. We have to stop any armour from getting through and we need to kill as many Germans as we can."

"Kill sir?"

"These are hard core, Hugo, if we don't kill them now we will have to kill them later." I put the camouflage cape on. I suspected that I would need it soon.

The snow had stopped but the grey skies promised more. The weather forecast appeared to be accurate up to now. I hoped that it continued to be so. That would mean it would improve and we would have air cover. As I ran up the snow packed road I could hear the rumble of the tank. It was a big one and it was north of us. Even as I neared the emplacement I heard the first crump of a booby trap going off. The other three went off in rapid succession. I had set them as early warning. Now they told me precisely where the Germans were.

"Officer's call"

Hugo and my two senior sergeants gathered around me. "Captain Ferguson I want you to take charge here. The armour will head east, The

Germans will head down here. Keep their heads down and use grenades. They will be hungry and they will be cold. Unless I miss my guess they will be running out of ammunition. However, that makes them dangerous for they will do anything to take this village. Sergeant Armstrong you head to Alnwick Castle and make sure that it has a good sergeant. Then bring half of your men here to reinforce Captain Ferguson. This is where the greatest danger will be. When you have organized the men here you can go to the other two outposts and give them support."

"And you sir?"

"Gordy and I will take the PIAT crew and head into the forest. We know where the armour is heading and we will try to destroy it."

Gordy said, "Sir, the PIAT has to be within 40 yards of the target and have a side or rear shot."

"Then that is what we will get. We are wasting time." I looked at the PIAT crew. The two soldiers were also East Lancashire boys. "You two stick like glue to us. When I say drop then bury yourself in the snow! Right?"

"Yes sir." They had similar accents to Sergeant Parr.

"Come on Sergeant Barker."

Sergeant Armstrong grinned, "For England, sir?"

"For England, Sergeant Armstrong! Sergeant Barker, tail end Charlie."

"Sir!"

I led the way and ran between the two houses at the east of the hamlet. It was virgin snow. I kept up a steady pace. Behind me, and to my left, I heard the crack of branches as the tank made its way east. As soon as it broke into the road then the firing would begin. I suspected that the Germans would attack our front line first. They were in for a rude shock. There were sixty men dug in. They might be clerks and Engineers but they had ammunition. They were well fed and they had protection. Even the S.S. would struggle to dislodge them quickly. I just hoped that Hugo did not do anything stupid and that Sergeant Armstrong would do as I had asked and advise Hugo.

I put that from my mind as we plunged into the forest. I needed to get ahead of the tank. I intended to let it pass us and then fire at its vulnerable rear. To make that work we needed to be well into the forest so that they thought they were clear of danger. When we met the road, I ran parallel to it. I did not want to have tracks on the road. That would be a giveaway. I waited until I heard the two men with the PIAT and the rockets huffing and puffing. I deemed that we had come far enough and we could make our ambush.

"Stop here. Sergeant Barker, get the men to make a snow dugout and cover the back with branches." I walked to a place which was twenty yards from the track but hidden by two huge trees. "Make it here and facing east."

"Sir. You two drop the PIAT and rockets there. We are going to play in the snow!" Gordy pointed to the ground. "Scrape a depression all the way to the soil. Pile the snow up in front of you so that the barrel is hidden. You will be the card up the sleeve!"

I walked back down our trail and then cut across to the trees always ensuring that my tracks could not be seen from the path the tank would take. I listened. I could hear it now. It was getting closer. Although I could hear small arms' fire I could not hear the main gun. That had been my worry. I had feared that the tank would have turned its gun to blast the wooden emplacements into matchwood. Perhaps they had run out of ammunition. I heard the crump of grenades. As much as I wanted to be at the crossroads with the motley crew of men I had to trust Sergeant Armstrong and Captain Ferguson. I knew I was putting a great deal of faith in my belief that the tanks would try to get home. It was based on the attack at Trois Ponts. There they had held their armour off and let their grenadiers deal with infantry.

I heard the tank's huge engine's noise increase as it began to climb the slight slope. I saw smoke from its exhaust. That meant it had passed the road. I retraced my steps and made my way back to the snow dugout. They had done well in the short time I had been away. You could only see branches and snow. I had to walk around to the rear before I saw the two men.

I knelt down. "The tank will come up here. It will be noisy and you will think that is so close that it is going to drive over you. Don't worry the trees will stop that but it will be a terrifying sound. When it is thirty yards up the track fire two rockets in rapid succession. You can't fire any closer than that and I want to make sure you destroy it. That is why I want you to fire two. One may not do the job. If you can then fire a third."

"Where will you be sir?"

I pointed up the trail, "The Sergeant and I will be up there. If I think they are suspicious then we will draw their fire. They may have grenadiers. As soon as it is destroyed then take your PIAT and head back down the trail to the hamlet."

"Do we wait for you, sir?"

"No. Just get back. They will need you at Blackpool Tower. Don't run in a straight line and use the trees for cover."

"Right sir."

The tank was getting closer as it ground up the slippery snow-covered trail. The driver would have it in low gear to help with the grip and that made it noisier. It was not as close as it sounded. I could tell the two lads were nervous. "Are you two lads from Wigan as well?"

The Lance Corporal shook his head, "Us, pie eaters? Nah sir. We have a proper Rugby League team. We are from St. Helens. Lance Corporal Lowery and Private Shaw." He smiled, "Don't worry, sir. We won't let you down!"

"I know you won't. Good luck. Come on Sergeant."

We headed up through the forest. I squatted down just fifty yards from the PIAT. I could see it but only because I knew where to look. Gordy had done a good job of disguising it. I laid two of my grenades on the ground. I had my Mauser and the MP 34. With only one magazine left for the MP 34 I would have to save that for any infantry who were with the tank. I took the Mauser and adjusted the sight. I made a pile of snow before me and laid the barrel on it. I then piled snow over the barrel making sure that the sight was unobscured. My head was exposed and so I pulled the hood of the camouflage cape over my head. Gordy had his Thompson with the last of my ammunition and his. It gave him two magazines. He, too, laid out two grenades.

I peered down the trail. I saw the barrel of the tank rising above the snow. "Bugger!"

"What is it sir?"

"It is a long barrelled 88. This is a King Tiger or a Panther."

"Well you and the Colonel got one of those up the backside with an armoured car, sir. We know they are weak there."

I laughed, "Gordy Barker becoming the optimist!"

"Of course, sir, it is almost New Year!"

I peered through the sights as the tank came into view. As it turned the corner, a hundred and fifty yards from me I saw that it was not a King Tiger. It was the tank destroyer version of the Panther. It was a Jagdpanther. With a steeply sloping front they were almost impossible to be destroyed from the front as the shells bounced off them. I had never seen one before but I had seen the Panzer IV version. Colonel Devine had told me of these new tank destroyers. I was glad that this was the first one we had seen.

The sloping sides meant that the Panzer Grenadiers who normally rode on the tanks were having to cling on to the spare barrel and track just behind the immobile turret. There were six of them. Their white camouflage capes made them stand out against the camouflage paint of the tank destroyer. We would have to take them out. I glanced to my left.

178

Gordy had hidden himself too. The tank destroyer lumbered up towards us. What I did not know was the thickness of the armour on this one. However, as the gun could not traverse if the PIAT failed to penetrate the armour Gordy and I could disable it through the hatch or the visor. The tank destroyer was level with the PIAT when disaster struck. One of the Panzer Grenadiers glanced down and he must have seen the barrel of the PIAT.

I saw him point down and shout. As they were clinging on to the hull they had to release one hand to bring their weapons around. I fired the Mauser and shot the sergeant who had spotted the gun. Gordy let rip with the Thompson. Two men fell and the other three leapt from the back and took cover on the far side of the Jagdpanther. The tank destroyer kept coming up the slope and the machine gun in the sponson began to fire. We were lucky that it could not depress very far. The trees above our head were shredded. It began to turn to give a better angle. That would not do. The PIAT needed a square on shot to stand a chance.

We had to draw the Jagdpanther back on track. "Keep watch on the grenadiers." I rolled to my right and rose. I fired the rifle from the hip and the bullet clanged off the huge steel behemoth. It was just thirty yards from me. The machine gun and the tank both tried to turn to follow me. I knew that I would soon be under fire from the Panzer Grenadiers as well as any others who were heading up the track.

As I reached the other side I felt a tug on my right arm as they opened fire. I rolled into the snow. I rose and brought up the Mauser. I idly noticed blood on my sleeve. The nearest Panzer Grenadier was just twenty yards from me. He raised his MP 35 but my bullet took him in the chest, throwing him to the ground. I had another shell loaded as the second raised his hand with a grenade. My bullet also hit his chest and the grenade fell. Just as the grenade exploded the first PIAT rocket struck. There was a huge explosion. It deafened me. The massive monster continued to roll. Then there was a second explosion as the men from East Lancashire sent another one into the damaged rear. I was lying on my back and I saw the turret fly through the air. It landed thirty feet from me.

I jumped to my feet. I saw that the last of the Panzer Grenadiers had been killed by his comrade's grenade. I ran to the dugout. The two men from St. Helens were still there. "Well done but shift yourselves! We need you back in the hamlet. Go to the hall. We may need the PIAT there."

"Sir, you are wounded!"

"Don't worry about that. Obey your orders."

"Sir!"

"Sergeant Barker!"

Gordy appeared behind me. He had spare ammunition for my MP 34 and grenades from the dead Germans as well as the two M2 grenades. He dropped them when he saw my arm. He took out a dressing.

"Sergeant, we don't have time for this."

"Sir, we do! There are no more Jerries between us and the hamlet. You can hear them firing. They are trying to take it and we will need you if we are to hold on." He had torn my battle dress to expose the wound. He grabbed a handful of snow to both clean the wound and help the blood to coagulate. He had a careful look. "You have been lucky sir. It has gone straight through the fleshy part of your upper arm." He shook on the antiseptic powder and then tied the dressing tightly around it. Taking his dagger he slashed one of the camouflage capes from a dead German and fashioned it into a sling. "I'll take your guns, sir. You can use your Luger. Wait here. You can follow me this time! There are Jerries down there, sir. We are not out of this yet. Not by a long chalk."

The snow on the wound and the sling supporting my arm meant that I was not in pain. That would not last. As soon as the arm warmed up then it would begin to ache. I would have to endure sleepless nights. There would be no evacuation to a base hospital for me. As we descended the slight slope the snow fell once more. There were few flakes on us for we were in the trees but at the road it was falling heavily. It would make the visibility poor and that would suit the Germans.

The firefight sounded one sided as we headed down the slope. There were more Allied bullets than Germans. The Germans were conserving their ammunition. I saw that the PIAT crew had headed further left. They were making for the hall. They had obeyed their orders. We had defeated one enemy tank but there might be others. The PIATs were not the best of weapons but they were a weapon we could use.

Gordy held up his hand and dropped to a knee. I joined him. Below us, about sixty yards away were six snow covered figures. They were making their way along the treeline to outflank the defenders. I could see what Hugo's men had done. They had been drawn to the firing at their front and they had not looked to the side. They were firing blindly and in a panic. The six Germans were less than forty feet from them and were stealthily moving through the snow. I levelled my Luger. It was extreme range but we had little choice. Gordy took out a grenade and laid the MP34 on the snow. Neither of us said a word. We had no need to. We had been doing this for years. It was second nature and we could read each other's minds.

He pulled back his arm and hurled the grenade high. Its arc and our height meant that it would explode in the air. There was a risk to our men but it was a slight one. I fired slowly and methodically from right to left as

180

Gordy sprayed them with my MP 34. As soon as we fired they looked around but by then it was too late. Three fell to bullets and then the grenade scythed through the others. I saw one of the East Lancashire men turn in surprise as the grenade went off. We slithered and slid down to them.

Gordy shouted, "Parr, watch your flank! You would have been dead men then!"

"Sorry, Sergeant, but there are so many of them."

I dropped next to the Corporal, "They are running out of ammunition. Pick your targets and stop wasting bullets."

"Sir."

"Sergeant Barker, go and check on the crossroads. Leave my MP 34 here."

"Sir!" He gave me a disapproving look.

"I don't want to move too much and this is the critical point, at the moment." As he handed me my gun and the last magazine I added quietly, "These lads need someone to take charge." I pointed to Hugo who was on the other side of the emplacement. He was being the hero and firing with his men on the front line. He was not looking for the danger and organizing his resources. "Captain Ferguson needs help. You and Sergeant Armstrong should be able to deal with the crossroads. The greatest danger will be if they have any more armour trying to get through."

"Yes sir."

I holstered my Luger and picked up the machine pistol and magazine. The Corporal and his men were armed with a Bren gun and two rifles. "You three, echelon yourselves to be at an angle to the rest of the line. You have line of sight to the track. Your job is to watch for anyone trying to sneak around the houses and get into our rear."

"But what if there is no one here, sir? We should be fighting with the other lads."

"Corporal, obey orders."

"Yes sir."

The next six men were all from the Engineers. They had rifles. Their barrels were so hot that they had melted the snow. Even as I approached a private fell backwards with a third eye. The other five almost emptied their magazines in response. I crawled next to them raised my MP 34 and rested it on the log. I fired a burst of five bullets.

"Sergeant, you are wasting bullets. The smoke from your rifles is obscuring the enemy. That is how they got close to you."

"But sir, they are wearing white! You can't see them!"

"Their faces aren't white. There is no hurry here. We are going nowhere and they are running out of bullets. They want our food and they want the hamlet. They can find shelter here. They have to cover the open ground in front of you. Stop wasting bullets."

The sling was getting in my way and so I took my arm out of it. It was a mistake as a paroxysm of pain shot down my arm. I gritted my teeth and bore it. I supported the barrel of the gun.

"Now then look for targets." I could ill afford to spend too long here but I needed to train them on the job. If I did not then we would not survive. "Work in pairs. Only one of you fires while the other watches. It saves bullets and will stop you being surprised."

The Sergeant's gun bucked and I saw an arm fall backwards as he hit a German. "Like that sir?"

"Just like that. Calm and slow, lads, eh?"

I stared through the driving snow. It was hard to see the Germans. They were past masters at hiding in plain view. Their camouflage capes helped. They knew that, face down, they were invisible. Then I saw a snow drift move. It was a German. He was sixty yards from me and on the other side of the road in the trees. I followed him and saw them trying to set up an MG 42. I levelled the MP 34 and fired two short bursts. I waited a heartbeat and sent another burst in their direction. The gun clicked empty and I put in my last magazine.

The Sergeant said, "You got a couple, sir."

"Well keep your eye on the place they fell. They have an MG 42 and that can do some serious damage. Your Lee Enfields have the range. Now keep their heads down while I go and speak with Captain Ferguson."

"Yes, sir, and thanks!"

I crawled along to the emplacement. The Sergeant turned as I moved into it. "Sir, we are using a lot of ammo!"

"Then stop!"

"What sir?"

"Stop wasting it! There is no chance of getting more. Husband it and choose your shots. You have rifles, use them. Aim at the men you are trying to kill."

"But sir, Captain Ferguson said to make this a killing zone!"

"And I am telling you to save your ammo. Your rifles have a better range anyway."

One of his men said, "But sir, in the snow we can see bugger all!"

"Exactly. That means they can't see you. They can see the muzzles of your guns when you fire. Do the same to the Germans. Stop firing and then either fire when they move or when you see the muzzle flash."

"Yes sir."

I slipped back outside. The snow was getting worse. Hugo was firing as fast as any of his men. "Captain Ferguson, come here if you please."

He was grinning like a schoolboy, "I heard the explosion. Did you get the tank, sir?"

"Yes, I did but it will be for naught if you have the men wasting ammunition. Go around the men to the left and tell them that they must only fire when they have a target!"

"Sir, what if they rush us?"

"Then we will have won for they will have to be desperate to do so!" I sighed. It had been much easier with the Americans. They had been fighting men from one unit. This was a cobbled together concoction and it showed. "Hugo, they will wait until night and then they will creep forward and use cold steel to kill us. When they have our guns they will slaughter us, eat our food and sleep in the houses. The road to the East is open. They could head through the woods and get home. They are hungry, cold and have little ammunition. All that they do have is the ability to kill. Sadly our men do not." He looked deflated, "Sorry Hugo, but this is war. I would stick to being a staff officer. Pins on boards do not fight back." He nodded and holstered his Webley. "I will stay here with your chaps."

I had been cruel but he needed a dose of the truth. Gordy and I had been made the way we were from St. Nazaire, through Dieppe, North Africa, Sicily, Italy and Normandy. I was not the same soldier who had run to Dunkirk. Now I was a Commando and, as Corporal Parr had said, a killer. Hugo was better off being what he was. A nice bloke.

"You chaps, stop firing. You are doing no good. I want you to wait until you see a target. That is an order." I picked up the rifle of a dead Royal Corps of Transport trooper. He lay with a hole in his shoulder. I took the spare ammunition from his webbing and laid them on the top of the breastworks. I used the wood to support my rifle. My arm still ached and I knew that blood was seeping from the wound but the cold would slow it down and it would stop. I peered down the sight. The Germans had not advanced across the road. Traffic along the road had piled up snow and it meant they could shelter behind it. That gave me an idea. I waited until a German popped his head up to see if we were firing. He ducked down straightaway. I aimed the rifle where his head had appeared and then fired into the snowbank below. I fired two shots. I saw the two men next to me look as though I was mad. I saw the snow through which I had fired begin to redden.

I risked looking at my watch. It was afternoon. The blizzard would bring night early and then they would come. If the weather forecast was correct then the snow would stop and we would have a clear night. The Germans might find it harder to approach then. They would come at dusk before the snow had stopped.

I fired at another head which appeared. I had no idea if I hit anyone but my bullet brought a fusillade of shots from the enemy. My men had heeded my orders. There was less firing from them now. That did not mean that no one died. Our men were still hit and I heard cheers as my men's bullets found flesh. Hugo returned as did Gordy.

"The crossroads is quiet sir. Sergeant Armstrong has it under control."

"Good, Sergeant. Get back there. I am expecting an attack on all fronts at dusk. They will try to break through. If you get the chance then booby trap no-man's land. We can't do it here but if there are no Germans there yet then you should be able to give yourselves early warning."

"Right sir. The sling!"

"It is fine, Sergeant. Stop fussing!"

Hugo sat next to me with his back to the timber wall of our defences. "Sorry sir. You are right. The men are running out of ammunition and it is my fault."

"Stop feeling sorry for yourself. Listen, they will come at dusk. Our problem will be that they will be hard to see and we have neither Very Lights nor flares. It will be close in fighting. You and I will have to be on hand. We have pistols and they are perfect for close in work. You look after the western section and I will look after the east."

"Right sir."

"After dark and after they have attacked, Gordy and I will slip out and have a look see."

"But your arm...."

"I have my pistol and I am right handed."

"Right sir. Good luck!"

"And to you, Hugo. Remember, no matter how black it looks do not give in. These are good lads. They might be rusty but they are made of the right stuff. We owe it to them to lead them."

He nodded. I headed back to the right-hand side of the machine gun. I put my head inside, "They will come after dusk. Keep your bayonets handy."

"Cold steel sir?"

"It will be close work and that means your machine gun will be useless. Don't worry, I will be close by. If you need me give me a shout. They know where we are."

Over the next few hours the Germans kept probing. Three more of our defenders were wounded. I had them taken back to Buckingham Palace where we had based our medic. We had no idea how many men we were facing or how many casualties we were causing. At least we were not using as much ammunition as we had been. It was towards dusk that the bad news came. A runner came from Sergeant Barker, "Sir, Sergeant Barker is at Alnwick Castle, he says that he can hear armour heading up the road!"

"He has all the anti-tank weapons. Tell him to pull the defenders from the south of the hamlet."

"Yes sir!"

I stood and shouted, "Jerry is attacking from the west. We have to hold here. No matter what they throw at us, we hang on!" There was silence. "I can't hear you. Am I here on my own?"

Then there was a roar, "No Sir!"

"That's better! Buddy up with a mate and keep a close watch. The only ones in front of you are Germans. They are the enemy! Kill them before they kill you!"

It was not Henry V's speech from Agincourt but it would have to do. There was an ominous silence from the German positions and that allowed us to hear the rumble of armour. It sounded like a lone tank. Then the small arms fire began. I heard the sound of German machine pistols and then the sound of .303 rounds. Thompsons fired; that would be the Americans and Gordy using the last of his precious bullets. Grenades exploded. I heard our two mortars as they lobbed shells at the Germans. I put Gordy and Sergeant Armstrong from my mind.

I levelled the Mauser. I had little ammunition left for the MP 34. I had my last grenades ready. My Luger and Colt were loaded. My Luger was in my right-hand holster and my Colt in the one on my left hand. My left arm ached but it would not stop me using my hand to support the Mauser. I peered through the sights. Magnified, I saw the Germans as they began to creep forward.

"Here they come!"

I sighted on the nearest German. He was a hundred yards away. His head filled the sight. I fired and loaded another bullet. The German's head exploded as the bullet entered his face. I moved right and fired at the next man. I was aware that, thanks to the telescopic sight, I was the only one who could see the enemy. Each time I fired I moved either to the left or the right to put them off. I moved down the line shooting as many as I could. Some I only wounded but, as they drew closer, then every bullet hit. They began to fire and my men fired at their muzzle flash. Bullets zipped over my head. There were just fifty yards away when my men saw them and they opened fired. It was too late for, by then, they were firing at my men from close range and these were good soldiers. They did not waste a bullet. The Engineer next to me pitched backwards with a bullet in the chest. The machine gun cut them down but we had only the one.

I reloaded my magazine. In the time it took for me to reload the Germans were less than forty yards away. I fired four quick shots and then dropped the rifle. I took my first grenade and hurled it. I used a German one and when I threw it I used the detonator cord to throw it. I gained both height and distance.

"Grenade!"

The shrapnel ripped through the air. As I looked up and readied a second grenade, an M2, I saw Germans falling. I hurled the second grenade. I just managed to bury my face in the snow before pieces of metal flew over my head. I rose and fired the last round from the Mauser at a German Panzer Grenadier who was preparing to spray his MP 35 at us. He fell clutching his shoulder.

Behind me I heard the crack of a 75 mm gun. The German tank was still firing. There were cries and shouts. Grenades exploded and machine guns duelled. I could do nothing. We were in desperate straits. The machine gun to my left had stopped firing. There were the sounds of guns and grenades to my left and right. This was their final assault. The Mauser clicked on empty and I drew the Luger. I peered over the tip of the piece of timber and aimed at the white clad German figures who were racing towards us. The Germans must have been desperate for food. They ran at our lines, seemingly oblivious to the bullets flying in their direction. I was proud of Hugo's rag tag army. They stood their ground and did not fall back. They fought for our tiny piece of England.

My gun clicked empty as the German Panzer Grenadier stood over me and pointed his MP 35 at me. He also clicked empty and threw the gun at my head. I used the Luger to deflect it as he drew his knife and leapt at me. He was a big man. He had not shaved for some days and he stank. I am amazed that I registered those facts. I punched my Luger at his face and he slashed at the gun with his dagger. The gun flew from my hand as his blade ripped against my fingers. I grabbed his wrist with my right hand. I was not certain if my left arm would stand up to the rigours of hand to hand combat. The German put his left hand on top of his right. He grinned, evilly, as he pushed down. I forced my left hand down. Even as he tried to force his razor-sharp dagger against my throat I was trying to undo the flap on the holster of my Colt.

He hissed, "You are a Commando and you shall die. My Fuhrer will give me an Iron Cross when I take your head back to him."

All around me was the sound of men fighting and men dying. All of us were in a personal battle for survival. This was not war. This was a primeval fight for those most basic of necessities, food and shelter. I undid the flap of the holster and reached my hand in to grab the pistol grip. The pressure on my right hand was growing as he added his weight to his two hands. The edge of the blade was a hand span from my throat and the weight of his body was forcing it towards my throat. I clicked off the safety on the Colt and pushed down on the grip to take the barrel away from me. I felt the edge of the blade touch my throat and I pulled the trigger. I was not certain if I would shoot myself or the German. His body lifted as the bullet drove into his groin. His grip relaxed and I turned the pistol up and fired a second time. His body was thrown from me. I held my gun out and looked for more enemies. There were none. As I came to my knees there was an eerie silence in front of me. The firing was all coming from the crossroads. Here, on the northern corner of our outpost there was silence. As I listened I heard the groans and moans of the dead, dying and the wounded.

I holstered my Colt and put another magazine into my Mauser. I half rose and peered into the dark. The snow had stopped and I could see no Germans. Certainly, there were none left alive. I sensed a movement in the woods ahead of me and I fired. If someone had moved I was not sure that I had hit him.

"Captain Ferguson!"

"Sir!"

He came over to stand beside me. I spoke quietly and calmly to him. "Take charge here. See to the wounded and make sure these bastards are dead! Send the wounded to the hall. It is as safe as anywhere. Have our dead taken there too. We don't want these lads to see their dead comrades."

"Sir."

"Collect any ammo. Repair any damage to the emplacement and go around all the men. Speak to them. They have lost friends and fought the deadliest killers in this part of the world. They need you to be calm and cheerful. We might think it is hopeless but we can't let them know that. I will go to Alnwick Castle!"

"Yes sir!" He said, "You know I don't regret this. I know I have not covered myself in glory but, if I stay on and have to lead men at least I can speak from experience."

"Wait until you are back in England before you make such statements. The men will tell you it is bad luck."

"I know sir but I wanted you to know that I appreciated what you have done for me. Just in case anything happens to me now. You are a superior officer but you are a friend and that is important to me." He turned and was reloading his gun as he wandered over to the nearest men. "Right chaps, let's see if we can make our little fort even stronger, eh? We have some bloody rude neighbours!" The men laughed. Hugo had grown. I hoped he would survive.

I used the Mauser's stock to push myself to my feet. The fight had made my wound leak even more. I put it from my mind. As I headed down the road I could hear the sounds of fighting from the crossroads. The night was lit up by the flash of muzzles and the sudden flaring as grenades, mortars and shells exploded. Even as I approached a 75 mm HE shell hit the house next to the one we had been using as a Command Post.

Sergeant Armstrong's voice had become even more Geordie, "Get down sir! Sergeant Barker has been hit!"

I threw myself sideways into the timber gun emplacement at Alnwick Castle. An American was applying a field dressing to Sergeant Barker's shoulder. Gordy looked up and gave me a thin smile. "Bit of a bugger eh sir? We will both be going back crocked."

I nodded, "Aye Gordy, but we will be going back. I do not intend to lose this hamlet. These lads have fought like veterans and we are not going to give it up." I looked at the American. "Get him back to the hall."

"Yes sir."

"I am fine, sir!"

"Then obey the order. Have your wound dressed and take charge at Buckingham Palace. If this falls then that becomes our Alamo."

"Yes sir." The medic helped him from the dugout.

"Situation Sergeant?"

"We managed to hit the tank sir. It was a Mark IV. The lads did well. It took six rockets but they stopped it. They hit the track and the turret but the beast can still fire." He pointed. The tank was eighty yards away. They had done well to hit it. I saw that the gun could not depress because of the damage but that it could traverse through eleven or twelve degrees. It explained why it was limited in its targets and why they were not firing wastefully. It was the machine gun which was the danger. No one would be able to approach without being cut down. The tank itself was at the bottom of the slightest of slopes. "We have Jerry pinned down but we have no more PIAT rockets left."

"What else do we have left?"

"We have a Browning .30 Calibre and two Bren guns. We are down to fifty rounds for each of them. We have the two mortars with ten rounds for

188

each one. I have stopped using them. Who knows when we might need them."

"Good decision. Where are the grenadiers?"

"They are using the tank as shelter. They know that we can't budge it. They are saving their machine gun ammunition. We are pinned down."

"Right. Let's think how we can destroy that tank. If we get rid of that then they will have no machine gun and nowhere to hide." The answer was staring me in the face but I was tired and the loss of blood must have affected me. I almost slapped myself when the idea came to me. "Can you hold on here, Sergeant?"

"Of course, sir but what do you have in mind?"

"A little trick that worked quite well once before."

Chapter 17

I knew what I needed and it was all back at Buckingham Palace. The two East Lancashire soldiers who had fired the PIAT now sheltered behind the emplacement. "You two, follow me."

As we approached the house I saw that the jeep was still intact and parked next to the south wall of the house. "One of you grab the can of petrol and bring it inside."

"Sir."

When I went in I saw no sign of Gordy. They must have taken him upstairs to use the beds. I saw, on the floor, some of the bodies of our dead. They were covered by their greatcoats. I shook my head. They had done their duty. The Corporal was back on duty on the radio. "Anything?"

"There is a major German attack sir, in the south; somewhere called Alsace, south of Bastogne."

I nodded, "Then we can't expect any help any time soon. Corporal, wear your tin lid. The Jerry tank can still fire. It might well start firing here. We need you."

"Yes sir. We have had a bit of plaster down already."

I turned to the private, "Shaw isn't it?"

"Sir."

"Go upstairs and find a sheet, a towel, anything like that. Bring it down." As Private Lowery came in I took the brandy bottle and poured its contents into the four mugs that were there. "Fill this with petrol." As he did so I took one of the bottles of wine and, taking a corkscrew, opened it. Private Shaw came down. "Tear strips off the sheet, Private. Private Lowery go and empty this wine down the sink."

"A waste sir."

I smiled. I did not think that he would have drunk anything other than sherry in his life. I handed him the bottle. "Here Private, have a swig."

He grinned, "Yes sir! Bottoms up!" He took a large drink. His face showed his displeasure. God sir that is disgusting! How the hell do the French drink it? No wonder you are pouring it away sir!"

He went into the kitchen at the back. Private Shaw came down. "Tear two strips off the sheet and give them to me."

"Sir."

He handed them to me. I took the strips of cloth and put them in the can of petrol. When they were soaked I rammed one into the brandy bottle. "Now fill the other with petrol and put one of these in the neck."

It did not take long and I took the two petrol bombs with me. "Bring the can of petrol too."

Even as we left more wounded were being helped into our makeshift hospital. Private Shaw said, quietly, "It is rammed upstairs, sir."

"I know. We will have to try to end this then, won't we?"

Just then Sergeant Barker came down the stairs. He saw the bottles in my hand. "Petrol bombs sir?"

"They worked before."

"You aren't going to throw them are you, sir? There are others who can..."

"Sergeant, we are all in the same boat. No one is more important than anyone else. Take charge here and see if you can let someone know that we are under siege."

"Yes sir."

"Give me your lighter, eh? It is lucky." He handed me his precious petrol lighter.

The snow had stopped and it was getting colder. Our breath misted as we walked. We ran the last forty yards crouched for the machine gunner in the tank could see us. Even though we zig zagged the machine gunner sent a short burst in our direction. The bullets sparked off the bricks of Buckingham Palace.

Once in the emplacement we were safe. Sergeant Armstrong sniffed. "Is that petrol sir?"

"It is. Let's see if we can make it a little hot for our German friends, eh? Shaw, do you think you can take the can and sneak around to the front. Go to the side slightly. I want you to lie down and open the jerrycan. Pour the petrol so that it flows down the snow. There is a hollow near to the tank and I want the petrol to gather there. When it is empty then throw the empty can as far down as you can."

"What about the machine gun, sir?"

"They are using a spotter who is looking out of the driver's visor. I intend to draw their fire here."

He nodded, "Right sir."

"Wait until I fire before you go out eh, Shaw?"

"Yes sir."

I took the Mauser and checked it had a full magazine. There was a gap between two of the logs and I slid the barrel between it. I knew that as soon as I fired they would return fire from the machine gun. The range

191

was only eighty yards and realistically I didn't even need the telescopic sight but I used it anyway. I saw a face through the visor. I fired and the face fell back. It drew an immediate response. Bullets rattled against the wood. We all lay down. I had kept the gun in the same position and, without raising my head, I emptied the clip. The bullets would hit the tank and, with luck, one might rattle around inside. The Germans would keep firing at us and Shaw would be safe.

Shaw appeared behind me. "All done!" He looked like the cat which has had all the cream.

"Good lad. That is half the job. Now let's finish it." I handed the petrol bombs to him and his oppo. "Follow me." The machine gun had stopped. Once outside we hunkered down behind the emplacement. "Private Shaw you know where the petrol is. When we light your bomb throw it as far down the slope as you can but you have to ignite the petrol, right?"

"Yes sir."

"Private Lowery you are insurance. When Shaw's bomb sets off the petrol then you throw your bomb as far as you can. If it does not work then give it to Shaw and he can have a second bite of the cherry."

Private Shaw now looked worried. "And if that doesn't work sir?"

"Then Private, I will crawl out and I will set fire to the petrol with the lighter."

Private Lowery shook his head, "Bloody hell, Stan, how hard can it be? You poured the bloody petrol! Christ you can smell it!"

"I am just saying, Phil, that is all. Light me, sir!"

I lit the cloth, "Don't hang around!"

He stood and hurled it high. He had ducked back down before the bullets were fired from the tank. Then we waited. A few moments later there was a whoosh as the petrol ignited. Private Lowery said, "Now me sir!"

The German machine gun had stopped firing. There was a crack and I saw a flame leap up in the air. I guessed it had reached the jerrycan. Private Lowery ran around the side of the emplacement and he threw it high. He had a good arm. I saw it arc in the night sky. It landed and there was a second whoosh. As Private Shaw threw himself to the ground there was an almighty explosion as the tank was engulfed in flames and both the fuel tank and ammunition were ignited. Flying pieces of metal hit the emplacement and even Buckingham Palace. The air was filled with the smell of cordite, burning petrol and the unmistakeable aroma of burning hair and human flesh.

Private Shaw looked at me and grinned, "So you won't need to be a hero then, sir."

"Well done, lads You both did well. I shall mention you in my report."

Private Lowery shook his head, "I just want to get home, sir. When I joined up I thought it would be like playing cowboys and Indians. It isn't. I will leave all that hero stuff to Errol Flynn in the pictures."

I shouted, "Sergeant Armstrong, take charge here. Dawn is just an hour away. Let's be ready to repel them if they come again. I'll go to Shenandoah and see how they are there."

"Right sir. Keep your head down though, eh?"

"Yes Sergeant."

I still kept my head down as I ducked out of the back of the emplacement. The Germans were still out there. We had destroyed their most offensive weapon but they were still cold and they were still hungry. They would come again. These were the S.S. and they would not surrender.

The Engineers looked up as I approached, "Dawn is on the way sir." I nodded. "We heard an explosion."

"That was a tank but Jerry is still there. How is it here?"

The M.P. Corporal said, "Quiet as the grave sir. We have been feeling guilty hearing all the firing going on and we still have full magazines."

"You have done the job I asked you to. Well done. Look, as there are six of you could three of you go and sort some food and a brew for the chaps."

"Of course, sir."

"You go with the Corporal, Ben, that way we might get some decent coffee." The American Sergeant handed a hessian sack with what looked like coffee beans to a Pfc. "Connor here makes the best coffee in the regiment."

The M.P. Corporal shook his head, "I wouldn't thank you for it. A nice Sarn't Major brew for us!"

I left them debating the merits of coffee and tea. I went in to Buckingham Palace. "Any news Corporal?"

"Just the same sir. The Americans are hanging on and they are trying to reinforce them. Sergeant Barker has passed on your message."

"Where is he?"

"In the kitchen sorting our food. He said he could do that with one arm."

Corporal Winterton, the medical orderly, came down the stairs, "I thought I heard your voice sir. Time for me to have a look at that wound."

"I am fine Corporal."

"As senior medical officer I feel obliged to have a look at the wound sir. We can't have the Commanding Officer collapsing, now can we? Come on, sir. It will take no more than five minutes."

"Very well but make it quick."

He took off my battledress and cut away the shirt. Using a pair of scissors, he cut away the dressing. The wound was bleeding. He shook his head, "I thought so." He reached into his bag and took out a couple of tablets. He handed me his canteen. "Here sir, take these Sulphadiazine Tablets." I swallowed while he washed and dried the wound. He took some Sulphanilamide powder and sprinkled it on the wound. It stung but I kept a still face. He did a better job than Sergeant Barker had with the dressing and he made it tighter. He replaced my battle dress and then put my arm in a new sling. He saw me about to object. "Sir, you need to support this or the wound will keep bleeding. You are an intelligent chap. If you lose blood then you will become weaker. You can still use your right hand."

"Very well."

Gordy came back in. He had a piece of ham sandwiched between two toasted pieces of bread. "Here y'are sir. Five-day old bread but they had some olive oil. I fried the bread and put some cheese and ham in. You eat it."

"What about the men?"

"Those lads you sent have made a stew. The men will have hot food but Winterton here reckons you need food so eat this sir and be a good chap. If you don't I shall tell Mrs. Bailey and your mother that you were a bad lad."

"You are assuming we are going to get out of this, Sergeant."

"With you in command sir there is never a doubt. Now eat. I found some mustard. That should be tasty as!"

He was right and I did not know just how hungry I was. One of the M.P.s gave me a mug of tea and I left feeling better than I had done for some time. A mixture of drugs, a hot sandwich and a nice brew did the trick. By the time I reached Blackpool Tower the sun was peering from behind the hills to the east. The darkness had hidden the blood but now we saw the puddles and patches which marked the fights to the death which had taken place. The German bodies lay where they had fallen. Hugo and his men had not risked their lives to move them.

"What is the roll call, Captain?"

"We have twenty here fit and well. Ten of those we sent to Buckingham Palace should be able to fight at a pinch."

"We did well. Now if the Air Force can get a few sorties in the air then we might stand a chance."

"Surely they are beaten now!"

Just then a rifle sounded and one of the East Lancashires fell clutching his shoulder. "Take cover! This is not over! Keep your eyes open for

194

Germans! They are still out there." I turned to Hugo, "See what I mean? I will send a mortar and crew. Let's see if we can put the wind up them. Keep the men on their toes, Hugo. Don't let them take chances. The Germans are a hundred and twenty yards in that direction." I pointed to the woods. "Let's keep them there, eh?"

Keeping low I ran back to Alnwick Castle. The fire had died down and there was sporadic fire from the Germans. "Sergeant I need one of your mortar crews."

"Right sir. Nobby, take your mortar to Blackpool Tower."

"Righto Sarge." The two men to the left of us began to pack away their mortar.

"Put it behind the emplacement but don't fire until I am there."

"Right sir."

As they left I took out my binoculars. I could see movement half a mile away. There were more German troops arriving. "Sergeant I think you will have company soon." I handed him my glasses. "There, about half a mile away from the burned-out tank."

"Bugger sir!"

"Food should be on the way soon. Go around and ginger up the troops, eh? I'll try and shift the ones from Blackpool Tower and then we can reinforce here."

"Sir, have you not thought that they might be heading for the track."

"It had crossed my mind. In which case you might have to reinforce us."

Sliding out of the back I crouched and ran to where the two men were setting up the 2-inch Mortar. With a range of five hundred yards and a charge which weighed two and half pounds it was a good weapon. Sadly, with just ten rounds it would not win the battle for us.

I knelt next to the two men. I pointed to the track. I want you to lob two shells forty feet beyond the tree line. They should be about fifty feet apart."

"You are asking for pinpoint accuracy sir."

"A few feet either way won't make much of a difference. I want to stir Jerry up. Wait for my command."

"Righto sir."

I slipped inside the dugout. Sergeant Ashcroft of the East Lancashires was there with two of his men and the only Vickers we had. It was the one weapon for which we had plenty of ammunition. All of the men had lee Enfields and they used the same bullet. The abundance of snow meant we could keep replenishing the water which cooled it. Hitherto we had not fired it very much. Now I intended to use it to its maximum effect.

"Sergeant, in a moment I am going to start lobbing mortar shells beyond the track."

"There are Jerries there. We have seen them moving but it would be a waste of ammo to fire at them."

"I know. That is why I am going to use the mortars. They should start to shift. Open fire as soon as the first mortar lands. Use a whole belt of ammo if you have to. I want to shake them up." I pointed north. "There are more Jerries on their way Sergeant. We will have eight mortar rounds left after this. I intend to save them for the last attack. How many belts do you have?"

"We have four sir but we have plenty of bullets to reload." He nodded to the gunners. "You heard the Major. Let's see how many Jerries we can send to hell!" They cocked the gun and nodded. "Ready sir!"

I took out my glasses and shouted, "Nobby, open fire!"

There was the familiar crump as the mortar round sailed high. The Vickers began to chatter. It made so much noise that I did not hear the second round being fired. The first one exploded. I saw limbs fly through the air and then the machine gun began to decimate their numbers as the Germans rose to run away from this unexpected attack. When the second shell exploded I saw men running east.

I slipped out of the back of the emplacement. I heard Corporal Parr and his men firing. I ran to them. "Sir, Jerries broke and they are heading up the trail."

"Watch them. Make sure they don't double back."

Private Shaw suddenly appeared, "Sir, Sergeant Armstrong said Jerry is attacking and in numbers."

"Tell him I will be there presently." I hurried to the mortar crew. "Well done. Be ready to lay down a barrage on the road."

"When do we fire sir?"

"When there are enough Germans to make it worthwhile." Hugo appeared, "We have broken them here but you will have more coming your way very soon. Don't let them flank us. If we break this attack then it will be over."

I took out my Luger. Both hand guns were reloaded. The dead Germans had yielded enough bullets for me to have four magazines for the Luger. It would have to do. The gunfire from Alnwick Castle was fierce. As I hurried to it I saw the explosions from the mortar shells and heard the chatter of the three machine guns. As I neared the defences I saw an Engineer pitched backwards by submachine gun bullets. The Germans were gambling on this one throw of the dice. I saw a German twenty yards from our defences. He pulled his arm back. I fired two shots. My sling unbalanced me and I wanted to be sure I hit him. He was pitched backwards and his grenade exploded in front of his advancing comrades.

I took the place of the dead Engineer. One of his companions said, from the side of his mouth, "You ought to have a tin lid sir!"

I laughed, "It would spoil my hair. I'll take my chances."

"Good on you, sir. I'll say one thing for Jerry. He is persistent."

"He is hungry and wants what we have."

The mortars scythed through the enemy. Then a voice shouted, "That's it sir. No more mortar ammo."

"Use your rifles!"

I noticed that the rate of machine gun fire had diminished. It allowed the Germans to edge closer. The machine guns were not Vickers. They were not air cooled and they needed to be fired in short burst. The Germans were using every inch of cover to get close. Disaster struck when a grenade exploded in the front of the dugout. The machine guns stopped altogether. I saw an officer raise his hand and shout something. I fired two bullets and he fell. The damage was done. He had ordered his men forward and a wave of Germans raced towards us. This was not as it had been in the night. It was worse because we could see the numbers.

I emptied my magazine and then put the gun in my sling. I took out a grenade and used my teeth to pull out the pin. I threw it high. "Grenade!"

It exploded behind the advancing men but the ones close kept closing. Changing a magazine one handed is never easy and I forced myself to be calm. Our men were dying as the Germans closed with us. I had just reloaded when the Engineer I had been speaking with was spun around as a bullet took him in the throat. There were just four of us left. I fired the Luger non-stop. I saw a German sergeant stand on top of the emplacement and smash the porcelain on his grenade. I dropped the Luger and pulled the Colt. The German was thirty feet from me and .45 slug knocked him from the top. The grenade exploded and took out four advancing Germans. It was a drop in the ocean. More were coming.

Suddenly mortar shells began to land amongst the Germans. I looked over my shoulder and saw a grinning Nobby firing it. Then there was a cheer from behind me. I heard Gordy shout, "Charge! We have food needs eating!" He was firing his Colt and leading the walking wounded.

The Virginians and the M.P.s were with him. They had disobeyed my orders and I was grateful. To my right I heard the Vickers as Sergeant Ashcroft slaughtered the Germans who were trying to get up the track. I climbed up to the firing step and began to aim at the Germans who were still advancing. They had heard the machine guns fall silent and thought that we were finished. The reinforcements broke their back. With a fully manned line we poured fire into them. Sergeant Barker had found more grenades and they were hurled into their serried ranks. They ran. Some of the men had blood racing through their heads for they were keen to follow. Gordy and I had to restrain them.

"Well done! See to the wounded and reload. They may be back."

I did not think that they would be but I was taking no chances. As the Vickers was still firing from the north I knew that the battle was not over. "Well done Gordy! See to the wounded. I'll go and check the emplacement."

I did not know what I would find and I was dreading entering the dugout. It was not quite as bad as I had thought. Private Lowery lay dead. He had borne the brunt of the grenade which had ended the defence of Alnwick Castle. Sergeant Armstrong had a badly bleeding face and appeared to be unconscious. The other four were all wounded but not as seriously.

"Get the Sergeant out of here. Carry him, carefully, to the Medic. He is a priority!"

"Right sir." I heeded my own advice and reloaded my Luger. My hands were shaking. They had not done that since 1940. I was getting too old for this.

I wandered over to Hugo. The firing had stopped by the time I reached him. The track had a dozen or so dead Germans lying on it. He pointed up the trail. Sorry, sir, but fifty or sixty got up the track. Sergeant Ashcroft and Corporal Parr said that they saw more heading through the forest."

"Don't worry about them, Hugo. Most won't make it back. Look at those skies. There is not a cloud in sight. They will freeze to death tonight. We won't relax our grip but the worst is over. Now we just have to see what the butcher's bill is."

The hot food revived everyone but we had the grim task of laying out the bodies of the dead. We left the Germans where they lay. As darkness fell I ordered one man in two to sleep. I could not rule out a night time attack but the men needed sleep. I was tempted to ask Winterton for something to keep me awake but I did not. He came, at midnight to speak with me. "Sir, we have the bill. "We lost twelve men today. There are twenty-five with minor wounds and ten who need a doctor and soon."

I nodded, "How is Sergeant Armstrong?"

"His lucky sir. He has lost an eye but he will live. He was asking for you." I rose. He shook his head. "I gave him something to make him sleep. It will keep until morning."

"Thank you Corporal. You did well today."

"We all did, Major."

Dawn brought the sun. Overhead we saw aeroplanes both German and Allied. We heard, on the radio, that the Germans had launched an air offensive. They had not yet given up the fight. The good weather also meant relief. We heard that a column was on the way from Verviers to relieve us. We had held.

I went to see Sergeant Armstrong. He had a cigarette hanging from his lips. It looked strange because the rest of his face was bandaged, all except for his left eye. He took it out with a heavily bandaged hand, "I'd get up sir but…"

"You stay there Sergeant. You did well."

"Aye, well I look like Lon Chaney in a horror film don't I sir? This face will scare me mam when I get home."

"Surgeons can do great things these days. You will be alright. I suppose this means you will be leaving the army then?"

"I guess so sir. I am glad. I have done my bit. I can look my old comrades in the face now. I felt a fraud hiding at Headquarters with Monty. I am proud to have served with you, sir."

"As am I Sergeant."

"Sir, could I ask a favour of you?"

"Of course."

"Could I shake you by the hand?"

I held out my hand, "I am proud to."

"If I ever get married and have bairns then I can say I shook hands with a real hero."

"Then shake the hands of every man here, Sergeant, for they are all heroes."

Epilogue

Antwerp

Gordy and I were sent to the same hospital as John Hewitt. For once I could not use my rank to get out of it. A senior doctor insisted that I be hospitalized. Hugo came with us. He had a spring in his step these days. We were even visited by Field Marshal Montgomery. I suspect it was to see his old sergeant but he was effusive in his praise of all of us. He had the press with him and he was all smiles as they took photographs of the heroes of Monts. The cynic in me wondered if this was so that he could have his own Bastards of Bastogne. On the day we were supposed to leave, January 8th 1945, Major Foster arrived. He looked pleased with himself. He sat on the end of my bed.

"Well Tom, you have surprised me again. I get you a nice little number talking to people and you manage to get involved in a major offensive."

"Toppy, do me a favour."

"Yes, Tom?"

"Don't do me any favours."

He laughed, "Well the Americans are very pleased with you. There is a Colonel Devine who is making a lot of noise about you needing another medal."

"I don't need a medal."

"I know but politically it is a good thing. The newspapers will be clamouring for the story of how British soldiers fought alongside Americans to throw back a German Offensive once the doctors release you."

"Please, Toppy! I do not want this in the newspapers. Sneak me out or something. I just want to go home for that leave you promised me and see Susan and my family. That is not too much to ask is it?"

He suddenly looked sad, "No, Tom it is not. Well I will do my best to keep the press away from you."

"And Hewitt and Barker! They don't need this either."

"You drive a hard bargain. Very well. The press seem keen to interview this Geordie Sergeant and Monty does too. He already has the photos."

"The photos I can live with but not a story."

"It is a good story, Tom."

Major Foster had changed since I had first met him. He was still a good chap but he had different priorities these days.

"Thanks and then I will get back to my unit. That will be a relief."

"Actually, Tom, it is not the same unit you left. Sergeant Poulson is now Lieutenant Poulson and Beaumont and Fletcher have been promoted. You also have another ten men in your section. The lads have been training them up while you were enjoying the snow. Anyway, you have a three week leave coming to you. You report to Falmouth on the 1st February." I nodded. "Anything else I can do for you?"

"There is one thing. Get the three of us on a flight back to England! If we only have three weeks we shouldn't have to waste two of them on a troopship."

"You don't ask for much do you? Very well. Oh by the way, the brevet rank has been confirmed. You are a Major now and your pay has been backdated to November. Well done Tom."

To Major Foster the promotion meant everything. To me it was not important. What was important was the sacrifice by the men I had led. They had not been Commandos but they had been soldiers and I was proud to have known them. That was better than any promotion, medal or newspaper report. The war might end soon but the memories would last a lifetime. For those who had died the living would have to live their lives for them. It was a great responsibility.

The End

Glossary

Abwehr- German Intelligence

AP- Armour Piercing Shell

ATS- Auxiliary Territorial Service- Women's Branch of the British Army during WW2

Bisht- Arab cloak

Bob on- Very accurate (slang) from a plumber's bob

Butchers- Look (Cockney slang Butcher's Hook- Look)

Butties- sandwiches (slang)

Capstan Full Strength- a type of cigarette

Chah- tea (slang)

Comforter- the lining for the helmet; a sort of woollen hat

Conflab- discussion (slang)

Cook-off- when the barrel of a Browning .30 Calibre overheats

Corned dog- Corned Beef (slang)

CP- Command Post

Dhobi- washing (slang from the Hindi word)

Ercs- aircraftsman (slang- from Cockney)

Ewbank- Mechanical carpet cleaner

Fruit salad- medal ribbons (slang)

Full English- English breakfast (bacon, sausage, eggs, fried tomato and black pudding)

Gash- spare (slang)

Gauloise- French cigarette

Gib- Gibraltar (slang)

Glasshouse- Military prison

Goon- Guard in a POW camp (slang)- comes from a 19thirties Popeye cartoon

HE – High Explosive shells

Hurries- Hawker Hurricane (slang)

Jankers- field punishment

Jimmy the One- First Lieutenant on a warship

Kettenhunde - Chained dogs. Nickname for German field police. From the gorget worn around their necks

Killick- leading hand (Navy) (slang)

Kip- sleep (slang)

Legging it- Running for it (slang)

LRDG- Long Range Desert group (Commandos operating from the desert behind enemy lines.)

Marge- Margarine (butter substitute- slang)

MGB- Motor Gun Boat

Mossy- De Havilland Mosquito (slang) (Mossies- pl.)

Mickey- *'taking the mickey'*, making fun of (slang)

Micks- Irishmen (slang)

MTB- Motor Torpedo Boat

ML- Motor Launch
Narked- annoyed (slang)
Neaters- undiluted naval rum (slang)
Oik- worthless person (slang)
Oppo/oppos- pals/comrades (slang)
Piccadilly Commandos- Prostitutes in London
PLUTO- Pipe Line Under The Ocean
Pom-pom- Quick Firing 2lb (40mm) Maxim cannon
Pongo (es)- soldier (slang)
Potato mashers- German Hand Grenades (slang)
PTI- Physical Training Instructor
QM- Quarter Master (stores)
Recce- Reconnoitre (slang)
SBA- Sick Bay Attendant
Schnellboote -German for E-boat (literally translated as fast boat)
Schtum -keep quiet (German)
Scragging - roughing someone up (slang)
Scrumpy- farm cider
Shooting brake- an estate car
SOE- Special Operations Executive (agents sent behind enemy lines)
SP- Starting price (slang)- what's going on
Snug- a small lounge in a pub (slang)
Spiv- A black marketeer/criminal (slang)
Sprogs- children or young soldiers (slang)
Squaddy- ordinary soldier (slang)
Stag- sentry duty (slang)
Stand your corner- get a round of drinks in (slang)
Subbie- Sub-lieutenant (slang)
Suss it out- work out what to do (slang)
Tatties- potatoes (slang)
 Thobe- Arab garment
Tiffy- Hawker Typhoon (slang)
Tommy (Atkins)- Ordinary British soldier
Two penn'orth- two pennies worth (slang for opinion)
Wavy Navy- Royal Naval Reserve (slang)
WVS- Women's Voluntary Service

Historical note

Readers of my books know that I incorporate material from the earlier books. Some of my readers have joined the series half way through and I think it is important that they know the background to my books. If you have the first books in this series, then you can skip down to the section marked Battle of the Bulge. It is 20 pages down.

The first person I would like to thank for this particular book and series is my Dad. He was in the Royal Navy but served in Combined Operations. He was at Dieppe, D-Day and Walcheren. His boat: LCA(I) 523 was the one which took in the French Commandos on D-Day. He was proud that his flotilla had taken in Bill Millens and Lord Lovat. I wish that, before he died, I had learned more in detail about life in Combined Operations but like many heroes he was reluctant to speak of the war. He is the character in the book called Bill Leslie. Dad ended the war as Leading Seaman- I promoted him! I reckon he deserved it.

'Bill Leslie' 1941
Author's collection

I went to Normandy in 1994, with my Dad, to Sword Beach and he took me through that day on June 6th 1944. He pointed out the position which took the head from the Oerlikon gunner who stood next to him. He also told me about the raid on Dieppe as well as Westkapelle. He had taken the Canadians in. We even found the grave of his cousin George Hogan who died on D-Day. As far as I know we were the only members of the family ever to do so. Sadly, that was Dad's only visit but we planted forget-me-nots on the grave of George. Wally Friedmann is a real Canadian who served in WW2 with my Uncle Ted. The description of Wally is perfect- I lived with Wally and his family for three months in 1972. He was a real gentleman. As far as I know he did not serve with the Saskatchewan regiment, he came from Ontario but he did serve in the war. As I keep saying, it is my story and my imagination. God bless, Wally.

I would also like to thank Roger who is my railway expert. The train Tom and the Major catch from Paddington to Oswestry ran until 1961. The details of the livery, the compartments and the engine are all, hopefully accurate. I would certainly not argue with Roger! Thanks also to John Dinsdale, another railway buff and a scientist. It was he who advised on the use of explosives. Not the sort of thing to Google these days!

I used a number of books in the research. The list is at the end of this historical section. However, the best book, by far, was the actual Commando handbook which was reprinted in 2012. All of the details about hand to hand, explosives, esprit de corps etc. were taken directly from it. The advice about salt, oatmeal and water is taken from the book. It even says that taking too much salt is not a bad thing! I shall use the book as a Bible for the rest of the series. The Commandos were expected to find their own accommodation. Some even saved the money for lodgings and slept rough. That did not mean that standards of discipline and presentation were neglected; they were not.

The 1st Loyal Lancashire existed as a regiment. They were in the BEF and they were the rear guard. All the rest is the work of the author's imagination. The use of booby traps using grenades was common. The details of the German potato masher grenade are also accurate. The Germans used the grenade as an early warning system by hanging them from fences so that an intruder would move the grenade and it would explode. The Mills bomb had first been used in the Great War. It threw shrapnel for up to one hundred yards. When thrown, the thrower had to take cover too. However, my Uncle Norman, who survived Dunkirk was demonstrating a grenade with an instructor kneeling next to him. It was a faulty grenade and exploded in my uncle's hand. Both he and the Sergeant survived. My uncle just lost his hand. I am guessing that my uncle's hand prevented the grenade fragmenting as much as it was intended. Rifle grenades were used from 1915 onwards and enabled a grenade to be thrown much further than by hand

During the retreat the British tank to Dunkirk in 1940, the Matilda proved superior to the German Panzers. It was slow but it was so heavily armoured that it could only be stopped by using the 88 anti-aircraft guns. Had there been more of them and had they been used in greater numbers then who knows what the outcome might have been. What they did succeed in doing, however, was making the German High Command believe that we had more tanks than they actually encountered. The Germans thought that the 17 Matildas they fought were many times that number. They halted at Arras for reinforcements. That enabled the Navy to take off over 300,000 men from the beaches.

Although we view Dunkirk as a disaster now, at the time it was seen as a setback. An invasion force set off to reinforce the French a week after Dunkirk. It was recalled. Equally there were many units cut off behind enemy lines. The Highland Division was one such force. 10000 men were captured. The fate of many of those captured in the early days of the war was to be sent to work in factories making weapons which would be used against England.

The first Commando raids were a shambles. Churchill himself took action and appointed Sir Roger Keyes to bring some order to what the Germans called thugs and killers. Major Foster and his troop reflect that change.

The parachute training for Commandos was taken from this link http://www.bbc.co.uk/history/ww2peopleswar/stories/72/a3530972.shtml. Thank you to Thomas Davies whose first-hand account of the training was most illuminating and useful. The Number 2 Commandos were trained as a battalion and became the Airborne Division eventually. The SOE also trained at Ringway but they were secreted away at an Edwardian House, Bowden. As a vaguely related fact 43 out of 57 SOE agents sent to France between June 1942 and Autumn 1943 were captured, 36 were executed!

The details about the Commando equipment are also accurate. They were issued with American weapons although some did use the Lee Enfield. When large numbers attacked the Lofoten Islands they used regular army issue. The Commandos appeared in dribs and drabs but 1940 was the year when they began their training. It was Lord Lovat who gave them a home in Scotland but that was not until 1941. I wanted my hero, Tom, to begin to fight early. His adventures will continue throughout the war.

M1A1 Rocket Launcher Courtesy of Wikipedia and the Smithsonian

PIAT courtesy of Wikipedia and Canadian War Museum
Courtesy of Wikipedia

Hawker Typhoon- this has the D-Day markings
Courtesy of Wikipedia

King Tiger

Weight   68.5 tonnes (67.4 long tons; 75.5 short tons) (early turret) 69.8 tonnes (68.7 long tons; 76.9 short tons) (production turret)

Length   7.38 metres (24 ft 3 in) (hull) 10.286 metres (33 ft 9 in) (with gun forward)

Width   3.755 metres (12 ft 4 in)

Height   3.09 metres (10 ft 2 in)

Crew   5 (commander, gunner, loader, radio operator, driver)

Armour   25–185 mm (1–7 in)

Main armament   1× 8.8 cm KwK 43 L/71 "Porsche" turret: 80 rounds

Secondary armament   2× 7.92 mm Maschinengewehr 345,850 rounds

Engine   V-12 Maybach HL 230 P30gasoline 700 PS (690 hp, 515 kW)

Power/weight   10 PS (7.5 kW) /tonne (8.97 hp/tonne)

Transmission   Maybach OLVAR EG 40 12 16 B (8 forward and 4 reverse)

Suspension torsion-bar

Ground clearance 495 to 510 mm (1 ft 7.5 in to 1 ft 8.1 in)

Fuel capacity   860 litres (190 imp gal)

Operational range Road: 170 km (110 mi) Cross country: 120 km (75 mi)

Speed   Maximum, road: 41.5 km/h (25.8 mph) Sustained, road: 38 km/h (24 mph) Cross country: 15 to 20 km/h (9.3 to 12.4 mph)

Source: File:SdKfz182.jpg - <https://en.wikipedia.org>

Cutaway of a Sherman tank.

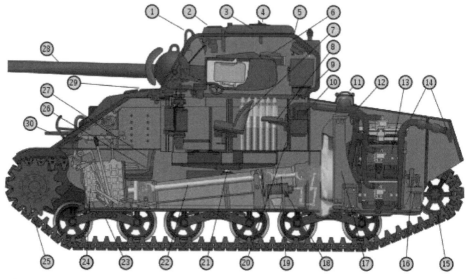

M4A4 Sherman Cutaway:
1 - Lifting ring, **2** - Ventilator, **3** - Turret hatch, **4** – Periscope, **5** – Turret hatch race, **6** – Turret seat, **7** – Gunner's seat, **8** – Turret seat, **9** – Turret, **10** – Air cleaner, **11** – Radiator filler cover, **12** – Air cleaner manifold, **13** – Power unit, **14** – Exhaust pipe, **15** – Track idler, **16** – Single water pump, **17** – Radiator, **18** – Generator, **19** – Rear propeller shaft, **20** – Turret basket, **21** – Slip ring, **22** – Front propeller shaft, **23** – Suspension bogie, **24** – Transmission, **25** – Main drive sprocket, **26** – Driver's seat, **27** – Machine gunner's seat, **28** – 75 mm gun, **29** – Drivers hatch, **30** – M1919A4 machine gun.

Jagdpanther

Source: File:Jagdpanzer V Jagdpanther 1.jpg -

Just to give an idea of size- top is a Sherman, then a Tiger and finally a Jagdpanther. They are all the same scale and are my collection. Sadly I do not have one of a King Tiger. You will just have to use your imagination! It is bigger than the Tiger!

The incident with a Greyhound destroying a King Tiger with three shells is a fact. It happened at St. Vith. Colonel Devine and Colonel Cavender were real people. I have fictionalised some of their achievements but Colonel Devine did hold the German advance up for a day. The German paratroopers were not as effective as the High Command expected. Like the British at Arnhem and the Americans in Normandy, they were spread over a wide area. They still caused a large number of casualties and massive disruption. The massacres of the soldiers at Malmedy and Wereth happened as did the torture of the Afro American soldiers. Many soldiers escaped the massacre at Malmedy and it was they who told their comrades

Kampfgruppe Peiper which was spearheaded by the 1st S.S. were the most successful. It was they who captured the fuel dump. It was they who almost made it to Dinant. They might have succeeded had the supplies drop they requested been dropped in the right place but SS-Brigadeführer Wilhelm Mohnke decided that Peirper's coordinates were wrong and the supplies were landed behind American lines! They were not as efficient as they thought they were. Eventually the Germans ran out of fuel and ammunition. Kampfgruppe Peiper abandoned their vehicles and made their own way back to Germany.

The siege at Bastogne is famous and does not need me to tell my readers how brave and resilient the airborne defenders were. What is less well known is the fact that the defence of the Elsenborn ridge was the factor which saved Antwerp and therefore stopped the German Offensive.

The 106th Division suffered the greatest number of casualties in one unit. Between 7-8,000 men were either killed or captured.

The weather played into the German hands and it was only when the skies cleared the American Air Force and R.A.F could send in their aeroplanes. Even so it was still a close-run thing. The narrow roads and the extensive forests did not help the Allies. It also hurt the Germans. A single wrecked tank could block a road. This happened on numerous occasions.

The German offensive did not end when their initial attack stalled. On January 1st Hitler sent another Division to attack in the south and he almost succeeded. General Bradley had to send the men who had just beaten off the first offensive to help them. At the same time the Luft3waffe bombed and attacked allied airfields. It was a Pyrrhic victory. They stopped Allied Air cover but they were destroyed themselves in the process. As the Allies could replace all of their losses in a couple of weeks it was one of the costliest mistakes Hitler ever made.

The Battle of the Bulge or Battle of the Ardennes as the British called it was the last serious offensive in the west. For the next few months, until their defeat in April, the Germans were just trying to stop the Allies. This was the beginning of the end.

Reference Books used

- The Commando Pocket Manual 1949-45- Christopher Westhorp
- The Second World War Miscellany- Norman Ferguson
- Army Commandos 1940-45- Mike Chappell
- Military Slang- Lee Pemberton
- World War II- Donald Sommerville
- The Historical Atlas of World War II-Swanston and Swanston

Griff Hosker March 2017

Other books
by
Griff Hosker

If you enjoyed reading this book, then why not read another one by the author?

Ancient History

The Sword of Cartimandua Series (Germania and Britannia 50A.D. – 128 A.D.)
Ulpius Felix- Roman Warrior (prequel)
Book 1 The Sword of Cartimandua
Book 2 The Horse Warriors
Book 3 Invasion Caledonia
Book 4 Roman Retreat
Book 5 Revolt of the Red Witch
Book 6 Druid's Gold
Book 7 Trajan's Hunters
Book 8 The Last Frontier
Book 9 Hero of Rome
Book 10 Roman Hawk
Book 11 Roman Treachery
Book 12 Roman Wall
Book 13 Roman Courage

The Aelfraed Series (Britain and Byzantium 1050 A.D. - 1085 A.D.
Book 1 Housecarl
Book 2 Outlaw
Book 3 Varangian

The Wolf Warrior series (Britain in the late 6th Century)
Book 1 Saxon Dawn
Book 2 Saxon Revenge
Book 3 Saxon England
Book 4 Saxon Blood
Book 5 Saxon Slayer
Book 6 Saxon Slaughter
Book 7 Saxon Bane
Book 8 Saxon Fall: Rise of the Warlord
Book 9 Saxon Throne

Book 10 Saxon Sword

The Dragon Heart Series
Book 1 Viking Slave
Book 2 Viking Warrior
Book 3 Viking Jarl
Book 4 Viking Kingdom
Book 5 Viking Wolf
Book 6 Viking War
Book 7 Viking Sword
Book 8 Viking Wrath
Book 9 Viking Raid
Book 10 Viking Legend
Book 11 Viking Vengeance
Book 12 Viking Dragon
Book 13 Viking Treasure
Book 14 Viking Enemy
Book 15 Viking Witch
Book 16 Viking Blood
Book 17 Viking Weregeld
Book 18 Viking Storm
Book 19 Viking Warband
Book 20 Viking Shadow
Book 21 Viking Legacy

The Norman Genesis Series
Hrolf the Viking
Horseman
The Battle for a Home
Revenge of the Franks
The Land of the Northmen
Ragnvald Hrolfsson
Brothers in Blood
Lord of Rouen
Drekar in the Seine

The Anarchy Series England
1120-1180

English Knight
Knight of the Empress
Northern Knight
Baron of the North
Earl
King Henry's Champion
The King is Dead
Warlord of the North
Enemy at the Gate
The Fallen Crown
Warlord's War
Kingmaker
Henry II
Crusader
The Welsh Marches
Irish War
Poisonous Plots

Border Knight 1182-1300
Sword for Hire
Return of the Knight
Baron's War
Magna Carta

Struggle for a Crown 1360- 1485
Blood on the Crown

Modern History
The Napoleonic Horseman Series
Book 1 Chasseur a Cheval
Book 2 Napoleon's Guard
Book 3 British Light Dragoon
Book 4 Soldier Spy
Book 5 1808: The Road to Corunna
Waterloo

The Lucky Jack American Civil War series
Rebel Raiders
Confederate Rangers
The Road to Gettysburg

The British Ace Series
1914
1915 Fokker Scourge
1916 Angels over the Somme
1917 Eagles Fall
1918 We will remember them
From Arctic Snow to Desert Sand
Wings over Persia

Combined Operations series 1940-1945
Commando
Raider
Behind Enemy Lines
Dieppe
Toehold in Europe
Sword Beach
Breakout
The Battle for Antwerp
King Tiger
Beyond the Rhine

Other Books
Carnage at Cannes (a thriller)
Great Granny's Ghost (Aimed at 9-14-year-old young people)
Adventure at 63-Backpacking to Istanbul

For more information on all of the books then please visit the author's web site at http://www.griffhosker.com where there is a link to contact him. Or you can Tweet me at @HoskerGriff

32759957R00129

Printed in Poland
by Amazon Fulfillment
Poland Sp. z o.o., Wrocław